PEOPLE WERE TALKING EVERYWHERE ABOUT THE YOUNG LADY FROM NOWHERE

All fashionable Regency London was abuzz about the sudden emergence of Julia Edgeworth as the brightest beauty in the social firmament.

Rakes like Sir Vincent Fitzgerald skillfully planned her seduction.

Rivals like Maria Sutherland subtly plotted her destruction.

Idle tongues and busy brains speculated on who was financing her splendid townhouse, her enchanting gowns, her magnificent carriage and steeds.

But no one could guess that even Julia did not know who lay behind her dazzling debut—and no one could ever dream what she would do when she found out. . . .

The Reckless Orphan

The
Reckless Orphan

by
Vanessa Gray

A SIGNET BOOK

NEW AMERICAN LIBRARY

PUBLISHED BY
THE NEW AMERICAN LIBRARY
OF CANADA LIMITED

PUBLISHER'S NOTE

This novel is a work of fiction. Names, characters, places, and incidents are either the product of the author's imagination or are used fictitiously, and any resemblance to actual persons, living or dead, events, or locales is entirely coincidental.

NAL BOOKS ARE AVAILABLE AT QUANTITY DISCOUNTS WHEN USED TO PROMOTE PRODUCTS OR SERVICES. FOR INFORMATION PLEASE WRITE TO PREMIUM MARKETING DIVISION, NEW AMERICAN LIBRARY, 1633 BROADWAY, NEW YORK, NEW YORK 10019.

First Printing, December, 1981

3   4   5   6   7   8   9

SIGNET TRADEMARK REG. U.S. PAT. OFF. AND FOREIGN COUNTRIES
REGISTERED TRADEMARK—MARCA REGISTRADA
HECHO EN WINNIPEG, CANADA

SIGNET, SIGNET CLASSIC, MENTOR, PLUME, MERIDIAN AND NAL BOOKS are published in Canada by The New American Library of Canada, Limited, 81 Mack Avenue, Scarborough, Ontario, Canada M1L 1M8

PRINTED IN CANADA

COVER PRINTED IN U.S.A.

1

Brightoaks, the country seat of three generations of the Edgeworth family, sat on the brow of a hill, commanding a fine view of the undulating country called the South Downs. Built of rough native ragstone, the large and comfortable house seemed as permanent as though grown out of the land itself.

The young lady sitting at the table in the breakfast room at the back of the ground floor of Brightoaks wore, however, an appearance of transience. Her bottle-green duffel cloak and matching bonnet lay on a chair near at hand, and a pair of worn bandboxes stood ready in the foyer, just inside the front entrance.

Lost in thought, Julia Edgeworth, chin in hand, gazed out of the window. She was oblivious of the sloping lawns, frost-covered in these last days of December 1813. She was alone in the house, except for Mrs. Meggs, the last of what was once a large staff, and Aunt Becky Moray, upstairs packing the last of her effects. The silence of the empty rooms was distinctly lowering to the spirits.

Julia considered the earth and all its inhabitants as though they were treats spread on a tray for her enjoyment. Not that she was exclusive about it—on the contrary. Life, to this point in her seventeen years, had been so bountiful in opportunities for delight that she longed to share her own enjoyment with everyone.

Of course, she mused this very morning, there were bound to be disappointments, like recognizing a fly when one had considered it at first to be a plump raisin. One of these setbacks, in fact, bore every indication of becoming a permanent flaw.

How else could one perceive the imminent arrival of agents for the new owners of Brightoaks?

Papa's gambling, while seemingly harmless except for momentary reverses at Watier's, had taken an unfortunate turn less than a year ago. It had taken only six months of Papa's ill luck at an establishment not quite *comme il faut* for the whole of Papa's not immense fortune to be whistled down the wind. Brightoaks had been the last counter the late Sir Philip Edgeworth, baronet, had placed on the table, and when that was gone, Sir Philip had quite simply blown his brains out. Since Lady Edgeworth had been dead these five years, Julia was left alone.

Except for Miss Rebecca Moray.

"And why your aunt," sniffed Mrs. Meggs, "calls herself *Miss* and wants to be a Moray again when that was the trouble in the beginning, I'll never know!"

"I don't see any reason why she shouldn't," said Julia with an air of reasonableness. "She was a Moray lots longer than she was a . . . whatever his name was."

"There!" cried the housekeeper in triumph. "You can't even call his name to mind! She wanted him bad enough at the beginning! I was just a parlormaid at the time, before I came here with your mother, and what a coil there was!"

"When my mother came?" asked Julia dutifully, even though she had heard the story often enough to be able to speak the words in unison.

"No, when Miss Becky took a fancy to the dancing master—a havey-cavey affair if there ever was. And I said at the time, mind you, that if nobody paid any attention to her, she would have settled down and married Sir Matthew, as everyone knew was the best thing."

"Pray get your information correctly, Mrs. Meggs," said a cool voice from the doorway. "My late husband was not a dancing master."

Mrs. Meggs, caught in the midst of her gossip, colored, but stood her ground. She had a snug post waiting for her near Chiddingfold, a fact that gave her sufficient ground to stand on.

"Near as nothing!" she snapped.

"An impoverished Italian count," said Becky, as though repeating a lesson, "who was forced to teach Italian and French for a living."

If the impoverished count had been born a peasant near Perugia, and had left his widow with towering and unsuspected debts, now paid off by unremitting toil and resourcefulness, Miss Moray was not free with the information. "Is the coffee hot, Mrs. Meggs?"

"My coffee is always hot," muttered the housekeeper, and reached for the silver pot.

Becky sat erect and at her ease, as though her only niece were not on the point of eviction from her ancestral home. She had doubts as to whether her irrepressibly impulsive relative would fit well into the boardinghouse on Queen Anne Street, but surely the elderly residents would be grateful for the sight of a fresh young face, framed bewitchingly in curls the color of a raven's wing, with deep violet eyes sparkling with curious interest in all and sundry.

But what about a husband for Julia? She would not let the girl marry beneath her station—she had had enough experience of that. But no one would look for a baronet's daughter without a sovereign of dowry on Queen Anne Street—a fact of life that Becky had not yet found a solution for.

But first of all, they must get to London, leaving Brightoaks behind for the new owners.

Finishing her Spartan breakfast, Becky smiled at Julia. "We must hurry, or we'll miss the stage."

Mrs. Meggs followed them into the foyer. "I never thought I'd see the day!" she mourned in valedictory. "The young miss is much too young and trusting to be set out into the world alone." Grudgingly she added, "A good thing, Miss Becky, she's got you to do for her."

Struck by an unexpected emotion, Becky turned to the housekeeper and, to their mutual surprise, hugged her. "We all have to do things we don't want to do, Mrs. Meggs," said Becky, straightening her bonnet. "I don't know how we shall go on, but something will turn up, I am sure of it."

Mrs. Meggs watched Becky, a slim erect woman, move gracefully to the door. She was attired modishly in a traveling costume of puce, carrying over her arm a warm woolen pelisse, and wearing a pair of black velvet half-boots. No lack of money there, thought Mrs. Meggs. Maybe he *was* an Eye-talian count.

But her eyes rested longest on her dear Julia. The child was the sunshine of Brightoaks, she thought in a flight of fancy, always dancing instead of walking, always with that bright friendly look. Julia knew and cared about every villager, every farmer on Edgeworth land, and they adored her in turn. A trusting, sweet-natured child like her mother . . .

Mrs. Meggs set aside her tears for later. She would not mar Julia's last hour, even though she saw the child through a mist. She took refuge in tartness.

"How the child will do when she gets to London passes all!"

Becky gave one of her rare chuckles. "I should, myself, worry about how London will fare!"

The hired carriage was at the door, and they mounted into it. The carter would come later in the day to take Julia's few possessions up to Queen Anne Street.

The road wound down from the summit of the hill, and then curved away toward Cuckfield. It was a gentle land of soft wooded slopes and well-kept fields. The winter winds were tempered here, and the cold was seldom cruel.

Julia turned in her carriage seat and watched Brightoaks unwinkingly until a turn in the road hid it from her view. Then, as though she had committed the sight to memory, she set her face ahead to the unknown future. She said no word until they reached the King's Head in Cuckfield.

"Oh, good, we're on time!" she exclaimed, seeing the expectant air of the ostlers at the inn when they drove up.

"Not long to wait, miss," said the landlord, helping Becky down to the ground. "Already they've winded the horn from South Hill."

Her heart sank. How could she ever leave Brightoaks? The dear house she had never looked at until now, the friendly stable boys, the farmers . . .

Becky noticed only a tightening of Julia's lips. Truly sympathetic, she chose to mistake the cause of Julia's misgivings.

"The stage is perfectly safe," she told her bracingly. "There is no danger."

"Not unless the weather changes," agreed the landlord, glancing over his shoulder at a bank of metal-gray cloud rising in the west.

4

Two days earlier, in London, Lord Charles Langley, the second son of the former Duke of Knebworth and brother of the present duke, stood before the mirror in an upstairs dressing room of his elegant house on Mount Street.

Brimm, his valet, hovered in unaccustomed anxiety. Lord Charles was not unreasonably demanding at the best of times, and Brimm had never felt the sharp edge of his lordship's tongue. But Lord Charles had become—to Brimm's horror—completely indifferent to his appearance. Neat, well-tailored, elegant—yet Lord Charles had lost interest in his neckcloth, allowing it to fall in most decorous and unoriginal folds. He had turned down a new delivery of fancy gold-thread waistcoats, firmly declining to introduce the new fashion to the *ton*.

Just now, Brimm held the French brocade dressing gown, one of Schweitzer and Davidson's most handsome creations, in maroon with silver lapels, which Lord Charles had just removed.

"I think, my lord, the dark green today?"

"What? Oh, yes. Not the dark green, Brimm. I go to visit my sister, who has an unaccountable aversion to green."

Brimm was understandably taken aback, since he had never heard of Lady Harriet Minton's dislike for green, and in fact he had himself seen her no longer ago than yesterday, entering her carriage after shopping in Henrietta Street, wearing a smart new walking costume in Pomona green, covered by a sable-lined pelisse in the same color, matched by a bonnet with an upstanding poke front.

If Lady Harriet did not like green, it must have been an overnight miracle of change, Brimm thought. Then, more sedately, he remembered that his lordship had been restless and out of temper for some days now, and properly dismissed the matter from his mind as a footling excuse.

Once clothed in subdued elegance—dark blue tailcoat with brass buttons, buff waistcoat, and light-colored pantaloons—Charles left his Mount Street house and made his way on foot toward Lady Harriett's house. He was indeed, as Brimm knew well, in a restless mood. The busy winter season in London had left him with a taste as of

5

dead ashes on the tongue. Turning from Mount Street onto Audley, oblivious of the frequent pedestrians he met on his way, he found himself on the south side of Grosvenor Square without quite knowing how he got there.

Forming his words in his mind, he was admitted to Lady Harriet's salon without delay. Harriet was stretched out at leisure on a Grecian sofa with boldly curved head-piece, the scrolled end curving elegantly at her feet.

Glancing up, she gave a crow of pleasure and rose to offer him both hands in welcome.

"Charles! How good it is to see you! After that rout last night, I had not expected to see you before the week's end! How you manage to rise so early . . ." A dismaying thought struck her, and in an altered tone she added, "Is something wrong?"

He kissed her hand and helped her to sit again on the sofa. "Not at all. That is," he added, careful to be accurate, "nothing unusual."

He sat beside her, conscious of her anxious gaze on him, but reluctant to launch out on the purpose that had brought him out at an hour when the fashionable world, having opened one eye to the daylight, promptly closed it again and burrowed deeper under the eiderdown.

"I always liked this room," he said at a tangent. "You make it very homelike, my dear."

"Homelike, Charles? You mean like Knebworth Castle? I should die if I thought so."

Grasping at conversational straws, Charles smiled. "Perhaps it is not you, my dear, but Minton who keeps a firm hand on the house!"

Lady Harriet gurgled in laughter. "Remember the time I thought I must have an Egyptian Room? Like the Regent's, of course, and Lady Patton had been the first to follow his lead. Minton was aghast!"

Charles roared with unaccustomed laughter. "I shall never forget the look on Minton's face when he set eyes upon that pair of chairs. Dark green——"

"Those lion feet, so realistic!" gasped Lady Harriet. "In gilt paint, too!"

"I don't wonder at him," said Charles, more self-possessed now. "They were truly ugly, dear sister."

"He sent them back at once," reminisced Lady Harriet.

"And quite rightly. I should have died of disgust at them long since."

They fell silent. Lady Harriet cast furtive glances at her handsome brother, now contemplating the floral design on the Turkey carpet. She was excessively fond of Charles, and had been aware, as had Brimm, that something was sadly amiss with him. Not that he had failed in courtesy, nor that he had turned his back on the social whirl—no, indeed! But it was almost as though Lord Charles Langley were represented by a mere shell, looking like him, talking like him, but somehow without the essence of his personality.

As though, she decided with a sinking heart, the real Charles had gone somewhere, far, far away. She hoped she could call him back before he moved beyond her reach.

"Charles . . ." she said, stretching out her hand to him as though to tether him.

He took her fingers in his and held them. "Harriet," he said, "I'm going to get married."

"Married!" she cried. "Charles! You didn't tell me!"

"I'm telling you now," he said with a wry smile. "But don't worry. There is time enough to order your gown for the wedding."

"When is it?" she demanded, thinking quickly about Desirée's quick fingers, in the new shop opened recently just off Oxford Street. "Not before May, I hope?"

"Actually, my dear, I don't know."

"The date not set? Well, that is understandable. But you have not told me who."

"That's understandable, too. I don't know."

This addled answer brought Harriet to her feet. She stood before Charles, a smallish figure trembling with emotion, and glared down at him.

"This is outside of enough, my dear Charles! You are bamming me, and I tell you I won't have it!"

"Scold Minton, if you will," said Charles lazily, "but pray don't ring a peal over me!"

She hesitated. "But, Charles! What is this japery?"

"No jape, I promise you. Now, sit down, my dear, and stop hovering over me like an avenging angel."

Slowly she sat down beside him. He took her hand

7

again, and held it as though to keep her from leaping again to her feet.

"My dear," he began, "we must take notice of facts."

"Won't she have you?"

He turned a blank expression to her. "She? Who?"

"Whoever you have asked to marry you," said his sister ungrammatically.

"The *facts*, Harriet, are that our brother has failed the family. Therefore, there is no hope for it but for me to marry."

Harriet began to see the trend of his thoughts. Anxious, though, to be fair, she pointed out, "But it is not his fault, Charles."

"You think not? Who was it, I wish to mention, who insisted on marrying that vinegar-jug Eugenia? I could have told him—indeed, all of London could have told him—that a woman with seven sisters and no brothers was not precisely the wife to produce a half-dozen sons."

"True," said Harriet enthusiastically. With a rush of confidence she added, "I have never been able to develop the least fondness for her."

"Very sensible of you. Nor, as far as I can see, has our dear brother, Edward. So, you see, since he has failed, it is up to me to secure the family line."

"And you must marry, then. But, Charles," said Harriet after a long thoughtful moment, "who do you fancy?"

He gave a bark of unamused laughter. "Anyone presentable enough so that I don't have to get blind drunk before I remember my duty."

"Well," mused Harriet, "that eliminates several. Eleanor Paget, for one."

"Paget? Good God, she was never in the running."

Harriet was pursuing her own line of thought. "Maria Sutherland? She would leap at the chance. She turned down Brookfield, you know. Everyone said she was waiting for you."

"The Langley nose," said Charles obscurely. At his sister's look of inquiry, he added, "The Langley nose is prominent enough, without adding the Sutherland nose to it. Our children would be monsters!"

Harriet, with an air of great helpfulness, said, "Elizabeth Gore?"

"You wish to leg-shackle me to a constant carper? In another ten years, she'd be just like her mother."

Harriet agreed. Lady Gore was noted for making every gathering of which she was a part miserable by her whining monologues.

"Not the Mimms girl, surely," said Harriet judiciously.

Charles did not answer at once. Then he said slowly, "Maybe. Just quite possibly you are right. The Mimms girl."

Harriet, hiding her dismay, said, "Such a wisp of a girl. She fades away into nothing when you speak to her."

"Biddable, at least, you must admit."

With intent, Harriet said musingly, "I imagine she will work out well. Eugenia will show her how to go on."

Charles burst out indignantly, "I shall not marry to oblige Eugenia!"

After a short silence Harriet said in an altered tone, "I have heard no word about obliging yourself, Charles."

"That does not matter."

Oh, Charles! she thought she said, but realized that it was an inward cry. Tears stung the back of her eyelids. How could she bear to see Charles unhappy?

"I'm off to Brighton in the morning," said Charles.

"Brighton!"

"My dear, pray don't echo my every word!"

"Well," said Harriet with spirit, "if you insist upon saying such outlandish things, you must be prepared to meet with a certain amount of disbelief!"

He bowed in acknowledgment of the truth of her retort. "But I must consider my next step," he told her, "and I think Brighton will provide sufficient calm for me to make up my mind."

"Midwinter? Who will be promenading on the Steyne?"

"All to the good, my dear. If I see no one at all, I shall think better."

He rose to take his leave, and she went with him to the door. He bent to kiss her hand. "My dear Harriet," he said, a note of fondness clear in his voice, "don't fret about me. I shall do very well."

She hesitated, then made up her mind. "Charles, I really must tell you something. For your own good."

"Ominous," he said, steeling himself.

"Truly, I know you far too well to misunderstand you.

9

I know you are the soul of kindness, of thoughtfulness . . ." She lost her words in confusion. She had never spoken thus to him before. But so exercised was she by his clear unhappiness that she threw caution to the winds. Recklessly she said, "You truly must mend your ways, Charles, lest your apparent *haughtiness* bring all to naught."

"*Haughtiness*?"

"You truly do not know how you appear to others, to those who don't know you well. Please, Charles! Try not to give the impression that you know what is best for everyone!"

He lifted an eyebrow. "I should be an odd fish indeed if I did not know how to manage my own affairs, shouldn't I?"

"Surely, my dear Charles, no one could take possible exception to that! But *sometimes* you do give one the idea—I think it must be your very grave manner, Charles, and that habit of looking down your nose—"

"The Langley nose," murmured Charles.

Harriet lost herself in floundering words. She wanted him to be valued for himself, for whoever married Lord Charles Langley would be the luckiest of women. Except for herself, she added. Minton was the darling of her eye, and she counted herself fortunate beyond her deserts.

Charles had risen to his feet. With a wry smile he said simply, "Then my fortune must make amends for my person."

She watched him out of sight, biting her tongue and wishing she had kept her own counsel. But what she said was true, she told herself. No lady of her present acquaintance was good enough for Charles. Few persons knew of his many unheralded charities, his constant consideration for her, for his old nurse Sarratt, and his servants, all of whom loved him dearly.

But his superior air, born (she knew) of boredom and some queer unnamed hunger, turned people away, and made him more solitary than ever.

There was no trace of loneliness in his upright figure as he walked across the square and disappeared from her view. But there was indeed a tumult in his thoughts.

Harriet's words touched him on the raw. Not her accusation of haughtiness, for that seemed of no moment to him, and thus not worthy of consideration. But her suggestion that he had said nothing about obliging himself—that idea harrowed his thoughts.

There was indeed no one in London now who struck his fancy. It would be several months before a new crop of young ladies filtered into the marriage market, and he would be hunting them in earnest. He truly did not know what he wanted in a wife—the only thing he could hope for was a girl as far removed from Eugenia's pattern as was possible.

It was simple, he thought as he turned into Brook Street. I have a duty to perform, since Edward has not provided an heir for the Langley family. I shall marry, do my family duty, and have done with it all.

There was, not surprisingly, no comfort for him in that decision, either.

Lord Charles Langley's household was sufficiently acquainted with his vagaries that there was no consternation belowstairs when their master bade them travel to the Old Ship at Brighton with only the essentials for a stay of two weeks.

The chariot was sent on ahead, carrying Brimm; Samson, the footman; Diggs, a man for all purposes; and four trunks roped on behind. Charles himself traveled incognito—that is, he took his newest curricle, bearing no identifying markings, and, with Crouch, his groom, took the road out of London. His matched chestnuts were fast steppers, and soon London was left behind.

Within an hour the travelers were moving through true countryside. Beyond Croydon the land began to rise gently. Charles, handling the ribbons, was blue-deviled enough so that little caught his attention until they reached the North Downs.

The day was gray, wet, and gloomy. Charles was reminded of the words of some wit: "London is a fine place to live, if only for the pleasure of leaving it."

Given this kind of day, when London was sodden and sooty, Charles knew again that his true happiness would come to him if he moved to the country. He had estates in plenty, sufficient to choose from—but there was the question now of his marrying. All must wait upon the right moment.

The clouds lowered, and the breeze stiffened. Just beyond Purley, on the Brighton road, the storm began. He set his chestnuts a faster pace. A benighted road, at least, he remembered, not one for the storm-bound traveler. He cast an eye at the dark clouds. If he was not mistaken, there was worse weather to come.

2

The lowering clouds that caused Charles to touch the whip to his chestnuts darkened the sky at Cuckfield, where Julia and her aunt Becky waited for the stage. The clouds trailed misty fingers across the gentle, rolling hills, crowned by small coppices of trees, and softened Julia's homeland into a kind of scene seen in a dream.

To the south, toward Brighton, the sky was clearer, and the landlord had no doubt that the Brighton-to-London coach would be on time.

Becky cast an anxious glance at her niece. She was taking it remarkably well, Becky thought, considering that the child—no longer a child at seventeen!—had lost her father through a gunshot wound to the head, and had seen all her family possessions, under the hammer of the auctioneer, pass into alien hands. Becky herself had left home at Julia's age, but in Becky's case it had been a matter of going in pursuit of love and happiness. It had turned out badly, of course.

Julia turned to Becky. Reading her aunt's thoughts, she said softly, "I shall be fine. I knew Papa was in trouble with gambling, for there were many times we had to send all the servants away. But they always came back when Papa was in funds." She pulled the hood of her traveling cloak tightly and held it under her chin against the rising wind. "Of course," she added without a quaver, "I had no idea Papa would take such an extreme measure to balk his creditors this time. In confidence, dear Becky, I think he didn't mean to kill himself. It would be so like Papa to try to fob off the bailiffs with a sham attempt at suicide." Her eyes were bright with unshed tears as she finished, "But like many of Papa's ploys, it went awry."

Becky was saved from answering by the sight of the coach tooling up the road from the south. A faint cheer rose from the stable boys, more as a matter of custom than of enthusiasm.

The coach pulled up in the stableyard of the King's Head, and with a clatter of steps the door was opened and the passengers emerged to stretch.

"No time, no time," bawled the coachman. "Yon weather doesn't look good to me."

The passengers sorted themselves out into those who had reached their destination and the four who were to go on.

"No place, miss, but outside for you," said the groom, swinging down from the perch beside the coachman.

"I have paid," said Becky distinctly, "for an inside passage. And I shall have it."

Her unexpected defiance rattled the coachman and the guard to such effect that, over the mutterings of the coachman—"Illegal, that's what it is, against the law!"—she and Julia found themselves shut up inside the coach.

"Outside seats, indeed!" said Becky. "Not in this weather. It's the end of December, after all!"

Julia was not convinced that sitting inside, three to a seat made for two, was preferable to breathing the fresh air on the outside seats. But she forbore to question why she should feel trussed up like a fowl ready for the spit, and know that from now to London she would hardly be able to move a finger, to say nothing of easing a cramped leg.

It would only be for a little while, she believed. In that belief, she was more accurate than she knew.

Becky, as soon as the coach moved out on its way north, lapsed into silence. Soon the motion of the coach soothed her and she closed her eyes. On the contrary, Julia was more wide-awake than ever.

She had never ridden in a stage before. She had gone to London once, several years before, but then her father had taken her in the big coach with the family crest on the panels, two changes of horses, and a number of servants and outriders. A greater contrast to the stage could hardly have been imagined.

Julia smiled, and her dimple appeared momentarily. She was caught then by the fixed stare of the clergyman

14

just opposite. The expression on his face told her that he was astounded at his luck to have such a vision appear before him. She was forced to smile again at him, and the effect of her dazzling regard was all she could have wished for. The woman sitting between him and Becky leaned forward. "My brother and I," she said in a raspy voice, "are on our way to our new church. He is to take up his duties as curate before week's end."

"And you are escorting him there?" suggested Julia, "or will you keep house for him?"

"You're a child, miss," said the sour-faced sister. "And I should not expect you to understand the life of a curate. I count it a privilege to serve the church as well as my brother, by protecting him and taking care of him in every way, so that he may be free to pursue his onerous responsibilities."

It was an impressive speech, thought Julia, and would have been effective except for the curate's expression. Julia had seen just such a desperate look in the eyes of a leveret caught in a trap.

She smiled again at the curate, this time in mere kindly fashion. Far be it from her to cause discord in the new home of the curate. She repressed a strong desire to free the hare from the snare. It was not possible.

She became aware, then, of the smell of apples. She sought out the source, the couple on her right, a rotund farmer and his wife, who had managed to extricate from pockets a couple of red apples.

The tart aroma overcame at last the smell of greasy ham that seemed to exude from the very cushions, and the smell of damp wool. Did sheep on the hills smell thus? wondered Julia. If so, then no wonder the shepherds kept them in the open as long as they could. Maybe, though, it was the dye that sent its odor into the air when the cloth got damp. It was a minor puzzle, fit only to beguile the hours to London, to occupy the mind from thinking resentful thoughts about the sharp corner of a basket clearly pressing her ribs, and the deeper uncertainty of what might await her in London.

The coach at last lurched into Horley. The guard told them there was not time to get out for a stretch. Julia murmured, "We should probably never fit together as well again. Besides, it's raining."

The inn was one of the better ones on the London–Brighton Road, and prided itself on changing horses in under three minutes. After some shouted conversation, the coach took again to the road.

The farmer's wife, gulping the last of her apple, settled in for conversation.

"Our name's Applegate," she informed the others.

Encouraged by a murmured response, she continued. "Going to Redhill. New grandson we haven't seen. First one!"

Her husband, as though in deliberate contrast to his wife's cheerfulness, mumbled, "May never get there."

"Why not?" demanded the curate's sister, whose name was Miss Brassey.

"Did ye hear what ostler said back there? Said a wheel loose."

The curate cleared his throat in a most ominous way. "He was hired to do just that."

Julia marveled. "What do you mean? Hired to loosen the wheel?"

Mr. Brassey expanded under the sincere interest he read in Julia's violet eyes. Ignoring the disapproving glare of his sister, he informed Julia, "No. That would be quite beyond the law, even of decency. No, the ostler is instructed by the landlord to make such dire suggestions, so that the passengers, thinking better of continuing, will take refuge in his inn."

"For goodness' sake!" exclaimed Julia.

Applegate disagreed. "I shouldn't wonder if ostler was right. Don't like the feel of the ride."

Mrs. Applegate said forcefully, "Why didn't you notice it before, then, before you heard aught about wheel?"

Mr. Brassey, greatly daring, ventured upon a bit of slang. "A Cock and Bull story, in my opinion."

Encouraged to explain, he was not at all loath. "The Cock and Bull are two inns. On Watling Street, I believe, at the crossroads at Fenny Stratford."

Julia realized that Mr. Brassey was of a pedantic turn. Protected by his sister, he had only to speak to be favored with profound attention by his listeners. "Many habitués of the inns, of a volatile and irresponsible nature, I fear, found pleasure in setting at large certain wild stories without foundation."

16

"Stories about coaching accidents?" Julia prompted.

"That I am not sure of. I understood from my informant that the stories were of varied nature. An invention of the devil, of course, who finds work for idle hands. Or, in this case, of idle tongues."

A slight hissing at the leather curtains now began to make itself heard. The rain had now turned to little pellets of snow, and as if in answer to Julia's doubts, the coach began to move more slowly.

"Ice on the road, doubtless," said Mr. Applegate. "We'll chance our luck if we keep on."

"Applegate, you're the limit!" frothed his wife. "What else would we do? There's no inn for miles, I'll be bound."

She spoke for them all. Uneasiness stirred in each passenger. Julia took especial notice of the squeaking of the wheels. The noise had been an uncomfortable undercurrent since they had left Duckfield, but now, her senses honed by anxiety, it seemed to her that the sound had reached an unwarranted volume.

She could feel the coach slowing, laboring along. The passengers in their anxiety fell silent, and in the sudden quiet she heard the horses blowing as they toiled ahead.

Becky stirred, moving the leather curtain to peer around the edge. "Good God!" she exclaimed. "Are we only at Three Ash Hill? We won't be in London before tomorrow at this rate!"

The prophetic words had scarcely left her cold lips before the coach reached the top of the hill, and started, disastrously, on the downward slope. The weight of the coach on the slippery road was too much for the six horses, struggling with their own uncertain footing. The coach began to slip to one side, and in seconds was out of control. The horses, feeling the coach too close on their heels, neighed in fright, and in less time than it took Julia to recognize trouble, the coach canted to the left, a great heavy bump on the road—was a wheel off?—the door sprang open by itself, and the passengers spewed out of the coach onto the frozen grass.

Julia, sitting next to the door, was propelled by the weight of the Applegates behind her to the farthest edge of the verge, where she found herself, stupidly, on hands and knees in a state of stunned disbelief. Dazed by the force of her impact with the ground, she didn't move.

Behind her she heard, as though from a vast distance, recriminations between coachman and passengers. All were jumbled together on the cold verge and the slushy road. She could hear broken phrases:

"They *told* you about the loose wheel—best have looked to it, *I* say!"

"Shut up, Applegate!" That was his spouse's voice, rich with exasperation. "Always know best, don't you, after it's all over!"

Julia turned her head toward the sound of the voices. Where was Becky? Suddenly Julia couldn't see. She was blinded! She gagged over her heart unaccountably risen into her throat. She sat up and put her trembling hand to her eyes.

It was only her hood, fallen forward over her face.

Thus encouraged, she got to her feet, sliding slightly on the hoar-coated grass, and climbed to the slippery road. The accident was worse than she thought. The coach canted crazily into the ditch, one wheel lying at a distance, as though disclaiming all responsibility for what happened.

The horses, broken loose from the shafts, stood in a steaming clump a little way off, clearly frightened, the guard standing shivering at their heads to hold them.

Fist raised in the air, the farmer bawled, "My stableman would be sent packing at such a fool trick!"

But the coachman had a different line for his thoughts to travel, equally distasteful. "Six insiders. Ought to have four. Two of you should have been outside. Too many insiders."

"Outside passengers," pointed out the curate, "would have been killed at once."

It was true, Julia thought. Since they were all so tightly packed inside, there was little room for being tossed to and fro, at peril to limb.

"If company finds out I got six insiders," mourned the coachman, "they'll kill me!"

"If I don't do it first!"

"Shut up, Applegate!"

But where *was* Becky?

Becky was stretched out on the grass on the opposite side of the road, eyes shut . . .

"She's dead!" shrieked Julia.

She ran to her, frantic to help and not knowing just how to do it. She knelt beside her aunt. "Please, Becky, open your eyes. Say something. Tell me . . . where are you hurt?" Julia turned agonized eyes upon the others, who, now aware of serious trouble, hovered around the supine figure and her distressed niece.

"Poor lady," murmured Mrs. Applegate.

"She's freezing to death!" cried Julia, chafing her aunt's hands. She glared at Miss Brassey, wrapped in a warm merino shawl. That lady, doubtless conscious of her duty to provide an example of selfless Christian womanhood, slowly removed her shawl and dropped it into Julia's hands.

"Thank you, Miss Brassey," said Julia meticulously. "She must be kept warm until she gets to an inn."

"No inn," said the coachman. "Not for miles. Horley's half a dozen miles behind. Dunno how far Crawley is ahead."

"But what are we to do? She'll die if she stays here!"

A low moan from the victim gave emphasis to Julia's words. There was not a soul other than the ill-fated stage party on the road. No friendly farmhouses sent their welcoming light through the growing dusk.

Applegate, ignoring his wife's invitation to "close his trap for once," said sarcastically, "Well, coachman, may as well start walking!"

"You're daft!"

"You're right," said Applegate. "Never make it, fat as you are."

"Only clothes!" retorted the coachman, stung.

"Someone's for it," pointed out Applegate, with a semblance of reasonableness. "You, or the guard, or—"

"My brother is not well!" came the raspy voice of Miss Brassey. "I forbid him to go."

"But, Lavinia . . ." The curate's protest was mild.

The coachman had moved away, and stood looking at the wheel in the ditch. "Maybe," said the coachman, "we could put the wheel into place." The coachman, a devoted chapel-goer, addressed the farmer. "You could help, and maybe we could get it fixed. Instead, if you'll pardon the allusion, of roaring like the Bull of Bashan and getting nowhere."

"I'd get somewhere if you weren't such a dumbhead!"

The curate, removing himself from mundane affairs such as a disabled coach, knelt beside Becky's body. It was too much for Julia. Ordinarily as optimistic as the first robin in spring, now she thought that the curate, more experienced than she, knelt to perform the last offices of the church. A pitiful moan escaped her, and Mrs. Applegate, a fat pillar of strength, moved to stand beside her.

"Is she . . . ?"

Before Mrs. Applegate could frame an answer that was truthful as well as kind—no mean feat—a hail arose from the coachman, standing in the middle of the road.

"We're saved!" he cried dramatically, pointing ahead on the road.

All eyes squinted to see the cause of his optimism. A black speck against a gray background of ground mist grew into a recognizable rig.

"What's a curricle doing out in this weather?" mumbled the coachman, his optimism fading. A curricle spoke of a member of the upper classes, and there was, in his experience, no help to be forthcoming from one of the nobs.

"No matter how he got here," pointed out Mr. Applegate stoutly. "He's saved you a long walk for help!"

Coachman mumbled some words that sounded suspiciously like "Not me!" but Mr. Applegate apparently did not hear them.

The curricle, smartly black with no identification of any kind on it—Lord Charles Langley was traveling incognito—pulled up at the scene of the accident. Indeed, he could hardly do otherwise, for the road was effectively blocked, full of baggage, the handful of passengers both erect and prostrate strewn over the road, the coach tilted crazily in the ditch.

Lord Charles suppressed a sharp word. He was anxious to reach the amenities of the Old Ship at Brighton, before the weather, already making travel difficult, worsened, as it gave every promise of doing.

Lord Charles surveyed the scene. The loose coach wheel canted against the far side of the ditch in which the coach itself had come to rest. Clearly it was incumbent upon any civilized person to take a hand in rescue operations.

Lord Charles rose to the occasion. Reining in his chestnuts, he said, "Crouch."

Obediently his groom descended to the roadway. It was immediately clear that a new factor had been added to the scene.

"What's all this?" demanded Crouch. "Anybody gone for help? What's amiss with the lady?"

Nearly at once Crouch had infused an air of hopefulness into the situation. Coachman, strongly exhorted to move his fat self, forgot to worry about what the company would say. Mr. Brassey and Mr. Applegate retrieved the errant wheel and trundled it to the coach.

Lord Charles, wrapped in his own gloomy thoughts, allowed the spectacle before him to fade from his view, while he paid heed only to the unattractive parade of his own thoughts.

He was brought back to the present by the sense of someone staring at him. With a slight start he saw a small figure on the ground looking up at him.

"You are," said the small figure, "quite possibly the most selfish person I have ever had the misfortune to meet."

"What?"

"You see my aunt lying at the point of death in the road, and you have not even the civility to offer to help."

"I am not a surgeon."

Julia surveyed him and his shiny black curricle, the matched pair of chestnuts—"a few pounds at Tattersall's for *them* cattle," as Applegate had said—and then looked again at Lord Charles. "It is clear," she said incisively, "that you have no gainful employment at all."

Lord Charles, unaccustomed to hearing such strictures, could barely refrain from gaping at the child. He saw, though, that she was more than a child. Her bonnet, not quite in the latest fashion, had slid to a position over one ear. There was a smudge—dirt or a bruise—on her left cheek. Her nose, not quite in the current mode, was nonetheless charmingly tilted, and her violet eyes emitted sparks. Something stirred deep within him, surprisingly, as

21

an unseen force moves the placid surface of a spring of water.

It was an uncomfortable feeling, he thought, and he took steps to regain his own composure. Never one accustomed to receive strictures submissively, not even years ago from his respected tutor, Charles allowed his features to assume an expression that had heretofore dampened and put to rout any impertinence that might be offered him.

His adversary was not in the least daunted. "One might think," Julia pointed out, "that even a gentleman with as little human feeling as you, my lord, would feel compassion for an injured lady—"

"Lady?" he murmured, and was instantly glad she hadn't heard him.

For this mite of a miss glaring at him was indeed a lady. No one without breeding could look at him in just such an unintimidated way, he considered rightly.

She was still looking up at him in expectant fashion, clearly waiting for him to do something. Her eyes, he thought, slightly bemused, were the color of violets—violets in the snow, he decided, noting their frosty expression.

"My aunt is in need—"

He stirred himself. "Crouch!" he said, hardly raising his voice.

Crouch knelt beside Becky on the frozen ground. After a moment, during which both Julia and Charles watched him intently, he said, "She'll do, my lord."

Crouch had cleared the road effectively for Charles's curricle. As they prepared to leave the scene, against a background of indignant protests, the lady on the ground stirred, and called, "Julia?"

Her niece, Charles's recent opponent, bent swiftly to her aunt's aid, and said, "I'm right here."

The curricle whirled away down the road, Crouch hanging on to the bar. "My lord?"

"Never mind, Crouch, we'll be in Horley in moments, and I'll deal with it there."

Crouch subsided, satisfied. If his lordship said he would deal with it, then the coach passengers were as good as tucked up before a roaring fire that instant!

3

Even though the haughty newcomer on the scene had not deigned to descend from his curricle, yet his powerful influence was evident to the coach passengers within the hour.

From Horley came carriages for the unfortunate passengers, wagons for their luggage, and sufficient muscular minions to set about at once, in the deepening dusk, righting the carriage, replacing the wheel, and gathering in the horses to put them in the thills once again.

More effective help could not have been wished for, Julia admitted. Indeed, as Becky pointed out sometime later, had not the unknown lord held firm his fractious chestnuts, the pandemonium on the slippery road might well have been compounded into disaster.

By morning Becky was restored sufficiently to resume travel toward London. Ready for departure, Becky and Julia were astounded to see standing at the door a private coach, with four horses in the traces, a coachman and footman on the box, and the landlord leaping forward to help the ladies mount.

"But," cried Julia innocently, "we cannot afford this . . ." Becky, still too shaken to keep her wits honed, said nothing, and Julia believed she understood. "But then, the coaching company does things handsomely, do they not?"

Since the coaching company had naught to do with the private coach, the landlord did not find it necessary to agree. In fact, he wished nothing to interfere with the speedy departure of the coach-and-four with its two privileged passengers, before the other victims of yesterday's accident became aware of their own less desirable circumstances.

Lord Charles Langley had indeed made amends for his apparent indifference to Julia's suffering, but, being a man unused to explaining, whose actions were never subject to question, he had apologized in his own way, anonymously, and munificently.

The storm having blown away toward the southeast coast of England during the night, the roads were clear and the coach traveled smartly toward London.

How much more comfortable this coach was! thought Julia delightedly. Why couldn't the coaching company provide such luxury for all its passengers as a rule? She said as much to Becky.

"Where would they put the farmers with their smoked hams?" she demanded. "I thought I would be ill yesterday if I had another hour of that noxious air!"

"Well," said Julia practically, "I vow it was better than that icy slush we landed in!"

"I'm not sure," said Becky with a downward quirk to her lips. Her head still ached, feeling strangely filled with wet cotton balls, and she closed her eyes. Never one to suffer the motion of a carriage without illness, she had thought yesterday's journey to be quite possibly the worst experience of her life.

Julia glanced knowingly at her aunt. "You'll feel better when we get home."

It was a home that Julia could not look forward to. She was sure it would be nothing like Brightoaks—nothing in London could compare with the sprawling stone house where she had always lived. But there was no profit in looking ahead, so her governess, Miss Pringle, had always said.

So, with the optimism that was as much a part of Julia as breathing, she turned her attention to the passing scene. By the time they reached Croydon, the snow lingering on the ground was increasingly deep. But the closer they were to London, the dirtier was the snow, until it didn't look much like snow at all.

The coach, following directions furnished by Becky, turned on Bridge Road, and then Julia caught sight of the Thames, the fabled river that flowed through London to the sea, bringing the world beyond England right up to the wharves in the middle of the city.

Answering Julia's question, Becky said, "All the ships are downstream in the Pool. We'll go see them someday."

They crossed the river at Westminster Bridge. They turned right when they reached the other side. Westminster Abbey towered to the left, Becky told her, but just now the towers were shrouded in snow, falling again, and a kind of yellow swirling fog.

The coach turned on Oxford Street, then onto Wimpole, and then right on a short street named after Queen Anne. They drew up before a nondescript house whose only virtue, to Julia's disappointed eyes, was that it stood unmoving and gave every promise of remaining so. She had had a sufficiency of the rolling motion of the coach.

The house where Julia was to live was a drab building on a drab street, turning an indifferent face to passersby. But if the outside seemed indifferent to mere humans, the interior proved to be bursting with exuberant welcome.

The coach stopped, and the footman, bundled to the ears against the weather, hopped down from the box and let down the steps. The house seemed to Julia's eyes to erupt. The door was thrown open, and a small redheaded boy shot down the steps. He was enormously freckled, with an engaging grin that displayed a tooth missing. He looked half-starved, but his energy was unflagging. He hurried around to the heads of the horses, examining them as though he were prepared to spend a hatful of guineas at Tattersall's.

"Only job horses, they is," he pronounced judiciously.

Becky was on the sidewalk. "And why not?" she demanded. "The coaching company sent us home. The first coach had an accident, and I'm very short of temper, young Harry, so be advised."

Harry, the potboy, understood his mistress thoroughly. Without further ado he sprang to take care of the luggage, deposited on the snowy sidewalk by the footman.

A couple of maids had appeared on the steps by now, and they helped Becky up the stairs and into the house with tender hands. Becky was not as well as she had claimed.

Julia, picking up her own bandbox and Becky's reticule, followed, struck suddenly by shyness at entering a strange house with strange inhabitants. She was thus in a position to overhear Harry's pert remark to the coachman.

"Nary coach company I ever heard sent riders home in a private carriage," he pointed out, "even if them *be* only job horses."

The coachman opened his mouth to explain, but changed his mind. He contented himself with a broad wink at Harry, as from one man of the world to another. The potboy's freckles seemed to quiver as his face crinkled in gratified, if bewildered, amusement. A hail from the house cut short any questions that he might have had, and he galloped up the stairs with the heavy baggage.

Julia stopped just inside the door. Sally and Polly were fussing over Becky like rival hens over a lone chick. Sally, neat as a new pin, took Becky's cloak in her rough red hands. Polly, the upstairs and parlormaid, was an older woman, with a haunting sadness always in her worn face.

Julia watched, feeling more than ever an outsider. This was a feeling she had never had before, since her whole life had so far been spent in her own home with her own servants. Now, nothing made her feel the change in her circumstances as much as standing aloof and ignored.

But she was, as it happened, not at all unnoticed. The third member of the welcoming party in the hall stepped forward at last, but not to speak to Becky. Instead, she came directly to Julia.

"My dear child," she said, "how glad you must be to stop traveling at last!"

She reached for Julia's green duffel cloak. "Set your bandbox down. Young Harry will take care of it. If he ever gets around to it!"

She was a bustling, motherly person, round as an apple, dressed in a gray morning dress with white collar and cuffs, much like a superior kind of housekeeper. Surely she was not a servant?

"I'm Elsie Hastings," offered this very kind person, "one of your aunt's residents here. We're going to get along just fine!"

As a speech of welcome it did lack polish, thought Julia, but it could not be faulted for warmth and cordiality. She smiled gratefully. "We had an accident, you know," said Julia. "My aunt was hurt, but not badly."

"No wonder you didn't get here yesterday," said Mrs. Hastings. "Now, you just let the girls take her upstairs, and you and I'll have a nice cup of tea."

26

Julia was to learn that, like all members of her class, Mrs. Hastings believed in the total curative power of a nice cup of tea. While she was a resident in Becky's house, she had been a superior kind of housekeeper most of her life.

"Yes, indeed, I lived in Tring most of my life," she said. "Born in London, but it so happened that the position in Tring, that's in Hertfordshire, you know, just outside Hemel Hempstead, at least no more than ten miles from it, turned out to be more than temporary. Went there for six months, stayed thirty years."

"They must have been kind to you," murmured Julia, feeling the hot tea gradually restore life to her bones.

"That they were," Mrs. Hastings answered. "Have a scone, Mrs. Wilkes makes them, she's the cook here. Temperamental, but get on the good side of her and you're all right." She looked critically at Julia. "Need a little fattening up, if you don't mind my saying so."

Julia minded, but held her tongue. If Mrs. Hastings was an example of the other residents in Becky's boardinghouse, Julia believed it would be a long winter. But then, she thought, if they were all as kind as Mrs. Hastings, she would be grateful.

Before that first day was over, Julia had met the other boarders:

Mrs. Prince sat all day by the fire and yet was never warm.

Old Miss Rachel Owens embroidered constantly. She had, so Elsie Hastings whispered, a massive trunk upstairs, full of the most exquisite work. She sold a piece now and then, in order to meet her rent.

The fourth boarder was Margaret Cooper, a former lady's maid who had a way with hair.

All of them seemed, in their various ways, delighted with Julia. "A breath of fresh air," said Miss Owens kindly.

Only when Julia retreated to her white-painted room, containing a narrow bed and presenting a view of the chimney pots of London, did she feel her heart sink. The rest of her years with these elderly women, their lives clearly behind them, and nothing for them to look forward to, was not a bright prospect. Julia was hard put to hang on to her usual cheerfulness. Even a born optimist must have at least something to hang bright thoughts on.

A fortnight after she arrived in Queen Anne Street, Julia ventured out on her own for the first time. Becky, recovered from her accident, was still short of temper.

The winter had been cold. London chill was far more penetrating than was the cold of Brightoaks. Whether it was the proximity of the river, Julia did not know. But she was unpleasantly aware of the gusting winter winds puffing out the thin summer curtains hanging at her one small window. The room at the top of the house had, of course, been occupied in previous days by one of the maids—surely two could not have slept in such a tiny cell!—and it did not matter to the master whether or not the windows fit tightly.

It was beyond even Julia's ability to deal with the window frame, but at last, after two weeks of biting her tongue on her misery, she thought of a solution.

"Heavy curtains," she said to Becky. She had found her aunt in the small room off the dining room where her minuscule desk was covered with ledgers and a great many scraps of paper covered with figures. "There must be somewhere in the house a pair of heavy curtains. To put up at the window in my bedroom." Seeing the blank look on her aunt's face, she added, "To keep out the drafts."

Becky threw down her pen, unmistakably exasperated. "Drafts. If that's all you have to think about, I wish you well. I suppose even a drafty room is better than sleeping in a hedgerow with a bit of bread for your breakfast?"

Julia shrank away, stricken. Becky, instantly repentant, leaped to her feet and embraced her niece. "Julia, I'm sorry. I just don't know what made me say that. I don't mean it. Julia, I didn't mean it!"

Julia, incapable of harboring a grudge, forgave her on the instant. But even with Becky's coin in her hand, and the commission to purchase sufficient material so that heavy curtains could be made, Julia could not forget her aunt's outburst.

Becky had been kindness itself all through the ordeal of her dear papa's death, and the departure from Brightoaks. Surely she could not have spoken and acted so fairly if she resented Julia's presence?

By the time Julia, clad in her serviceable bottle-green duffel cloak, and wearing lined half-boots on her feet in country fashion, had reached the shops lining Oxford Street, she guessed the truth. The ledgers, the stacks of papers, a large packet of what she recognized from Papa's affairs to be unpaid bills—the answer leaped to her mind and she stood stock-still on the walk. Becky's establishment tottered on the brink of bankruptcy, to put it plainly. And Julia was the tiny shove that was about to send Becky over the edge.

And there was nothing that Julia could do. She had at first attempted to help with the household chores, but it was kindly borne in upon her that the maids feared she would take away their jobs, and she abandoned the attempt.

Wrapped in her own pessimistic thoughts, Julia hardly knew how she found herself in front of the shop of Layton and Shear's, just off Oxford Street. She hesitated, thinking she should go back to Queen Anne Street with her coins unspent. But she caught sight of a handsome royal-blue damask in the display window, and without volition she was inside the shop.

The shop assistant was engaged with a woman, not quite of the *ton*, Julia saw, in spite of her sage-green walking dress in the latest fashion. She spoke in a penetrating voice, and Julia, ostentatiously not listening, turned away.

She was entranced by the great bolts of cloth, so many and of such varied hues that it was like being set down in the middle of a rainbow. There was English poplin, and Irish poplin, the latter being much too dear at six shillings the yard, but the texture was so creamy one could eat it. On strawberries, thought Julia, letting her fancy run.

A voice spoke at her elbow. "Going to buy it, miss?"

Julia turned quickly, expecting to see the shop assistant, but instead saw a girl—perhaps ten years old, but with eyes that held an adult shrewdness.

"No, I shan't buy it," said Julia, smiling. "It is much too dear."

"My mother could buy it for you."

"Oh, my goodness, no!" exclaimed Julia, shocked. The child was precocious, and Julia was not quite sure how to deal with her. She improvised swiftly, "I have no place to wear a gown like this, besides."

"My name is Fanny," said her new acquaintance. "And I shall have places to wear lovely dresses, one day. I shall have a million gowns when I go to Paris."

In spite of the child's rudeness, Julia was drawn to her, most likely because the shrewdness in her blue eyes did not hide a kind of hunger that Julia guessed might never be appeased. Besides, Julia was curious.

"Oh? You are going to travel widely? How interesting! And you will start, of course, in France?"

With calm assurance Fanny informed her, "I shall be a *smash* in Paris."

Julia's imp of mischief made itself felt. "*Vous vous amuserez beaucoup, sans doute.*"

Fanny was, quite simply, overwhelmed. Round-eyed, she breathed, "Is that French?" When Julia nodded, she said doubtfully, "Shall I need to know how to speak it?"

"Well, of course you will. You will need to give orders to your servants, won't you? How embarrassing to tell them to take you to church, and you find yourself in the vegetable market!"

Fanny giggled. Mrs. Skinner heard her, and called, "Fan, how many times have I told you not to bother people! I declare, you'll be my death!"

"No bother," said Julia, but her words did not reach Fanny's mother, for Fanny's sharp voice overrode them.

"She *speaks* French, Mama. I never knew anybody who spoke French before. Mama, I wish she could teach me."

Mrs. Skinner glanced briefly at Julia, but Julia had the feeling that her cloak had been appraised, her wet boots had been dismissed with contempt, and even her black curls disapproved of. Without thinking, she drew herself up to her full height and favored Mrs. Skinner with a look that Miss Pringle had assured her would daunt the most persistent suitor. Mrs. Skinner wilted.

But Fanny's persistence, like that of a gadfly, could not be ignored. "Mama, ask her, ask her." She turned to Julia and demanded, "Will you teach me French? My mama will pay you."

"Fanny! Don't insult the lady."

Julia hesitated, lost in a dream of *earning money*, of

handing over coins to Becky, to repay in a small way Becky's generosity. She hesitated only a moment. "I am not insulted, Mrs. Skinner. Your daughter is eager to learn, and I am willing to teach her."

Seeing a gleam of cupidity in Mrs. Skinner's pale blue eyes, Julia added firmly, "For a price, of course."

In the face of Julia's obvious quality, even Mrs. Skinner did not try to bargain. The fee was settled, and Julia felt a leap of her heart. She was employed! At the back of her mind was a doubt: What would Becky say?

She could say nothing, thought Julia stoutly, on the way home, the purchase of heavy curtains forgotten. I can't run a boardinghouse, but I can do this.

In the event, Becky was shocked, but not fatally. As though to make up for her sharp tongue, she bestowed one of her rare words of praise.

"I'm proud of you, child," she said.

"*Je te remercie.*" Julia giggled.

4

Julia backed into the kitchen, bearing the remains of Miss Owens' dinner on a tray. She set it down on the table, and looked around her.

The kitchen was quite the most comfortable room in the house. Mrs. Wilkes saw to that. There was always a fire in the grate, the floor was spotless, and almost invariably something in the oven filled the room with a spicy, tantalizing aroma.

Harry, the potboy, sat on a stool in the corner, scouring the bottom of a cooking pot. He had clearly been working for some time, for there lay around him various utensils, clean and sooty.

"Why do I have to scrub the bottoms?" he complained. "They just go on the fire again."

"Cleanliness in the kitchen gives health and happiness to the home," pontificated Mrs. Wilkes.

Harry muttered something that sounded like, "Let the home clean 'em up, then," but Mrs. Wilkes chose not to hear. Instead, she attacked on another front.

"Look at 'im, then, Miss Julia. A disgrace, what I calls it—coming into my kitchen with a great black eye. Mind me, young 'arry, fightin'll bring ye to an early grave."

Harry protested stoutly. "Not me. I'll make me fortune."

Julia, greatly interested on her own behalf, demanded, "How?"

"Bully at t' fair," said Harry. As an explanation, she decided, it lacked clarity.

"What?"

"Bully," he said. "Fella who can fight Bully and lay 'im low gets the cheese. Or even a sovereign!"

"And you expect to win?"

"Ought to," sniffed Mrs. Wilkes. "He practices enough. But he didn't win no cheese this time. Worst shiner ever I saw."

Harry's gap-toothed grin shone through his tousled red hair, falling over his face as he scrubbed. "Other guy's got two," he explained modestly. "I'da got the cheese, all right."

"I've never been to a fair," Julia remarked wistfully.

"Oh, it's a treat, miss. They've got a bear, stands high as a man, he does, and dances." Julia's skeptical expression led him to add indignantly, "Proper dancing he does. And there'll be a barrow race, the chaps pushing 'em with kerchiefs over their eyes so they can't see where they go. And *eat*! I'll lay you this, Miss Julia—a king couldn't feed no better!"

Julia expressed admiration, but her thoughts were shot through with the darker image of serious consequences of fisticuffs. She sat down on a kitchen stool and, chin in hand, contemplated young Harry.

"Wouldn't you rather," she said at last, coaxingly, "be a coachman?"

Harry's hands, apparently, could not work at the same time as his brain. He stopped, scrubbing brush in midair, and repeated, wondering, "Coachman?"

Detecting a spark of interest, Julia set out to fan it into a small flame. "You'd sit up high on the box, where you could look down on everybody, even nobs in curricles," she said, borrowing his cant. "Six horses, and you'd have the ribbons in your hands—you'd be master of them, I just know you would."

Half-convinced, Harry allowed his mouth to drop open. "I dunno, miss. Think I could?"

Julia exclaimed, "I know you'd be better than our coachman on the way here. He didn't even think to look at his wheels, and one of them fell off, you know, rolled right down the road ahead of us."

"D'jever get it back?"

"We all flew out of the coach and onto the road!" said Julia, her violet eyes kindling again at the recollection.

"Coachman saved you all, then?" demanded Harry, his eyes shining at the thought of such heroics. He'd do a good deal better, he knew that much.

33

"Coachman was an idiot," pronounced Julia. "A real top-of-the-trees came along then, in his curricle."

Mrs. Wilkes edged closer. She hadn't heard this version of the mistress's accident. Now she spoke. "And he took Miss Moray to safety, I'll be bound."

"Not quite," said Julia with scorn. "He didn't even dismount from his curricle. He sent his *groom* to inquire, and then drove *away!*"

The incident had developed complications that quite daunted the potboy. He frowned, and his hands began their rhythmic scrubbing motions. Finally he put the cap to it all. "Rather fight t' Bully!"

The prospect of fighting the Bully or of enjoying any other of the manifold delights of a traveling fair seemed as remote to those in the Queen Anne Street boarding-house as a Druid celebration on Midsummer's Eve.

The snow began again on the twenty-fourth of January, and continued. It snowed, and snowed—a great white curtain of white that hid the houses across the street as though with a gauzy veil.

The cruel weather forced most Londoners to stay within doors, but not everyone allowed the weather to keep them home. Two days after the snow started, an event occurred that reduced Becky to fruitless disappointment.

"Drury Lane," she said, in answer to Julia's question. "We could have attended the theater that night, but no, we had to pretend that the snow was too deep to venture out!"

Elsie Hastings pointed out, "Worst snow of the winter."

"But other people were out," said Rebecca, whirling to face her boarder. "An event of this kind—and I was not there!"

"I don't understand," began Julia.

"I'll tell you," said Becky, "if you'll give me a chance."

Since her audience had sat mute for some time, it was a most unfair statement. But neither Elsie nor Julia protested.

"Kean, that's what! A new actor named Something Kean, first time in Drury Lane. He played Shylock in a *black wig.*"

Elsie exchanged a swift glance with Julia. Had the snow addled Miss Moray's mind?

"He was a triumph!" cried Becky. "A black wig and beard, when always Shylock has had hair as red as . . . as Harry's there!"

"But—"

"I know, I know. We can see him when he repeats. But to be there at the first . . ." She pounded her fist into her other palm. When she turned to look again at Elsie and Julia, she burst out laughing. "All right, so I have become demented. I know you think so. But truly, I dearly love the theater. I do believe this is why I stay in London. The *Morning Chronicle* critic called Kean a *portent*, if you will. A new comet lighting up the stage.

"Hazlitt, that's the critic, you know, William Hazlitt, is not easily pleased, either."

"Well," said Elsie prosaically. "I'm glad it's no worse. I thought old Bony had routed the Czar again."

"If it's snowing in France as much as here," laughed Becky abruptly, "the Czar will be as much at home as in Saint Petersburg!"

The newspapers had been crowing about the Grand Campaign that was just starting—a campaign that put thousands of men in the field against Napoleon, on his own ground. Opinion was sharply divided as to whether the French would rise against the invaders, or whether the population was heart-weary after twenty-five years of war. Julia gave world affairs only a passing glance.

She was engrossed in her tutoring of Fanny Skinner. If indeed Napoleon were defeated, Fanny might well travel to Paris with her parents before she had quite mastered the language. Julia had no doubt that Mrs. Skinner would do well enough in whatever country she found herself.

On Julia's second visit to give Fanny her hour's lesson, she was surprised to find three girls instead of one. Jessica and Genevieve, she learned, were to share Fanny's lessons. The hour passed pleasantly enough, and the girls did their best in high good humor, but when the end of the lesson arrived, Julia was dismayed to see that the amount of her stipend was not increased.

"But . . . there are three girls now," she pointed out.

"But the lesson is the same," said Mrs. Skinner with triumphant logic. "So it's no more trouble to you."

It was Julia's first encounter with what she called later

a "real penny-pinching *Cit*." She smiled brightly at Fanny's mother. "Too bad," she said. "I had hoped—"

Mrs. Skinner's eyes narrowed. "I'm sure, miss, you'll see I'm fair enough."

"Of course," agreed Julia with an air of innocence. "But Fanny would have benefited so greatly . . ." She allowed her voice to trail away regretfully.

"You mean you're giving her up?"

"Oh, no," protested Julia. "I gave my promise to teach Fanny French, you see. But I'll be able to give her only a third as much attention now."

"But I'm paying, and I'll expect you to teach Fanny . . . !"

Julia eyed her pleasantly, but said nothing. Mrs. Skinner was, in the long run, no fool. She recognized the advantages of having her daughter taught by a "real lady," and if it cost an extra bit of gold, then it was well worth it. But what she'd say to Mr. Skinner didn't bear thinking on!

So Julia returned home to Queen Anne Street feeling rich as Croesus.

January departed, and February arrived, in heavy snow and bitter cold. Never before had the likes of such cold been felt in London! At least, so everyone said.

At length, young Harry burst in and shouted, "The river's froze over! Froze all the way!"

Suddenly Becky was a girl again. "Such fun! Julia, let's go!"

They went, along with, so it seemed to Julia, the entire population of London. They stopped short on the bank.

"Where is the river?" asked Julia at last. The ice stretched between the new Blackfriars Bridge and old London Bridge, and no doubt farther, but Julia could not see beyond the bridge piers. Besides, there was a sufficient spectacle directly before her to engage her attention.

Lining the ice next to the riverbanks were stalls and booths. Bakers and booksellers, toy shops and printing presses. And through the middle, where the river current would be, was the passage called Freezeland Street.

Julia found herself bewildered by the myriad treats in store. She could not look at them all. No sooner had she become entranced by tumblers, clad in red and yellow tights, flipping themselves into the most intricate movements, than she was caught by the novelty of a newspaper published on a press right out on the frozen surface of the Thames River. *The Freezeland Street Gazette*, making the most of its short existence, bore at the top of the single sheet its motto: "Hot off the Press!"

She was tantalized by the aroma of pork roasting on a spit, and bought a slice. How good it was to have money in her pocket! She glanced around for Becky, but she had moved out of sight. No matter, thought Julia, savoring the meat.

Time flew by. She was hungry again, and found a booth selling brandy balls. She bought some as a treat for Becky. She sampled one, but the taste was too sweet on her tongue.

She lingered, watching a family squabble over a darts game. A Punch and Judy show, surrounded by squealing children, tempted her for a while. She looked once in a while for Becky, in vain. She had never seen so many people, and to think the river current ran deep under their feet! Mostly the people of London had come to make merry at the Frost Fair, but once in a while someone of obviously higher class could be seen. A pair of gentlemen on a snow knoll near the bank, for example, watched the lower orders through quizzing glasses. Julia ignored them.

A voice spoke in her ear. "Ow abaht a hoyster or two?"

The cockney oyster girl was young, thought Julia, no older than herself. "I'll take some!" exclaimed Julia. "This cold air makes me so hungry!"

" 'Ere's harf a doz for the lydy. Too bad them pretty peepers don't have a gent to look at!" said the girl, struck by Julia's violet eyes, her red cheeks, her sweet smile. Nothing of the nob about her!

Julia laughed. "I'm perfectly well satisfied without a gent." Then, giving way to her intense interest in her fellow creatures, she asked, "You have one?" The girl nodded. "What's he like?"

The oyster girl beamed. "He's a one! Beats me proper, 'e does!"

Julia's questions burned on her lips, but the girl was surrounded suddenly by the same family who had fought over the darts game. Apparently they had worked up an enormous appetite. Julia moved away slowly. *Beats* her, did she say?

A short time before, Lord Charles Langley and his friend, Sir Matthew Morrison, the pair of gentlemen watching the scene through their quizzing glasses, were bored. Since this was Charles's usual state of mind, Sir Matthew did not notice. Certainly this was an event of such rarity as to go down in the history books, thought Sir Matthew—not that he read widely, but he was tickled in his vanity to think of being a spectator at such a notable occasion.

Charles at his side scarcely heeded him. Such a tumult over nothing, he thought. The river was frozen, indeed. But such a natural phenomenon required only that he note it, and pass on to more rewarding diversions. He had no intention of joining the rabble in their happy pursuit of the novel, no more than any gentleman would enter into the jollity of Bartholomew Fair.

He had now had a sufficiency of the Frost Fair. He was on the verge of saying so to his companion when he caught sight of a young girl who moved with such grace that she might well be dancing the cotillion at Almack's. His curiosity stirred, and a strange sense of familiarity crept upon him. He had seen her before—he would swear it. But no lady of his acquaintance would venture out upon the frozen river entirely alone, with not even a maid within call.

He watched the slight figure, clad in a bottle-green duffel coat with a hood. She moved from bookstall to sideshow. She stopped, bought oysters. She exchanged a few words with the oyster wench, and then stood a little apart, eating her purchase with every sign of enjoyment. Charles shuddered.

He didn't like puzzles, he told himself. That was the only reason he watched the girl. Clearly she belonged to the exalted sphere in which he spent his own leisure hours. But equally obviously, she was acting in a far less inhibited fashion than any lady of his acquaintance.

It was at that moment that he became aware of an unaccustomed sensation stealing upon him. He was a man up to the mark in all the nice forms of behavior—none of which, for example, included munching oysters in public without the slightest appearance of embarrassment. In truth, the girl's reaction to the Frost Fair—and the cause of his having watched her progress for some minutes—was one of sheer exuberance. Every step was light and quick. She almost darted from one attraction to another. The tilt of her head as she spoke to the oyster girl indicated unaffected enjoyment, even though he could not see her face.

He knew, but did not know how he knew, that he was a witness to a zest for living that he had long forgotten existed. He was conscious that a wellspring had been touched in him, a need that had until now been obscured.

"Matthew," he said, striving to make his voice casual, "what odds that young miss moans on her bed before nightfall?"

"Where?"

"That one, eating oysters. It quite turns me up to think of it." He eyed Matthew speculatively. "Do you know her?"

Matthew searched the crowd obediently. "I don't see . . . Oh, that one with the hood, in green. Or is it the one with her?"

While Charles's attention had wavered, Julia had been joined by Becky. He was relieved, almost as though he himself had arranged that the girl have some sort of protection.

"By Jove!" Sir Matthew's eyes lit up with pleasure, and, quite possibly, something more. "It's Rebecca!"

The pair, unaware of being observed, turned toward them, and Charles knew at once where he had seen that tip-tilted face before—on the road to Brighton, and, most unaccountably, twice in his dreams.

"Rebecca!" repeated Sir Matthew. Always a stickler for the conventions, and disapproving entirely of stuffing one's mouth in public, to say nothing of delicately licking crumbs from the fingers with the point of a pink tongue, he added, "If she's in charge of that minx, she has her hands full!"

Surprisingly, Charles felt a stirring of anger. Minx, indeed! But he was essentially a fair man, and he had to admit that an impartial observer, noting the girl's progress from stall to stall, drinking in the smells and sights—and most obviously the tastes—of what was after all an entertainment for the lower orders, would dismiss her as beneath serious notice.

But it occurred to him, with the force of an unexpected blow from ambush, that he was not quite impartial.

"No," said Charles, memory returning with a rush. "Not Rebecca. *Julia.*"

"Julia," her aunt had called feebly, supine on the road.

He was at once wary. He had much to lose—reputation, to name only one item—and he must walk with great caution. Like a bather, he thought, testing the water lest it be too cold. But his training came to his rescue. With every appearance of disinterested inquiry he said, "Rebecca? Matthew, I've never heard you speak of a Rebecca. You sly dog, you've been keeping her hidden? I never suspected you of a secret dalliance."

He was talking too much, but Matthew paid no heed. "I thought she was dead. Charles, you'll have to excuse me . . ." He started down the slope with the clear intent of approaching the pair. The crowds were thicker now, and before he reached the surface of the ice, the pair had disappeared. Disappointed, he motioned to Charles. "Come on, I've lost her."

Julia was unaware of the eyes on her, as was Becky, or she might have recognized one of them. As it was, Becky said, "I'm going to find some more brandy balls, and then we'd better go home."

"I'll be along in a minute," Julia agreed, cheerfully enough, although she was loath to leave the excitement of the fair.

Charles joined Matthew at the edge of the ice. The snow had been shoveled into high uneven banks to make a flat surface for the booths and the sideshows. "Too bad, Matthew, but you'll be able to find her again. You know who she is."

"Rebecca Moray," said Matthew, still searching the faces of the crowd. "Youngest daughter of the old laird up in Scotland. She ran away, got married. Some artist fellow, I think. Nobody expected it."

Sympathetically Charles suggested, "Was it a blow to you?"

Matthew answered simply, "Thought she was going to marry me."

Charles hesitated. When Matthew did not continue, he asked, "Who is the girl, then?"

Matthew was apologetic. "Only got a glance, don't you know. But she looked enough like Lady Edgeworth to be . . . No doubt about it." He searched his memory. "Young Miss Edgeworth."

Charles was suddenly angry. "What are her parents thinking about, letting her sport down here in this kind of place?"

"No parents. Mother died long since. Rebecca's sister, she was. You must have been with Wellington then, not heard of it. Sir Philip Edgeworth gambled. Lost everything. Cheated the bailiffs at the last. Shot his head off."

Charles said slowly, "I seem to recall. Last summer, wasn't it?"

But Matthew paid him no heed. "I've got to . . ." Clearly emotion made him even more bereft of speech than usual. "Thought she was dead, you know. But she's *not!*"

Julia was, of course, not aware of the intense interest evinced in her affairs. She was reluctant to see the end of this day, but with good grace she accepted Becky's decision. But first, while Becky was supplying herself with sufficient brandy balls to see her through the next day or two, Julia wanted one last look at the fair. The surface of the river was flat, but the snowbanks along the shores provided a vantage point exactly to her taste.

She made her way to the top of a snow ridge. From here she could look out over the heads of the crowd and view the entire panorama of the breathtaking spectacle. The bridges arching over the frozen flood, the brightly colored canopies marking the stalls where the merchants had set up their wares, the happy shouting people—oh, it was the most wonderful sight she had ever seen! It was like market day at home. Even the comforting aroma of roast meat, the snatches of song, reminded her of home. A scuffle broke out in the throng not far away, and she stood on tiptoe, the better to see. She felt her feet slipping . . . she tobogganed down the slope and landed at the feet of Lord Charles Langley.

Without conscious thought, as though it were the most natural thing in the world, he reached down to take her hands. A part of his mind told him: *Minx, for certain!* He

41

pulled her to her feet, and she looked up, and recognized him. She wished she were dead.

"Are you hurt?" he inquired anxiously.

She thought she had sustained some real damage, for why else would her blood pound in her head? Even her skin felt warm. The cold around her, the touch of snow on her legs where her velvet boots had scooped it up in her slide down the slope, were as nothing. Inside her clothing she could feel warmth mantling her body.

His strong hands held hers as tightly as though the two of them were bound together for a limitless moment, or forever. She clung to him, for unaccountably her limbs had suddenly grown weak and quivery.

The sensation lasted only a moment before the spell was broken. Julia was truly exceedingly well-brought-up, but the strange feeling somewhere inside her, demanding her undivided attention, had never been mentioned by Miss Pringle, that peerless governess.

"No, thank you, sir. I'm quite all right." It was as though she listened to a voice from far away, one she did not recognize as her own.

Matthew, intent upon his pursuit of Becky Moray, began, "I say—" but he was too slow off the mark. Charles, his thoughts buzzing like honeybees, seized his arm and all but dragged him away.

Julia stared after them, her cheeks flushed with embarrassment and a rising anger. How deadly he was! He made no secret of his loathing for her—he did not even attempt a civil manner. What a fool he must think her! Always she appeared at a disadvantage—first on the road, mussed from her forceful encounter with a muddy ditch, and now, sliding in the snow like a tomboy, in the most ramshackle manner possible!

She pulled her hood more closely about her face, and retrieved her muff, wondering why she thought her appearance would make a difference to that haughty aristocrat, anyway!

She strove to regain her composure after her noble rescuer had incontinently fled the scene, pulling his companion with him. Strange, she thought, I don't even know his name. Nor does he know mine. But then, she reflected, there was nothing to say to him that she hadn't already tried to say: Thank you for the timely rescue, my lord. She set off to look for Becky.

"You look queer," said Becky bluntly, when she finally caught up with her at a bookstall close to Westminster Bridge. "Is something amiss?"

"Nothing at all," said Julia. It was not truly a lie, for nothing had happened. The tingly feeling when her rescuer had looked into her eyes was gone, to be replaced by an odd queasiness in the pit of her stomach. The sparkle had gone out of the day. It's the oysters, she told herself. Very upsetting to the stomach, especially when added to a variety of other delicacies. Even a healthy digestion like Julia's might be expected to rebel, and even account for that queer breathless feeling when she had encountered the man she loathed beyond all for his arrogance.

They could not find a cab, and walked home through the gathering blue dusk. The lamps shining from the windows of houses they passed sent soft yellow light into the twilight, giving patchy illumination on the snow.

When they reached home, Elsie Hastings was full of her day in charge of the boardinghouse. "Easy as pie," she told Becky enthusiastically, if not tactfully. "We never missed you at all. Mrs. Wilkes made us a fine fish pie for dinner, and afterwards I let Sally go to the fair." She eyed Becky with a dubious air. "I hope you'll agree—I promised Polly she could go tomorrow afternoon. It's something to see, I'll be bound!"

Becky was not quite pleased with Elsie's reordering of the household. "After all," she told Julia later, "we were only gone a few hours."

It was clear that Elsie suffered from idleness. She had spent some years as housekeeper in a large establishment in Hertfordshire. They were not unhappy years, but they were shot through with longing for her beloved London, where she had grown up. At length, the longing for the bright lights and hubbub of the capital grew too strong for her and she gave in her notice.

"Sorry to see me go," she had told Julia. "*That* sorry. She—that is, the mistress—begged me to stay. But I'd studied on it, and made up my mind."

"Were they kind to you?"

She sniffed. "No more than they had to be."

Although she had been overjoyed to breathe in the unsavory aroma of London, to walk the streets in sheer happy nostalgia, yet her hands were unaccustomed to leisure. It had been a blessing when Miss Moray had left her in charge, first when she went to fetch Miss Julia, and now this day of the Frost Fair.

A small idea was born: If she could run her own boardinghouse, life would hold no higher bliss!

Just now she watched Miss Julia climb the stairs with leaden feet. "What happened to her?"

Becky gave Elsie a swift glance. "I asked her that myself," she confided. "She said, nothing." She chuckled suddenly. "Nothing, Elsie, except an inordinate amount of oysters, and gingerbread, and a meat pie from the pieman, and brandy balls, and—I am not sure, but I *think*—a double portion of roast ham."

Elsie said simply, "Good God."

"And then she capped it all by sliding down a snowbank."

Elsie was speechless.

"Somebody picked her up," explained Becky. "I did not see it, but her cloak was snow-covered, and I inquired."

"That explains it," said Elsie comfortably.

Julia sought comfort in her room, but in vain. The ceiling pressed down, and the walls seemed to close in. Was this how it was to be for the rest of her life?

She was oddly overset. What would she ever do? She had no way of meeting any man of her own class to provide her with a future. She was well aware of what her life would be had her parents lived, or even had her father been less improvident.

Now she was left without any resources. There was not even a friend of the family to care what happened to her. She had dear Becky, of course, and she counted herself blessed on that score. But there was a world of society in London to which her birth would, under better circumstances, provide her entry. But no more. Without money for dress, and for at least some kind of dowry, she would have no chance at all.

There could be no husband in her future, not even one who would "beat her proper." Her mood was all the fault of the man who set her on her feet in the snow. He was quite the most odious creature under heaven. She had so

44

decided that gray day on the Brighton Road. Today's encounter had not given her the slightest reason to change her mind.

He could not depart swiftly enough, she recalled. But then, she also remembered the queer breathless feeling she had when his powerful hands pulled her up and she had looked into his anxious gray eyes. Cold, they must have been, but she could not now remember anything but the odd sensation she had of being adrift on a strong current. He had unsettled her, perhaps, but—she told herself—he was nothing to her.

It must have been the oysters.

5

But in the morning, Julia's natural good sense came to the fore again. She threw herself—perhaps with not quite so much enthusiasm as before—into her teaching.

Fanny Skinner was by far the most intelligent of the three pupils. Jessica Matson followed slavishly where Fanny led, stumbling valiantly with *la plume de ma tante* and *le chien de mon oncle*, far in Fanny's wake.

Genevieve Fisher, however, was a ten-year-old who had every trait of twenty years. She had long dark lashes, and already knew how to peek provocatively through them. She had a dainty air, walking as though clouds lay beneath her feet. Her French sentences cast her aunt's pen to the winds. Her interests lay more along the lines of *donnez-moi des bijoux, s'il vous plaît*.

Julia pretended amusement at Genevieve's demand for jewels. But nonetheless, in the privacy of her small blue-and-white room she essayed the same piquant glances that came naturally to her precocious pupil. If only that very superior aristocrat she had met twice could see her now!

She burst out laughing. He was no doubt in the toils of far more experienced enchantresses than she would ever be. The thought did not recommend itself to her.

The Frost Fair had closed as the snows set in. For six weeks the snow fell. The sounds of traffic in the streets were hushed, and none of the residents ventured out for fear of falling. Colds and coughs plagued the household, and the enforced isolation from the world told on dispositions.

Even though affairs in the boardinghouse on Queen Anne Street were barely moving, the residents paralyzed by their longing for an end to the endless winter, affairs elsewhere were progressing more swiftly.

Lord Charles Langley had been stirred to his depths, much against his will, by the pair of frosty violet eyes that had weighed him at first in the balance and, notwithstanding his obvious wealth and breeding and experience, found him wanting.

The second time he saw her—on the frozen bosom of the Thames—it came to him that perhaps there was a chance that the long gray years ahead for him might be alleviated by a glimpse of sunlight.

A revelation had come to him, that day, as unexpected and as blinding as a bolt of lightning. Suddenly he had felt young again. He had had a sudden vision of himself and Harriet, when young, sliding on a pond near Knebworth Castle, and Edward, the oldest, watching with a snowball at the ready in his hand.

It was Julia's zest in her surroundings, the wonder that was in her at all she saw, and the contrast between her freshness and his own ennui that filled him with an uncommon sadness. Had his life come to this? Possessed of all advantages, he was strongly aware of a void in his life. It was not the first time the thought had occurred to him.

But now, for the first time, he knew precisely what he had lost, and the pert child, whose name he now knew, could be his salvation.

His means were sufficient so that his eccentric scheme, formulated at the Frost Fair and refined by serious thought, met no obstacles. In less than two weeks, all was complete, and it was left to Charles only to wait, possessing his soul with what patience he could muster.

The snows stopped in mid-March, and London became a blackened mudhole. As the year turned to spring, and Julia was worn to exhaustion by the unending trays to the sick upstairs, the nursing of colds, the ceaseless hacking of one cougher or another, the soot-colored slush and the heavy skies, her thoughts turned inevitably to Brightoaks, now lost to her forever.

The long gentle hills would soon be a mist of green. The dead leaves would be scoured away from the ground by March winds, and the breeze would turn soft upon the cheek.

The smell of wet, soiled garments forever drying on the fender, the extra work for Julia when Sally fell victim to the common ailment, sorted ill with Julia's recollections of the heady fragrance of small Dutch hyacinths, the satisfying smell of newly turned earth, of spring rains.

Becky, as weary as Julia, demanded diversion. "Two tickets," she announced, brandishing the small pasteboards aloft. "For this very night. Kean is playing at Drury Lane, and we are going."

"But Sally still coughs dreadfully—"

Becky said grandly, "But Sally is not going. You and I are going, and there's an end to it."

Julia, delighted, protested no more. "I've never been to the theater."

Elsie broke in. "I have, and it's precious silly, if you ask me. All on the surface, it is, and you know it's not real. Give me a good penny-a-pitch anytime!"

Becky said, "Don't put her off, Elsie, before she even leaves the house. Harry shall get us a hackney, in good time. I don't want to miss a moment of the play."

They rode east on Oxford Street. When they turned onto curving St. Giles High, already the street was clogged with carriages. The *ton* had discovered Edmund Kean. Falling snow drifted past the lamps burning before the theater doors. At last Becky and Julia found their places within the theater.

Becky glanced at Julia. "Excited?"

Julia answered fervently, even if not with originality, "It's like fairyland! All the lights, the people . . ."

Becky thought: This is the milieu where Julia belongs. Too late for me, for I'm contented enough where I am.

The bill at Drury Lane was to be a repeat of the successful performance of January twenty-sixth. Though Becky had missed the debut of Edmund Kean, this night burst upon her as though freshly minted for her ecstasy.

The theater was not two years old when Julia first saw it. Becky told her the previous structure had burned to the ground five years before, in a spectacular blaze that was seen for miles around London.

This night, Julia was not sure what to expect. But from the first moment that the slight figure of Shylock entered, even though he did not speak at once, she was captured by his magnetism. And a bit later, when he spoke with

48

contempt to Antonio—"Hath a *dog* money?"—she was enraptured.

During an intermission she gazed around her at the fashionable ladies. I'm like a village milkmaid, she thought, up to town for the first time. The gowns in particular caught her fancy. She must remember them all to regale Elsie when she arrived home.

She let her eyes roam, studying the ladies in the boxes as her glance fell on them. There, in a box almost atop the stage, was a splotch of color—an orange-blossom gown, made, judging from the way the folds of cloth lay across the low-cut bodice, of sarsenet. And next to it a water-green gown with a daring décolleté—how did those ladies keep from their death of pneumonia? Julia shivered in sympathy.

There were other gowns on other ladies that were too distant for her to see well. She was aware only of splotches of amber, rose, sapphire blue, punctuated with glancing rainbows from the jewels that Julia was sure were perfectly splendid. She turned to speak to Becky, but her aunt was far away, carried outside herself by the drama just concluded on the stage.

Julia believed Elsie Hastings had the right of it—real life was far more enlivening than even the noblest playacting. For instance, what of the ladies clad in gauzy rainbow hues? Where would they go after the final curtain—home to elegant little suppers of crab cakes and the delicious almond flavor of orgeat, gentlemen attentive to their slightest wish?

Or were the ladies, like their sisters in boardinghouses and in country rectories, subject to vapors and cold drafts and anxieties about their professed lovers?

Becky's elbow nudged her, bringing her back to earth, or more precisely the hard chair in Drury Lane. "Stop staring," she admonished her niece crossly. "Just because you're not sitting in a box is no excuse for forgetting who you are!"

"I'm sorry," murmured Julia. The thought crossed her mind: Who in truth was she? Certainly no longer Miss Edgeworth of Brightoaks! But she had been guilty of staring, quite rudely. When she realized that she was looking for a hawklike profile, a pair of cold gray eyes, she was struck by a lowering feeling. He would not deign even to

49

step around her were she collapsed on the pavement! He would quite simply not know she was there. Her spirits sank, unreasonably, and with determination she set her mind to enjoy the afterpiece without a backward thought.

Becky could—and did—dream for days on the strength of witnessing one performance. It was a revelation to Julia to see her tart-tongued aunt so much a prey to make-believe.

This new life was monotonous and quite unwelcome to Julia, even though she could, most of the time, remember her gratitude for having any kind of life at all, after all of Papa's wealth was sold up. She began to wonder about Becky. Did she regret the impulsive and wildly inappropriate elopement, the folly that had blighted her prospects? Perhaps illusion was more palatable than reality, after all, she thought, recalling the intense drama on the stage of the Drury Lane.

But before they came down out of the clouds of fantasy, the letter came.

It was directed to Miss Julia Edgeworth. She held it in her hand for a long time, looking at the name in the corner. "Ralph Clinton, Esquire," she read.

"Who is he?" Elsie poured another cup of coffee. She had lingered overlong at the breakfast table, and the pot had grown cold. Her curiosity was strong, and she drank the coffee without noticing.

"Somewhere in Chancery Lane, I think," puzzled Julia.

"Well, open it!"

Julia did so, and began to read: " 'The undersigned begs Miss Rebecca Moray and Miss Julia Edgeworth to call upon him at their early convenience . . .' " She broke off to look at her aunt, as mystified as she. "Whatever for?"

Becky reached for the letter. "You'll never find out at this rate. Let me." She glanced down the letter swiftly. "It doesn't say. But wait, here's something. He says, 'Some arrangement that will be profitable. . . .' "

"What can he mean? Who is he?"

"A lawyer, clearly."

Julia eyed her aunt. Shrewdly she commented, "You don't like lawyers."

"Don't trust them."

Julia said musingly, "But he said profitable."

Becky tossed the letter on the table. One corner fell into the marmalade, but she didn't notice. "Profitable to whom? Him, you may well believe."

"What shall we do? Refuse to come?"

"Better yet. We shall ignore the letter entirely."

Julia was not entirely satisfied with her aunt's decision. After all, the letter was addressed to *her*, Julia Edgeworth. But philosophically she conceded the point. "Whatever you think best, Aunt." They sat in silence for a bit, Becky still lost in memory of dealings she had had with the family lawyers that had resulted in her own exile with her ill-chosen husband. Julia still puzzled over the letter. After a bit, she ventured, "Suppose it's one of Papa's gambling friends who has remembered a chit he owes?"

Becky gave her bark of amusement. "More than likely it is one who has remembered your father owed *him*."

There was more truth in that, thought Julia, than she wanted to think about. Eventually Julia reached for the letter. "I just wonder . . . Here, Becky, look at this. He says, 'The client who instructs me is not entirely unknown to Miss Julia Edgeworth.'"

Becky struggled to be fair. "Well, then, it seems you are more closely involved in this than I. It is up to you what you wish to do."

Promptly Julia answered, "See what it's all about." It was clearly not the answer that Becky expected. Julia, watching her, added, "You don't approve."

Becky, in a matter-of-fact voice, said, "I do not like lawyers. Had it not been for one of that profession, I should not have been disinherited upon my marriage."

Disinheritance was indeed a catastrophic price to pay, reflected Julia.

Becky added, "But I will not stand in your way."

Julia, remembering Becky's kindness with gratitude, made up her mind. "Nonsense. There's likely nothing in it for us. The profit is doubtless, as you say, all for the lawyer. We won't go."

But the hand that held the letter shook in spite of herself. It might have been a way out of the grayness of their days. She didn't perceive just how, but it might be . . . She took another glance at Becky's cold face. Nothing would be worth more unhappiness for her aunt. She rose and tossed the letter into the fire. Murmuring an excuse, she left the room quickly, lest the tears that pricked her eyelids overflow.

Left alone with her thoughts, Becky stared into the fire. She noted absently that the letter tossed by Julia failed to reach the flames. It had landed at one side of the grate. Becky's conscience stirred. How dare she stand in the way of something that might, no matter how remotely, be of benefit to Julia?

The child had shown enormous courage in accepting the loss of parent and home, even being left with hardly more than the clothes she stood up in. She had accepted life in what was after all a dreary boardinghouse filled with rheumatic and peevish old women, and never once complained. Indeed, she found herself a handful of pupils, and insisted on contributing her wages to the household.

If Becky had set out to fashion a young lady in accordance with her dreams, she could not have done better than Julia.

If Julia could just come out into Society, if once she bent those devastating violet eyes on any eligible male, there was no doubt in Becky's mind that she could accomplish an advantageous marriage. Any marriage must be better than giving French lessons to impertinent daughters of vulgar Cits!

But Becky could not overcome her real fear of the legal profession. She had been no match for her family's man of affairs. She had tilted with the law, and ended up with nothing. She could not bear to see Julia harassed as she herself had been.

But suddenly, obeying an instinct she did not know she possessed, she swooped upon the letter, lying beside the grate, its edges already beginning to turn brown from the heat. She put the letter in a pigeonhole of her small slant-top desk, next to the ledgers which now showed a neat profit, but certainly no fortune.

If another letter comes, she decided, because this first one has not been answered, then is time enough to reconsider.

By the end of March, the first indications of spring had reached Queen Anne Street, even though no second letter from Mr. Clinton appeared. The tiny lawn at the side of the house, between it and the artist Mr. Turner's studio, turned an improbable shade of green.

With the turn of the season, Fanny's mother sent word that, while French lessons were all very well in the winter, she wished her daughter to be free of educational discipline during the summer months.

"Summer!" exploded Julia. "There's still snow in the areaway!"

But as Fanny did, so did Jessica; and Genevieve the Precocious apparently found other employment more suited to her talents. Julia did not wish to know what it was.

Finally, as the first balmy day came to London, teasing with the promise of spring flowers to come and the end of heavy boots and coats and mufflers to the eyes, Julia began to think again about the letter from Mr. Clinton. Suppose, her fevered fancy suggested, it meant that Brightoaks was not considered a part of Papa's assets and the sale was all a mistake! Suppose after all she could go home again!

Timidly she said, "I wish I had not thrown that letter away."

Like a conjurer at the fair, Becky went to her desk and brought out the letter. She flourished it before Julia's astonished eyes. "Rabbit out of the hat," she said.

"But I burned it!"

"Obviously," said Becky, relieved that the situation was well on its way to being clarified in spite of her own reluctance, "you didn't."

"We can at least see what he wants," Julia said. "No harm in that."

Young Harry was sent with a letter warning Mr. Clinton of Chancery Lane that Miss Moray and Miss Edgeworth would wait upon him at two in the afternoon, two days hence.

Now, all they had to do was wait, somehow, for the two days to pass.

6

On the fateful day, Julia and Becky mounted into a hackney coach summoned by young Harry, and they set out with varying degrees of apprehension for their interview with Mr. Clinton.

Suppose Becky were right? reflected Julia. Suppose this were simply a ruse by a hitherto unsuspected creditor of Papa's, too late to join the others in encompassing Sir Philip's ruin, but loath to be bilked of his money. It was possible, she decided, that a clever money-lender, a veritable Shylock, could devise such a plot.

What could she do?

The vivid recollection of all the trouble she had already seen with bailiffs, seeing Mama's little Queen Anne desk carried out of Brightoaks by rude hands, Papa's guns gone—she could still see Mama sitting at that desk, her own six-year-old hands tugging at Mama's skirt begging for a kiss, Papa's hands caressing the gunstocks. What a sham he was! He loved his guns, loved the intricate carving on the stocks, but he could hardly bring himself even to shoot a fox that was a reputed terror to his tenants' chickens!

Not for the first time, she wondered how Papa, hating even the most necessary violence, could have turned a gun on himself. It passed understanding, unless, as she strongly suspected, it had been another of Papa's ploys gone wrong.

If Sir Philip's luck had held, perhaps she herself would now have a wardrobe full of ball gowns, a box at the theater, and even, possibly, gentlemen always at hand to fetch cups of ratafia, to lead her on Wednesdays out onto the floor at Almack's.

She sighed wistfully, then glanced guiltily at her aunt. If Becky noticed Julia's preoccupation, she did not comment. Julia, feeling an odd pang somewhere in the region of her stomach, almost raised her hand to signal the coachman to return home. But then her common sense returned. Suppose Mr. Clinton really had good news? She might be able to be less of a burden on Becky.

Becky spoke her first words since they had left home. "We'll soon find out what this is all about. Here's Chancery Lane."

They were already turning off Oxford Street. As they stopped before the address given them, Becky remarked, "Let us pray that at least he provides us our hackney fare home."

Julia's curious glance showed her tree-lined walks, and gray hoary buildings, giving the majesty of the law of England a shape and form that was tangible. Reaching back for its foundations to the beginning of time, the Law stood as immutable as these massive buildings, thought Julia—as unchangeable, as immovable . . . and as unfriendly.

She wished they hadn't come.

Becky led the way to a door half-hidden in a gray stone wall. The clerk who let them in was a thin, lanky, awkward boy, ink-stained on fingers, as well as where his nervous hand had rubbed an itchy eyelid, giving him a rakish look. Also, thought Becky with sudden compassion, he looks chronically hungry!

Inquiry trembled on the boy's lips. Julia expected to hear him demand, "Wotcher?" But Becky's austere gaze awed him beyond his capability of speech. "Miss Moray and Miss Edgeworth," she announced. "We are expected."

Indeed they were. The clerk led them up a narrow dark stairway, smelling of recent application of soapy water. On the landing, he pointed to a half-open door. "There he is."

The first room they entered was of good size, and quite inviting. A coal fire burned on the hearth, quietly, as though not to disturb the enormous majesty of the law. The chairs were deep and comfortable, and there was little clutter. Bookshelves lined the room, reminding her of the library at Brightoaks. She wondered whether these books would be as untouched month after month as her father's. Somehow these books gave the impression that they enjoyed human contact frequently.

She was suddenly aware that she had crossed a line from a world with which she was familiar, into a world inhabited exclusively by men. Ladies were tolerated here, but only as one tolerates rainbows—a lovely sight, but not quite relevant to the real affairs of the world.

Even this hunched little man, welcoming them most courteously, was in a curious way superior to them. It was clear even in the charmingly condescending way in which he handed Becky to a chair.

He didn't fit her notion of a man of affairs. He was a wisp of a man, with an obsequious manner, but somehow formidable. Perhaps the power of the law stood behind him, making this little monkeylike man larger than life, and in a way dangerous.

As Julia sat quietly waiting, her glance fell upon a door open to what appeared to be an office behind this pleasant parlor. There were shelves to be seen, each loaded with large boxes of the kind that Julia knew were called deed boxes, holding secrets shameful and others simply private, of entire families. Somewhere, she thought, the affairs of Sir Philip Edgeworth, baronet, were all neatly folded, secured by miles of red tape and equally bright sealing wax. . . .

She came back to her surroundings with a start, to find Mr. Clinton proffering a cup of tea in a green Wedgwood cup, poured from a silver urn on a low table before the fire. Clearly, a part of her mind told her, they were being treated like honored clients, and not like destitute beggars.

At length Julia, having been very well brought up, smiled sunnily on the little lawyer with the clever eyes. "Delicious tea," she commented.

"China," he informed her, adding without modesty, "my own blend. George Berry makes it up to my order."

Becky set her cup down with a click. "I am sure you didn't ask us here simply to enjoy your hospitality, Mr. Clinton."

"Quite right, Miss Moray. I must say it is a pleasure to deal with a female mind of acuteness. That's what I like—to go right to the point. A rare quality, if I may say so, in one of your sex."

56

Julia cast a glance at her aunt. The man was not nearly so clever as she had thought, if he believed that flattery was a way to Miss Moray's favor. As she expected, Becky was not amused. Mr. Clinton cleared his throat, and turned to Julia. "Now to business, Miss Edgeworth. As I understand it, you have no close family ties?"

"You are aware that Miss Moray is my aunt?"

"Of course. But, if I may say so, Miss Moray is on what we may call the distaff side. I had in mind, more particularly, the Edgeworth family?"

"None that I know of, sir."

"Ah, just so." Was it her imagination that Mr. Clinton seemed relieved, even if ever so slightly? Becky's eyes were fastened on him.

"And no friends that come to mind?"

Where was all this leading? Julia, even though she was full of doubt, answered, "We lived an isolated life, Mr. Clinton. Papa thought only of gambling and preferred that I live at home—that is, at Brightoaks, with my governess."

"Oh, yes. It would have been lonely for you here in London, I should think."

He paused, reflecting. Sir Philip's career was well-known to him, gambling at Watier's at first, and then in increasingly less reputable places. It was no life for a child. But then, as he was uncomfortably aware, young Miss Edgeworth was no longer a child.

Becky interrupted his thoughts. "I quite fail to see, sir, your right to ask these questions."

Mr. Clinton, nettled by Becky's interruption, hid his thoughts. "I shall come, Miss Moray, to the point shortly." He had not expected the aunt to be such a dragon. He was to learn at once that he had even yet not plumbed the depths of Becky's character.

She reached for her cloak, placed on a nearby chair. "I think, then, my dear Julia, that we shall return home and wait until Mr. Clinton sees fit to arrive at the burden of his message."

Julia's curiosity was mingled with relief. "Of course, Aunt." She rose and pulled her cloak together under her pointed chin. She knew her duffel cloak was not quite the thing to wear in fashionable London, and bestowed a pang of regret on it. Her manners were flawless. "Thank you, sir, for the tea . . ."

Mr. Clinton was agitated. As Becky rose, so did he. The expression on his simian features was almost pitiful to see. "No, no, ladies. You must not go. I beg your pardon, Miss Moray. Pray do be seated again, ma'am, for you have not heard the reason for my letter to you."

Becky said wryly, "I had thought we were never to hear the reason, sir." She glanced at Julia. "Well, Mr. Clinton," she relented, "we shall stay a moment. But pray have done with these roundaboutations."

Mr. Clinton's relief was obvious, and sincere. His client would not have looked kindly upon a report of failure of any kind. It did not bear thinking on what he would say if Mr. Clinton had to confess he had not broached this confidential matter to them. He bowed.

"Miss Edgeworth," he said hastily, "I am pleased to tell you that you were in error when you considered that you had no friends."

"What?" cried Julia.

Becky exclaimed, "What!"

Mr. Clinton forged ahead. "An old friend of the Edgeworth family—no one you would know, Miss Moray—has just learned of your unfortunate circumstances . . ." He caught Becky's kindling eye and, clearly against his grain, hastened to the point. "The gist of the matter is that the friend, that is, my client, that is"—he foundered, then finally pulled himself out of the morass he had made of his words—"my client wishes to give you a Season in London!"

There, thought Ralph Clinton, it's out, and a more havey-cavey scheme I never heard!

When Julia could collect her wits, she faltered, "Wh-what?"

"A house has been engaged," he went on, "with a suitable address, on Green Street. The house itself is quite modest, but with everyone coming to town in a fortnight or so, it is almost impossible . . ." His voice trailed away, since his audience gave every sign of militant objection.

Becky exploded. "Sir, you take too much on yourself!"

He hurried on, as though she had not spoken. "Credit has been established. For clothes, you know. For milliners, at Gunter's, at Layton & Shear's—"

Julia said, forcefully if not grammatically, "It can't be me!"

"You are to purchase what you will, Miss Edgeworth, and send the bills to me."

Miss Edgeworth said icily, "No."

He quickly assessed her fiery red cheeks, and the frigid look in those remarkable violet eyes. "I act on behalf of my client, I assure you."

Julia told him with scorching scorn, "Pray do not think, because I am female, that I have no wits, sir. You may wrap it up nicely, but what you are offering me is out of the question."

Mr. Clinton's embarrassment stemmed in part from his own agreement with her position, no matter what his client wished. "It is greatly to your advantage, Miss Edgeworth," he told her. "And entirely within the law."

"Then," said Becky, "the law is a fool!"

Julia's wits were indeed sharp. She had already leaped to the question that Becky had not yet reached. "Mr. Clinton, how is it you chose *me* to receive such a shameful offer? We are not acquainted, I believe?"

Mr. Clinton bowed. "I shall hope to remedy that lack in the future."

Julia, surprisingly in control of the conversation, told him, "If I were you, I should not make too much of it, for I see no occasion for a repetition of this interview."

The lawyer grasped her meaning. "Surely you will not refuse?"

Julia echoed him. "*Surely* you would not expect any lady of breeding to accept a *carte blanche?*"

Desperately he pleaded. "Believe me, it is not what you think!" He hoped he was telling the truth. He approved of her, however grudgingly, but he had a duty to his client. "Surely no offer of such a shameful description would be made through a respectable lawyer as I am?"

"I have no experience along that line, I am glad to tell you."

"A young lady, of high birth, with no opportunities for a suitable marriage—"

Becky took a hand, even though Julia was doing very well on her own. "In place of a suitable marriage, then, you dare to make this offer to my niece? If I were a man, I should call you out for this!"

Mr. Clinton's thoughts were chaotic. *Lord forgive me, I've bungled it.* He had expected a swift acceptance of his offer, which was generous beyond his own experience. He was not prepared to have the gilded snare thrown back in his face.

He made a last throw of the dice. "You are included in this proposal, Miss Moray. Did I not make that clear?"

"Who is your client?"

"I'm sorry."

"Well, my good man, *you* cannot be the generous *friend* of whom you spoke," said Becky. "Who is your client?"

"Anonymous. My client insists upon that. But," he added cleverly, "it is only for one Season. It could make all the difference to your charming niece."

Julia had retreated in her mind. It had taken much out of her to defy this strange little man who was giving her her heart's desire. What she had dreamed of for years—clothes, furs, carriage, the gaiety of a social whirl—was now within her grasp. But it was presented in a way that made it completely out of the question. Tears of disappointment stung the back of her eyelids.

The lawyer grew confidential. "Miss Moray, I entirely sympathize with you. Appearances are misleading. But this is most likely your niece's only opportunity to leave Queen Anne Street, to make a marriage suitable to her station in life."

"With such dubious backing? I think not."

He could but silently agree with her. He had initially believed the offer to be just what Miss Moray called it—an "arrangement." But upon seeing Miss Edgeworth, he revised his opinion. Surely his client—while wealthy enough to be humored in whatever idiosyncrasy he manifested—was yet, at least up to now, a nobleman of impeccable integrity. He had, to Ralph Clinton's certain knowledge, indulged in the charms of certain of the Cyprian set, but never had he cast his net at a lady of breeding, especially one hardly out of the schoolroom.

"Come, Julia," said Becky, and this time she could not be coaxed into further discussion.

Mr. Clinton watched them down the stairs. The dragon had a strong sense of duty, he reflected. *She'll see what she owes the girl.* They'd be back, he was certain. He hoped they returned before he had to explain his failure to his aristocratic client.

Julia's tumbling thoughts on their way home made her oblivious of the traffic on Oxford Street, usually a delight to her. Becky's regrets over her own past, tinged with the idea of opportunity unparalleled for Julia, warred silently with the clear knowledge that such an offer could not be accepted.

At length Becky ventured, "Sorry?"

Julia replied, with too much heat, "What nonsense! It was out of the question. What was the use of raising our hopes, only to present such an idiotic . . ." Her voice broke in spite of her valiant efforts.

"You would really like," Becky marveled, "to accept such a shameful offer!"

"Not at all. What a low opinion you have of me! I assure you I am quite wide-awake on that score."

Had Becky prevented Julia's advancement simply because her own chances had been ruined? It was a lowering thought. She could have had her Season, except that she chose to run off with Alfred. Really, Alfredo—of the laughing eyes, at first, and the flashing white-toothed smile until it was really borne in on him that her family, even though connected with earls and dukes, were more tight-fisted than tradesmen when it came to him!

Had she had her Season—what then? Would she have married Matthew Morrison? She would never know.

The cab drew up before the house in Queen Anne Street before Julia spoke. She observed with diffidence, "The only question, dear Becky, is, who do we know who would make such an offer?"

"Or any offer, for that matter," agreed Becky tartly.

A little knowledge is dangerous. Julia had heard this adage many times, but now she knew it was true. Once the idea of a Green Street house had entered the mind, it was well nigh impossible to rout it out as though it had never been.

Elsie Hastings, quivering with curiosity, met them at the door. "What was it? A long-lost uncle left you a fortune? I dreamed of fat sheep last night. That always means money!"

Becky, unsympathetically, said, "Well, tonight dream of

running water. That means prosperity slipped through our fingers!"

Elsie still championed her dream. "Then it *was* money!"

Julia interposed, "At least it was not another of Papa's debts."

"A debt of another kind," Becky commented.

"Before I simply explode like one of those Roman-candle things," Elsie warned, "I wish you would tell me!"

Becky told her.

"House? And servants, and gowns?" Elsie's eyes rounded with wonder. "Some beau you've met, Julia, now confess. Try to think. Who?"

Becky said flatly, "No man who had any sense of honor would even think of such an offer."

Elsie pronounced, "Better a practical gentleman, like this one seems to be, than one with honor. Those honorables are too high in the instep."

Julia was struck by a thought from the blue. "Gentleman! But nobody said 'gentleman'! Now, did he, Becky?"

It was an idea so far unconsidered. "N-no," she said reluctantly.

Julia warmed to her theme. "It could be an ancient lady, too ill to move from her country home. Probably," she improvised, "in Norfolk, where news doesn't come for months!"

Elsie, perhaps seeing, in her mind's eye, herself at the helm of the boardinghouse in Queen Anne Street while Becky moved herself and Julia to Green Street to partake of the delights of the Season, exclaimed, "Then it's a legitimate offer! Of course, you'll take it!"

Julia's warm violet eyes sparkled.

Becky brought them both down to earth with a thud. "We accused Mr. Clinton," she reminded Julia, "of offering a *carte blanche*, and *he didn't say no!*" She surveyed them to judge the impact of her remark, and added, "Now, let's forget the entire incident!"

Hours later, Becky and Julia and even Elsie went to bed, but not to sleep. Each in her own bed was companioned by the oldest temptation in the world.

None contemplated acceptance for a moment, but . . .
What if they did?

7

Julia, resolute, put the unsettling interview out of mind. A phrase used often by the Brightoaks stableman, dear old Follick, echoed in her thoughts. "No use whipping up a dead horse." And Mr. Clinton's offer was certainly dead!

But, unaccountably, the idea, even though dead, refused to lie down decently. It slid furtively around the edges of her waking thoughts, and whirled in mad mazurkas through her dreams.

What if . . . ?

What if *nothing*! she told herself crossly. You need a good shaking, my girl—she continued scolding herself—to bring you to your senses!

The state of mind which could be called "in her senses" was, not surprisingly, uncomfortable. It was not gratifying to consider the unexciting, unvarying rhythms of the hours, from a chilly awakening in her austere bedroom right on down to the monotony of the long games of whist—not for money, at Julia's insistence—in the evening.

Not that Julia was not grateful—far from it. She loved Becky dearly, and knew she was fortunate indeed to be lodged and fed, and loved. She shuddered to think what her lot would have been without her aunt.

But, equally, she was uncharacteristically—for she was an optimist by birth if not by experience—daunted at the prospect of months and years of what she could only think of as dreadful humdrum.

She had not thought much of the future—not until Mr. Clinton, in the unlikely guise of a fairy godmother, had offered to wave his wand and transform the world for her.

What if she accepted? Her reputation could be irretrievably lost. But—so said a part of her mind—what good is a reputation if no one knows you have it?

The inhabitants of what passed for the servants' hall were not unaware that the atmosphere in the house shrieked of tension.

"Seems like a good fight'd clear the air between them two," sniffed Mrs. Wilkes.

"The mistress and Miss Julia?" said Sally.

"Who else? Haven't seen them even pass the time of day between them."

Always fearful, Sally whispered, "Suppose they got to let one of us go?"

Harry, with bravado, boasted, "Won't be me!"

Polly reproved him. "Don't be so sure. Providence may decide to teach you a lesson—all that fighting!"

Harry blinked. "Providence ain't going to pay attention to the likes of me."

"His eye is on the sparrow," his mentor pointed out, her own eye kindling with zeal.

Mrs. Wilkes said sharply, "Don't bring your chapel ways into this house, what with my late husband the sexton of St. Margaret's for half his life!"

Polly subsided grumpily, and the speculation on the trouble between the mistress and her niece died away for lack of fuel.

Elsie Hastings was as aware of the tension in the house as the servants were, but she had the advantage of knowing the cause.

She agreed with the lawyer—a more ramshackle scheme she had never heard of. But she was also a realist, and while she might not approve of the ways of the world, she well knew the rocky road traveled by persons of independent habit.

Look, for instance—she reflected—upon Miss Moray herself. For one bad judgment, she had paid amply and was still paying. Now a reprieve, at least, was offered, and Miss Moray shied at it like a skittish hunter at a five-barred gate.

At length Elsie Hastings made up her mind. Someone in this house needed to have an eye to the main chance, she believed, and if Miss Moray couldn't see it, then Elsie would oblige by pointing out her plain duty.

Her opportunity came swiftly on the heels of her decision. In the night, she heard a soft padding step on the stairs. At once she rose from her bed and, opening her door a crack, peered into the hall. Becky was already at the foot of the stairs.

Elsie, similarly arrayed in nightcap and flannel wrapper, joined Becky in the kitchen. Becky, without turning, asked, "Can't sleep either, Elsie?"

Over steaming cups of tea, the Russian Caravan blend from Becky's private store, Elsie fired her opening guns. "What's keeping you awake? The child?"

Becky's lips tightened. Elsie was far too inquisitive to please her. But "a burden shared is a burden halved" came to her, tinged with the Scottish burr of her old nurse. Now, simply, she said, "Yes." Then, making up her mind to confide, she looked earnestly at Elsie, who was after all the dearest friend she owned. Her eyes were brimming with painful appeal. "Elsie, what shall I do?"

Elsie, in this moment of honesty, rose nobly to the occasion. "Accept the offer."

"But—"

She interrupted. "What's ahead for our dear Julia, if you don't? Marrying a shopkeeper? Keeping her own house?"

Becky grimaced. "I know, I know. But what if this turns sour? I could not bear it if she joined the Cyprian set."

Elsie mused, "Her sweet innocent face would be something new, all right. But I can't believe a shameful offer would come in such a neat fashion, all bound up with lawyers and such."

Becky nodded slowly. "A house in Green Street is at least in a decent quarter." She frowned. "But I truly don't like it, Elsie. I'm responsible for her, and I'm afraid. I don't dare to take the chance."

Shrewdly Elsie countered, "Do you dare *not* to?"

Unaware of that midnight conference, Julia found her thoughts circling around Mr. Clinton's proposal like rooks around their nests at evening. Naturally, the prospective advantages to herself loomed large in her vision, but also, generously, she considered that she must not refuse a life of comfort for Becky.

In the end, the weather took a hand in the affair. It was

65

the very end of March. The weather, typically, was abominable. The wind turned gusty, sending smoke down the chimneys into the rooms, causing strong fits of coughing. Clothes, once wet from rain or snow, refused to dry. Even so, there was a hopeful touch of spring underlying the blustery winds. Julia ignored it.

Seeking refuge in her bedroom, she found no peace. She had brought up a small armchair to add to the comforts of the small attic room. But she must move it to open the drawers of the minuscule chest, and again to open the door to the hall.

"This is outside of enough!" she exclaimed aloud. "There must be another way . . ."

And, always, she returned to the temptations dangled before her by Mr. Clinton.

"At least," she told herself, "I can go look at the house. Perhaps it doesn't even exist—and then I can forget it!"

The next day she wrapped herself in her cloak, still wet around the bottom, and left the house on Queen Anne Street. She turned on Wimpole Street, and then again west on Oxford Street toward the park. She had learned her way around London, at least the west end of it, and knew that Green Street was a small short street off South Audley.

It was a matter of only six blocks or so, but the alteration was as pronounced as though she had landed in the Antipodes. From mere respectability—left behind when she crossed Oxford Street—to dignified superiority in less than a mile!

The geographic distance was one thing. Quite another was the actual leap from boardinghouse to member of the *ton*. Julia had all the requirements—almost. Birth and education, she had. Money and a sponsor, she lacked.

She turned on Green Street. She realized that she did not know which of the neat houses was the one Mr. Clinton had meant. She stopped, bewildered. She had been foolish in the extreme to come. All the houses appeared occupied.

Her disappointment was acute. She put out a hand to steady herself on an iron railing protecting an areaway, and blinked back the tears that stung her eyelids.

Her distress was real. It spoke to a servant passing

along the walk. He stopped. "Are you ill?" He manifestly disapproved of young persons walking alone. When she raised her speaking violet eyes to his, his masculine superiority quivered pleasantly. At the sound of her voice, however, the gulf between them perceptibly widened.

"Is there a vacant house on this street?"

He informed her in an altered tone, "Not to say *empty*, miss. Someone has already rented that one, with the black door. Just last month it was, but I cannot recall the name."

He left her, hurrying as though he had urgent affairs to attend. He looked back once, to see her still standing, but she had somehow lost her despondent look. A very odd affair, he thought, and promptly dismissed her from his mind.

She, on the other hand, clung to his words. Recently taken, he had said. The name he didn't recall. Well, then, that name might well be Miss Julia Edgeworth. Did she dare make further inquiries?

While she stood there, caught up in inchoate speculation, a carriage went by, and then a second passed her. The coachmen looked down at her, as she pressed herself against the railing.

She could have borne insolence in their glance. As it was, they didn't even see her. She was struck to the core. Miss Edgeworth of Brightoaks was not yet accustomed to being ignored by a mere coachman!

By the time she turned again into the shabby—even though most respectable—street she must now call home, she had decided there was really no reason at all for her to accept a coachman's clear disdain.

At Queen Anne Street, her welcome was as cordial as any could possibly be—in Green Street or any other street. When she entered the hall, young Harry skittered across from the parlor to the dining room, carrying a hod of coal for the fire. His gap-toothed grin lit up his freckles when he saw her.

"Back," he said with satisfaction, "and a good thing, too. Missus is *that* cross!"

"Cross? With me?"

"Feared you got kicked by a hansom horse, so she said. I knew you got more sense than that!"

He vanished into the dining room. Julia took off her

67

cloak. The snow-covered hem was unpleasantly clammy when it touched her ankles. It would take forever to dry. Gone were the days when one simply *wore another cloak* if one wished to go out again! And when this cloak wore out, as it gave every sign of doing in indecent haste, even her French-lesson sovereigns might not suffice to obtain a new one.

She sighed. After dinner would be time enough to explain to Becky where she had been.

When they were at last alone, Elsie having gone to her room to write letters, and the other boarders pursuing their own limited interests, Julia said, "I went to look at the house."

It was curious that both knew which house she meant, without further description.

Becky was indignant. "I thought we decided . . . You're behaving idiotish! What have we to do with the house or anything else? I must say you've taken a good deal on yourself!"

Julia, having expected this outburst, waited in some impatience till Becky had vented her disapproval. She was rewarded, at last, by Becky's sudden curiosity. Without warning, Becky's tirade stopped. In a much altered tone she asked, "Was there really a house?"

Julia, heartened, related the events of the afternoon. Becky was silent for so long that Julia feared she was once again summoning the angry words at command.

Julia ventured, "We could leave at the very first sign of anything not quite . . . of anything, well, *havey-cavey!*"

Becky nodded. Then, to Julia's surprise, she revealed her inmost doubts. Surprisingly, the matter of the social conventions seemed no longer a factor. Instead, she said wistfully, "I'm so out of fashion, I wouldn't know where to start." She finished briskly, "But enough of this. It's really out of the question." They spoke then on other subjects for the rest of the evening.

Out of the question or not, Julia had not finished with the proposal. Simply the sight of that house in Green Street—an actual building of stone and mortar, with a fashionable address—was sufficient to bring the entire fantastic proposal into the realm of the possible.

After all, she reasoned, the proposal was addressed to

her, not to Becky, and it should be her decision whether or not to accept it.

When she lived at Brightoaks, and Papa was in London for months at a time, she had learned one thing—from her governess, Miss Pringle; from Mrs. Meggs, the housekeeper; and even from Papa.

She might have called it Julia's Law, so inevitable were its workings: Presented with a request, the answer from Authority will doubtless be negative, quite likely accompanied by tedious scoldings. But presented with a deed already done, Authority grumped a bit and said no more.

It was not far to Chancery Lane, hardly a greater distance than that to Green Street. By the time she arrived at Mr. Clinton's door, she had convinced herself that Becky's fears were make-believe, of the sort to frighten children in the nursery.

Mr. Clinton bent over her hand, appearing more simian than ever. "Ah, Miss Edgeworth!" He looked over her shoulder, clearly expecting to see that dragon of an aunt.

"I came alone," Julia told him. "Your offer was addressed to me, as I believe?" At his somewhat surprised nod, she continued with all her considerable self-possession, "I should like to meet her."

Mr. Clinton appeared dazed. "Her?" Did the girl think he'd abducted her aunt? He shuddered inwardly at the thought. "I don't quite understand?"

"My benefactor," she said with an appearance of calmness. "The old friend of my family." She fixed her lovely eyes on him and waited expectantly.

Mr. Clinton was not proof against even the most innocent of feminine charms. "Her," he said, as he improvised swiftly. "Oh, yes, the *lady*. It is not possible—an invalid, don't you know, who does not wish to undergo the rigors of presenting you in Society, and chooses this way of helping."

Julia did not appear convinced. Hastily he added, "She is certain that Miss Moray will provide adequate chaperonage."

"And so she will," Julia assured him firmly. "Make no mistake about that." Suddenly, in a burst of confidence, she added, "Although I must tell you that my aunt feels sadly out of fashion."

Ralph Clinton was satisfied. Miss Moray's relayed confession told him that the aunt was weakening. He knew the bait was too glittering to turn down. He did not know precisely the details of his client's little game, but at least his own part in it was successful, thank God.

"Have no fear, Miss Edgeworth, that you will be ignored by what I may call the Polite World."

Julia's heart sank. In all her dreams she had not even considered the possibility of a concerted snubbing by the *ton*. Her lips trembled, but she pressed them firmly together while she studied her hands folded in her lap. When she could speak, she said, "How can you be sure?"

For answer, he extracted from a drawer a handful of cream-colored vellum envelopes and wrapped them in a parcel for her.

"Take them home," he advised kindly. "Pray advise me of the date of your removal to Green Street. As soon as possible, you know."

She did not know quite how she got out of his chambers, nor did she remember summoning a hackney to take her home. She moved as in a dream. She had crossed the bridge, so to speak, and only by the most vigorous efforts did she keep from burning it behind her.

Had she done right? What if Becky absolutely refused to go along? Becky was, in simple truth, her lifeline, and she could not do without her. All the way home she framed her speech, selecting reasons which might convince Becky that the deed was done.

Mr. Clinton had all but admitted that her benefactor was a lady—and therefore the proposal was entirely *comme il faut*. Julia was not sufficiently worldly to dwell on his unmistakable hesitation before he agreed with her surmise. Becky would have suspected, rightly, that Mr. Clinton spoke falsehood—but then, Becky had not been there.

In the event, none of Julia's carefully planned speeches was needed. She found Becky surrounded by copies of *La Belle Assemblée*.

Becky confessed, "I have not kept up with fashion." A wistful note crept into her voice as she added, "Even last year, so it seems, no one wore stays anymore. And rows of ruching seem very much *à la mode*, although I must say this gown looks like a hedgehog, all knots of ribbons and ruffles."

Julia could only falter, "New gowns?"

Becky colored. "Well, I thought . . . well, after all, if . . ." Her voice died away.

Julia broke the uncomfortable silence. "No *if*, Becky." To her aunt's wondering expression she added, "I've done it. I've said we'd accept." Impetuously she dropped to her knees and looked into Becky's frowning face. "It will be all right, I promise you."

"You went to Mr. Clinton?"

"I know it was wrong to go alone, but I had to. And he said our Family Friend is an invalid lady. So that's all right."

Her words might be vague, but her meaning was clear enough. No slip on the shoulder, no *carte blanche* with its degrading affluence.

"How do you know?" Becky whispered.

Julia told her Mr. Clinton's explanation. "Too invalid to undergo the rigors. Rigors, Becky? It sounded almost like a sea voyage in a hurricane."

Becky, more to herself than to Julia, murmured, "I don't know . . ."

"Oh!" cried Julia, "I forgot! He gave me a parcel. I'll fetch it."

The parcel contained no more than four cream-colored vellum envelopes. Two were addressed to Miss Julia Edgeworth, the others to Miss Rebecca Moray.

Becky seemed reluctant to open hers. She turned them over, to look again at the superscription. "Miss Moray . . ."

Suddenly she was aware of a jarring divergence in herself. Her younger days stood as close as her shadow, the days when she had been Miss Moray of Shepperton, with invitations by the dozen, and her days and evenings a round of quietly convivial amusements. There had been suitors in those younger days, both insouciant and serious, and as a poet once said, every prospect pleased.

She had thrown her prospects away and her cap over the windmill. For *Alfred*, who had deserted her in squalid rooms in Genoa with only her marriage lines and a handful of lire. He had opportunely died within the month. When she at last made her way to London to scratch out her living, she had taken her own name again.

How different her days would be, she reflected, had she

not defied the customs of her world for what she had thought was true love!

One thing she had learned, she reflected as she reached for the letter opener; her dear Julia would have every chance Becky could give her for a life of comfort.

Noticing Becky's abstraction, Julia said, "What is it?"

Becky laughed, somewhat shakily. "Invitations! These take me back!" she said cheerfully, now as thoroughly committed to the adventure as her niece.

"We can't do it!" Julia tossed a heavy card onto the table in disappointment. "Only a fortnight hence! We can't accept . . . there's no time!"

Becky studied the invitation. Her own was identical. "A ball, at Minton house. Lady Harriet Minton—one of the Langleys of Knebworth, as I recall. Never met any of them, of course." She looked steadily at Julia. "Lady Harriet has an impeccable reputation, my child. This invitation—if it is genuine—makes me much more easy in my mind."

"But . . . so soon!"

"There is much to do, I warrant you," said Becky, gathering up the invitation cards. "Best do it quickly"—her rare smile lit up her features—"before I lose my courage!"

8

The first two weeks of their residence in the house on Green Street flew past on wings swift as eagles.

The removal, under the aegis of Mr. Clinton, was accomplished without so much as a ripple disturbing the dignified purlieus of the fashionable street. One evening the house was without its mistress. By the time the sun rose the next day, Miss Edgeworth and her aunt had been installed in comfort, if not quite with ease of mind.

Only within the shiny black entrance doors, adorned by a gilt lion's-head knocker, were surprises at hand.

The first waited, that first evening, in the black-and-white foyer as the butler, Buell, closed the door behind the new occupants.

A tall angular woman greeted them without the slightest trace of subservience. "Good evening, Miss Edgeworth, Miss Moray. I am Miss Sparrow."

Julia, already at a high pitch of excitement, fought off an onset of unseemly amusement. A creature more unlike a sparrow could not have been imagined. If she had called herself Miss Giraffe, Julia could have accepted the name as evidence of a fitting regard for truth. Lost in her fancies, she missed the first explanation of Miss Sparrow's presence.

When Julia paid heed again, the woman was saying, with a crisp manner that would become familiar to them, "Mr. Clinton feels that you would be glad of my help."

Becky had not lost her composure, at least on the surface. "Pray how do you plan to assist us?"

"Mr. Clinton feels that you may be more comfortable with my counsel on dress." Failing to elicit a favorable response from Becky, she continued, "Mr. Clinton feels that advice on the best shops and"—here Miss Sparrow was clearly choosing her words with great care—"the current fashions."

Becky lifted her hand. "Very well, Miss Sparrow. We shall see. It may be that I shall be glad of your opinions, since I myself have been retired from the fashionable world for some time."

Miss Sparrow bowed her head in agreement. "But," continued Becky, "you will oblige me by deleting Mr. Clinton's name from our future conversations. Mr. Clinton's feelings are of no interest whatever to me."

Miss Sparrow opened her thin lips as though to protest, but clamped them shut again. "Very well," she said, "as you wish."

In the event, Miss Sparrow proved worth her salt.

Clerks or their superiors arrived, in such numbers as to be in danger of treading on each other's heels, bearing samples of a mind-wrenching variety of brocades, satins, India muslins, English poplins, in a bewildering array of colors.

Close behind them came a battery of seamstresses, and an army of glovemakers, plumassiers, and milliners.

Miss Sparrow ordered. She selected—with only token deference to her two charges—harried, threatened, and in less than two weeks, to Becky's stupefaction, wardrobes were comfortably full of gowns and cloaks, shoe racks were laden with satin slippers of colors to match a myriad of new gowns.

Gauzy spangled shawls and scarves lay neatly in drawers. A stunning variety of hats lay readily to hand in hatboxes.

But at length, the whirlwind died away, and Miss Sparrow professed herself satisfied.

Becky had lost her initial mistrust of this latest example of Mr. Clinton's obtrusive attention to their needs. Indeed, she was conscious of an unexpected pang of regret at the thought of Miss Sparrow's imminent departure. She said as much to Julia.

"And how she has kept Buell in line!" Julia exclaimed. The butler was quite the most intimidating person she had ever met. He was no more than middle-aged, but he gave the impression—carefully nurtured as part of his service—that very few of the *ton*, no matter how well-bred or wealthy, came up to his exacting standards. The first few days of their residence had been distinctly lowering to Julia's self-esteem, until Miss Sparrow, in the intervals of her other duties, had somehow given Buell to understand that his continued tenure in his veritable plum of employment was dependent upon a clear change in his attitude. Buell was nothing if not alert to the main chance, and Julia was much gratified in the alteration she saw in him.

"I am sure he doesn't approve of us above half!" she confided to Becky.

"He is quite right, you know. Even *I* don't approve of us!"

"Oh, Becky!" After a moment, Julia inquired timidly, "Do you truly wish we hadn't agreed to this . . . adventure?"

Becky smiled fondly upon her niece. "In for a penny," she pronounced, "in for a pound. Let us keep Miss Sparrow."

"How can we? Mr. Clinton told us, you recall, that she was simply to arrange to put us into gowns of fashion. He must have other duties for her when she has finished here."

"Mr. Clinton," said Becky grandly, "will have to seek out another person, if there is such another paragon in London, which I truly doubt."

"But," protested Julia, "if Mr. Clinton feels he has done quite enough for us—"

"What Mr. Clinton feels," Becky interrupted firmly, "he may refer to his client."

Miss Sparrow was summoned to the breakfast room, provided with a cup of hot chocolate, and made to sit down.

Becky began, "I am sure you are aware, Miss Sparrow, that we are deeply grateful to you. I can't think how we would have gone on without your help."

The paragon's cheeks grew pink. She mumbled a few inaudible words. Becky kindly overlooked Miss Sparrow's obvious embarrassment, and came to the point. "We should like you to stay with us."

Clearly Miss Sparrow had not expected this development. "But, I don't know . . . I can't—"

Julia burst in. "We are such babes in the woods, Miss Sparrow. We truly need you. Please say yes!"

It was quite possible that Miss Sparrow had never before been told that she was needed. At least, she was stunned now to the point that her lips opened to speak but no sound came.

"Not quite babes in the woods," corrected Becky dryly, "but I confess I should feel easier in my mind if you were to stay." Then she continued, "I'll make it right with Mr. Clinton." She hoped she could.

At length, Miss Sparrow found her voice. "Well, I must say . . . Yes, I'll do it!" she finished with a nod of her head that could have been the same gesture used by Julius Caesar when he gave the order to cross the Rubicon.

"Besides," said Julia mischievously, "no one else can keep Buell in his place!"

Miss Sparrow unbent. "It's simply a matter of economics," she confided. "I have told him that one step out of line will mean he can find his next position fishing in the Thames, for all of me!"

"Bravo!" cried Julia.

Miss Sparrow's energetic efforts had borne fruit. The household was in order and the wardrobes filled, barely in time for the first foray of Becky and Julia into Society.

The paragon's approval as she stood in the foyer watching them descend was obvious. Julia floated down the stairs, dressed most appropriately in marigold-yellow, with a draped tunic à la romaine, embroidered tastefully with small rows of seed pearls, while her duenna had chosen a cornflower-blue crape worn over a slip of white sarsnet. Becky reflected with satisfaction that she still had a fashionable figure. No one will look at me twice, she decided, once they have taken in Julia's ravishing beauty, and been struck by those speaking violet eyes. But that was the point, after all, she told herself—to get Julia well and truly launched.

Miss Sparrow watched them enter their coach—newly hired, of course—and be driven away in the direction of Lady Harriet Minton's. Now I know, she thought, just how a fairy godmother feels!

Julia was soon enveloped by an anxious dream. She could hardly believe her good fortune, gowned exquisitely, ready for an evening of the most delightful entertainment. But suppose she managed, in her inexperience, to perpetrate some dreadful *gaffe*, some reprehensible deed that would close the doors of Society, now only just ajar, in her face forever?

"Becky . . . ?"

"What is it?"

"I'm terribly afraid, Becky. Let's go home!"

Becky, who shared her feelings exactly, said stoutly, "We can't. Look at the crush of carriages! We'll never be able to turn around."

"Maybe," said Julia in a small voice, "there will be so many people they won't see us."

Her aunt, judging, quite correctly, that rumor had passed swiftly through fashionable circles concerning the mysterious new tenants of the house on Green Street, forbore to answer.

In the event, the party was a mad crush. The stairs were crowded, with guests waiting their turn at the receiving line. Julia thought at first the staircase was buried under a mass of feathers. Quite odd! But beneath the plumes were beautiful scented ladies in beautiful fragile gowns, and the hum of their conversation sounded like a hive of unduly energetic bees.

When their turn came to greet their hostess, Lady Harriet, quite surprisingly, took both Julia's hands in hers. "My dear, I am so glad you could come. How pretty you are! I am sure you will cut a wide swath through all our young men!" She turned to a tall, elegant man standing nearby. "Charles, I beg you take Miss Edgeworth, and see that she enjoys herself."

Julia stared, most rudely. For Charles was the insufferably superior gentleman she had seen before, and loathed quite strongly!

Strangely, he didn't seem quite so arrogant now. He bent over her hand and drew her with him into another room, where there was music and the promise of dancing.

"I must apologize for my sister," said her escort. "She failed to introduce us properly. I am Charles Langley."

Sister!

Julia was unaccountably relieved. For a moment she had feared—and "feared" was quite the right word—that the escort Lady Harriet had cavalierly summoned was her husband.

Lady Harriet had, for once in her life, forgotten her exquisite manners. Reluctantly she had sent invitations to the unknown Miss Edgeworth, and the equally unknown Miss Moray, simply on the strength of Charles's wishes. Now, seeing the winsome sweetness of Miss Edgeworth and noting with approval the undisputed quality of Miss Moray, she was satisfied. Charles had not imposed upon his sister.

She believed she knew what Charles had in mind. If he made either of these women her sister-in-law, Lady Harriet decided she would much prefer her to Edward's wife!

Julia, who had wanted to remember every slightest word anyone said to her, to take note of every gown and every jewel winking in the light from what must be thousands of wax candles, could remember none. It was like a dream, in which certain small incidents loom large in the memory, while whatever held the incidents together faded quite away.

She remembered that Lord Charles Langley, while grave and reserved, had yet kindly led her onto the floor for the first set of country dances. It was a mark of signal honor, had she known it.

She recalled meeting many persons whose names and faces whirled through her mind, not pausing long enough to be fixed. There was Napier Wood, a serious young man clearly smitten at first glance. She was introduced to Lady Keniston, and must have responded prettily, for the turbaned head nodded graciously, and young Aubrey Keniston was produced for an introduction, and a dance. Julia loved to dance, and this night her dream came true. She danced country dances without ceasing. A number of nameless men partnered her, and she was quite surprised to find that Charles sought her hand for the *second time!* An overwhelming honor, and one likely to give her a *succès fou!*

The rhythmic pairing was conventional, save for one very odd circumstance. When Charles came to her again, she could have greeted him like an old friend. She had seen him before, after all, even though she did not remember the occasions with much pleasure.

But in this sea of unknown faces, even one she disliked was welcome, because familiar.

"You dance well," he said as he propelled her through the steps.

"I was well taught," she said briefly. Then, deciding that she had been rude, she favored him with a smile that had dazzled many a man before, from the groom who had taught her to ride her first pony down to the apologetic bailiff who carried off the Edgeworth possessions. Charles, to his surprise, was no more proof against it than any other.

The evening was enchanted, she thought. She even was conscious of a kindly feeling toward Lord Charles, heightened by her disconcerting awareness of the titillating aroma of his shaving soap.

If Julia's attention was totally engaged by the necessity of watching her steps, Becky's nerves were stretched taut as a fiddle string. One tweak, she was positive, would send her up into the boughs. The tweak was provided. Becky, having been greeted most kindly by Lady Harriet, was now standing somewhat apart. Nearby she noticed a couple she did not fancy at all. The man was long of face and wild of eye. If he were a horse, Becky decided, she would consider him unsound and no bargain. His companion was a fair-haired beauty of statuesque proportions, clad in satin cunningly draped to show her truly magnificent figure. A glossy pair.

A voice spoke in her ear. "A charming child," said Sir Matthew Morrison.

Becky whirled, her heart unaccountably pounding. "Matthew!"

The years fell away, and she was sixteen again, on the bank of what was called a rushing burn, and this very man was holding her hand, so tongue-tied he could do no more than gaze calflike at her. His gaze just now was far from vernal. Instead, she realized that he was in truth a man of the world, sophisticated in the extreme. She felt the veriest green girl.

"It's been a long time," said Sir Matthew, upon realizing that she was speechless, "but I remember that you were the lightest dancer in all Scotland. Have you changed?"

"Greatly, I fear. Matthew, what . . . ?"

Sir Matthew's smile came readily. "We can dance and talk at the same time, m'dear. Come."

He led her onto the floor to make up a set with the couple she had noticed. He had barely time to make introductions before the music began. "Sir Vincent Fitzgerald, Miss Sutherland, Miss Moray."

Before Becky collected Julia—some four sets later—and called for the carriage, Becky had shed fifteen years and an encrusted disposition, at least for the present.

"When I wake up tomorrow," Julia said to Becky as they parted in the upper hall to go to their bedrooms, "or rather *today*, I'm positive that there will be a shattered pumpkin in the hall."

Becky agreed wholeheartedly. The entire evening had borne more than one resemblance to Cinderella's ball.

"I hope," she said in high good humor, "that Buell can deal with the Coachman Rat!"

9

Late the next morning, when Julia descended to the breakfast room to join Becky and Miss Sparrow, she had become an overnight sensation.

"Well, slug-a-bed," Becky greeted her fondly. "You must strive for more stamina, my dear. There will be many more nights like yestereve, I expect."

Buell had reluctantly, at Miss Sparrow's direction, been forced to restrain his curiosity and leave the dishes on warmers on the buffet. Julia poured herself a cup of hot chocolate and sat down at the table.

"Stamina!" she exclaimed presently. "I have a sufficiency of that, if only my feet didn't hurt so! I vow they were near dropping off my ankles last night."

Miss Sparrow was genuinely amused. "One must conclude, then, that you danced every set!"

"I did! It was such fun!"

Miss Sparrow, who had received little description of the first evening in Society from Becky, bent her search for vicarious entertainment toward Julia. "Even the first set after you arrived?"

"Oh, yes. Lady Harriet was so kind. She asked her brother to partner me, and do you know who he is?"

Miss Sparrow knew very well. "Lord Charles Langley, brother of the Duke of Knebworth."

Julia brushed aside such preciseness. "He was that odious man who came along when our coach overturned!"

Miss Sparrow, not having heard the tale, was mystified, and Julia informed her. "But," asked Miss Sparrow, "he did not abandon you last evening?"

"Oh, no, he was quite proper. After all, it was his sister's house!"

Curiosity prodded Becky. "What did you say to him? As I recall, you had a good deal to tell him on the road!"

"Nothing."

"*Nothing?*"

Surprisingly, Julia appeared flustered. "Nothing to signify. He did say I danced well."

Becky persisted. "Did he remember meeting you before?"

"No. But to tell the truth, he is not curious about me now!"

Becky's doubts, which had kept her intermittent company since Ralph Clinton's first letter, melted away. To see her dear niece so ecstatic as to float a few inches above the floor made it all worthwhile. No matter what might lie ahead, no matter the unsettling intrusion of Matthew Morrison into her own life again—at least, Julia was happy.

"I danced with so many," said that young lady now, dreamily, "there was someone named Poulteney, and Aubrey Keniston, and a young man named Wood, and . . . I don't remember them all. But Lord Charles danced with me twice! Wasn't that kind?"

Miss Sparrow twinkled with amusement. "Kind? I believe you told me he was haughty, and drove away in his curricle? Is this the same person?"

Julia nodded. "It does seem odd. But then, his manners are flawless, no matter how toplofty he considers himself."

"He can give you enormous credit in the world," pronounced Miss Sparrow. "It would be well to cultivate him."

Julia's thoughts so far had lain less along the lines of cultivating Lord Charles, and more along the lines of tilling him under like a crop of fall rye. But, ever practical, she promised to consider overlooking his many faults in the interests of her own enjoyment of her new life. Kindness was indeed a rare enough quality to be valued.

Julia was sure that happiness lay just ahead, as soon as she became more comfortable in her present circumstances. She was not as a rule given to much reflection, but she was not a fool, and she knew that, no matter how she persuaded herself that Mr. Clinton's arrangements were entirely acceptable, the truth was quite otherwise.

And, since she was not of a devious nature, she believed that, sooner or later, the truth would out. In that event—optimistically, far in the future—she would quite simply sink into well-deserved oblivion.

In the meantime, there was a certainty of routs and afternoon teas and dinners and card parties and levees at Clarence House to look forward to. And if she were not ecstatically happy, she told herself, it was very definitely her own fault.

A *succès fou*, Miss Sparrow had pronounced her, quite rightly.

Indeed, the hitherto unknown Julia Edgeworth was the subject of more than one breakfast-table conversation in London. As a result, cards of invitation began to arrive in a veritable flood. As well, callers came in person, leaving their cards on the silver tray in the foyer, to Buell's growing stupefaction. Quite the belles of Society, were the mistress and the young mistress, and who would have thought it, coming out of nowhere, as you might say. Certainly not Buell.

One privileged caller who was admitted to the small drawing room was Sir Matthew Morrison. Sir Matthew, up to now, had been, if not satisfied, at least resigned to his rather austere life. Not that he was out of pocket—on the contrary, a series of timely departures from this world of moderately remote but prosperous relatives had put him well beforehand with the world. To call him, in fact, a nabob would not have been far off the mark. Even so, his fortune fell short in comparison with that of Lord Charles Langley.

But he had been disappointed in his youth, when Miss Rebecca Moray had found the wiles of her Italian tutor beyond resisting. While Sir Matthew had endeavored to console himself, he had not found anyone whom he fancied. The reappearance of Miss Moray had struck him as by a thunderbolt. He was sufficiently Scottish not to delude himself. The plain fact was that he was as much in love with her as ever. This time he would not let her escape again.

He called on her the morning after Lady Harriet's ball. There was much to say. Becky's eyes were anxious. "You are limping, Matthew."

"A small souvenir of Valladolid."

"I didn't know."

"No reason why you should, m'dear."

"Is Napoleon truly out of it now?"

"So I believe. He abdicated early in April, you know. Half of London has gone to Paris already. Napoleon is going into exile, traveling in a British warship, of course, and the Bourbons are back on the throne . . . To the devil with this! Becky, what's happened to you? Are you forced to dragon this perfectly lovely child? Is there no one else to sponsor her?"

"No one at all. She is my niece, you know, dear Verbena's daughter, and I am quite overjoyed to see her in her proper sphere."

He asked, "What of yourself?"

She shrugged. There was no possible answer. He paused, before adding in an altered tone, "It is only that I feel you must put me at a distance."

Becky was conscious of a surprisingly coquettish feeling. Her youth seemed to surge back, even though ten years of hard living had taken their toll, and dear Matthew limped and had turned gray—a most distinguished gray, however—at the temples.

Lightly she said, "You don't enjoy being at a distance?"

"Nor will I accept it, my girl!"

"I'm not your girl."

With firmness, he told her, "You were once, and I see little change in you."

The gay mood left her as abruptly as it had come. Sadly she looked at her hands, folded in her lap. "But, Matthew, I have changed. You don't know me anymore."

Matthew forced himself to stay strictly apart from her, in order not to make haste disastrously. In the military terms with which he was familiar, he must be careful not to overrun his van. Apparently on a tangent, he inquired, "How long do you expect to subject yourself to this duenna life?"

"Subject myself? Matthew, I am not suffering. Indeed, I am more comfortable than I have been for . . . some time. And Julia is a joy always."

"After she marries, then?"

"You think she will?"

"I have every trust in your ability to arrange a marriage of peerless advantage."

"Now, Matthew, stop teasing."

"I have never been more serious, I assure you. And when that happy event transpires, what then?"

Becky's thoughts flew back to Queen Anne Street, quite without pleasure. But she could not share her past with Matthew, not yet at least, and quite likely, never. "Pray, dear Matthew, do not trouble yourself about me. I shall come out all right."

Matthew forebore to answer. *I shall see that you do*, he vowed. Talking of other subjects, he lingered for a proper ten minutes before taking his departure.

Matthew's belief in Becky's ability to bring off a suitable marriage for Julia raised her spirits inordinately. She would not have been so complacent had she been *au courant* with Dame Rumor. But, in truth, Julia was not at fault for the proliferation of Dame Rumor's more lively tales. She was just being herself at Clarence House when she curtsied to the grossly fat Prince Regent, and—instead of being courteously awe-stricken—she smiled in a most intimate way at him and allowed him to hold her hand while he kissed it lingeringly.

"A nice gel," wheezed Royalty. "If I were ten years younger, I'd take a chance!"

Lady Jersey, nearby, was heard to say, "*Thirty* years, more likely. *And* ten stone the less!"

Julia confided to Lord Charles, "Poor man, he has such unhappy eyes!"

It was mere ignorance that led her to exclaim to the seventh Earl of Elgin and eleventh Earl of Kincardine, formerly envoy extraordinary to the Porte, "What a benefactor of humanity you are—to bring such beautiful works of art to England as a gift to us all!" Since the Earl was currently engaged in acrimonious negotiations with Government over the enormous price he wanted for the Parthenon statues, he was more than indignant.

And the more kindly of her acquaintance called her simply a dear sweet girl for demanding with passion that the Keeper of the Tower Menagerie provide at least two loads of fresh straw for the lion's couch.

In due course, notwithstanding the gossip mill, vouchers for Almack's arrived in Green Street, to Miss Sparrow's unfeigned delight.

"I knew that Lord Charles—and of course his sister—could help you greatly!"

Becky demurred. "Julia beguiled the Countess of Lieven, that's the nub of it."

Miss Sparrow said no more, but she knew what she knew. Sir Matthew Morrison had called often enough to serve as escort to Miss Moray—and incidentally Miss Edgeworth—and to Miss Sparrow's way of thinking, it was no mere happenstance that Lord Charles occasionally accompanied his good friend.

But Lord Charles did not accompany Julia and Becky to their first appearance at Almack's. To be seen at the Wednesday-evening subscription balls in the Assembly Rooms in King Street was the pinnacle of social ambition.

The reasons for its reputation were flimsy at best. The refreshments were minimal. Bread and butter, or stale cake as a special treat, provided little temptation, even with a choice of lemonade or tea to follow. Even the dancing seemed overly decorous, to the point of dullness.

Julia was not at all loath to be drawn from the dance floor by Lord Charles, who arrived shortly after she and Becky had, and rest for a bit on a settee along the wall. She was content to watch the dancers in silence, and Lord Charles was equally satisfied to watch her from the corner of his eye.

At length, Julia turned impulsively to Charles. "You know, it's not quite what I expected. Not that I'm not most grateful to the Patronesses for inviting us, but . . . it's disappointing!"

Charles, much amused, wondered, "What *did* you expect?"

Promptly Julia told him. "An anteroom to Paradise!"

"It is certainly not that. But one must be seen, you know."

"I wonder why. Well, I don't precisely wonder. I am certainly aware that it is greatly to one's advantage to be seen here." She glanced shyly at Charles, whose kindness in noticing that she was just a bit tired of dancing had put her quite in charity with him. Her mischievous impulse provoked her to add, "You know it puts me much in favor, Lord Charles, to receive such marked attention from such a Corinthian as you. You are most generous!"

Charles, believing he was successfully concealing his immediate resentment, said, "Pray forgive my vanity in intruding upon your company. Believe me——"

Julia's violet eyes were at once full of remorse. "Oh, sir, I did not mean to injure your feelings! I do enjoy your company!"

Charles made as though to leave. But her eyes tethered him, and he could not move. He told himself that, only because he realized what damage would be done to her reputation, were he to leave her abruptly, did he force himself to remain with her. But in a few moments he found an opportunity to place her in the hands of Napier Wood, and left the Assembly Rooms, alone.

Later, Napier led her onto the floor for the next set. It seemed awkward to dance in total silence, so she ventured, "I have not seen Aubrey Keniston this evening. Does he not come here?"

"Lady Keniston is ill, I believe, and Aubrey does not leave her."

"I'm sorry. I trust she is not in danger?"

"I shouldn't think so. She was quite up to snuff in the park yesterday. Gave Fitzgerald quite a setdown."

Julia said warmly, "Oh, dear."

Napier, quite coolly, said, "No pity for him. He'll always land on his feet. Nine lives, like a cat. He is a gazetted fortune-hunter, you know."

"But I have no . . ." She broke off just in time. She almost gave the game away.

Napier didn't notice. Bent on protecting her, he warned her strongly, "He's one to stay clear of."

Before the set was done, a stir at the door announced the arrival of Miss Maria Sutherland, escorted by an assortment of young men. She appeared in need of their attention, for one held her cloak, another her spangled shawl. A third offered his hand to help her through the throng. Her vivacious laugh had the effect of an announcement of her presence to those assembled.

She caught up with Lady Norland and Amelia, who had arrived just before her. Lady Norland had no affection for Miss Sutherland. With intent, she said, "I do not see Langley with you?"

"No, I do not expect him," said Miss Sutherland easily, giving an impression of intimate knowledge of his plans.

Mr. Poulteney protested, "But he was here, don't you know." All eyes turned to him. Embarrassed, he could do nothing but forge ahead. "Danced with Miss Edgeworth. Seemed to enjoy himself." His evil genius prompted him to add, "For once."

Since in previous attendances at Almack's Langley had usually accompanied Miss Sutherland, the result of this remark was not happy.

Miss Sutherland looked long across the room at Julia, who was preparing to leave with Becky. Miss Sutherland laughed shortly and tossed her head. "He likes to be amused, you know!"

Julia's reflections upon her first venture into Almack's Assembly Rooms were mixed. She had truly enjoyed Lord Charles's company. He had put aside all his haughtiness for the evening, and in truth he could be most amusing company.

But Napier's instructions to avoid Sir Vincent Fitzgerald rankled. A gazetted fortune-hunter he might well be, but since she had no fortune nor the prospect of any, she was not at hazard with him. Nor was she grateful for Napier's well-meant advice. He took entirely too much upon himself. Just the same, she would be careful not to be alone with Sir Vincent. In any event, she saw him very seldom.

She did not reckon, however, with Sir Vincent himself. While he was no longer admitted within the portals of Almack's, he nonetheless was not ignorant of what came to pass in those august precincts.

The unusual event, then, of Lord Charles Langley's attention to the lovely, if somewhat mysterious, Miss Edgeworth and his departure before the arrival of Miss Sutherland, whose future as Lady Langley was expected by all who knew her, was known to Sir Vincent as early as the breakfast hour the next day.

Forking his scrambled eggs and ham, he also had food for thought. Sir Vincent was at best without sufficient funds. Born of an impoverished Irish family, he had gambled on making his fortune in London. The cards had run his way long enough for him to believe himself the darling of Lady Luck. Alas, his good fortune had ebbed.

He still had funds enough to enable him to live in decent circumstances on his meager estates in Ireland, but he had tasted the delights of the greater, glittering world, and he would be loath to give it up.

In fact, there was little he wouldn't undertake if it helped him avoid a return to the land of his fathers.

He had somehow failed to make an advantageous marriage. His soiled reputation kept him—to make use of a phrase of his homeland—beyond the pale of heiresses. Now, to his intense interest, swam across his horizon a new possibility.

Miss Edgeworth's breeding was *comme il faut*, he knew. Her father, however, had left her without a feather to fly with, and in the ordinary way, Sir Vincent would not give her a second look. But as he assessed his position, it was clear to him that Miss Edgeworth might well be his last chance. There was undoubtedly money somewhere in her background, for her address and her apparel spoke the language of lucre, and only that dragon of an aunt to guard it.

Sir Vincent's thoughts moved with purpose upon devious paths. At length, he was satisfied with the results. His first move was to call upon Miss Maria Sutherland.

That lady, secure in the knowledge of her own worth, and possessed of the experience of five years in Society, had no qualms about receiving him. Indeed, she was delighted.

She greeted him in a small salon just off the foyer of her Berkeley Square house.

"I trust I do not intrude upon your plans?" he began.

"My thoughts are poor company." She brought him to sit near her. "Tell me some gossip."

"I came to you for some. The newest comet in the heavens—who is she?"

"Miss Edgeworth, I suppose you mean." Her tone turned vicious. "A minx!"

Sir Vincent's voice purred with understanding. "I believe I have heard that even Langley is interested?"

"He can't be. An idiosyncratic aberration, that's all!"

"That's not quite what I hear. He went to Almack's—so my informant tells me—particularly to meet her."

Miss Sutherland believed she concealed her agitation well. "Nonsense!"

He was not deceived. He had caught the telltale tightening of her fingers on the arms of her chair. He was hot upon the scent! Silently he let her see that he did not believe her protestations. Aloud he said, "Wherein lies her charm? Is it money?"

She regained her poise. "Money? Langley needs none."

"But not all are so . . . fortunate."

Dimly, in the back of her mind, shapes began to shift vaguely. Later they might form themselves into a scheme, but just now she could not recognize them. She knew, however, she must do nothing to banish . . . whatever they were.

With guile, she agreed with Sir Vincent. "Miss Edgeworth must have funds. Where do they come from?"

"I confess I am much more interested in their ultimate destination."

"I wish you good fortune."

Smoothly Sir Vincent suggested, "Perhaps there is more needed than good fortune. Perhaps a nudge in the right place?" Having made his initial point, he was ready to leave. "Perhaps I may call on you again?"

Miss Sutherland, seeing her future, which she had considered certain, in danger of being whistled down the wind, said glumly, "At any time."

10

The month of May 1814 had completed its appointed rounds and handed over to June. While May had been eventful for Julia, it had also contained memorable moments for certain others.

Ex-Emperor Napoleon Bonaparte had spent all of the month save three days on an island he had not even dreamed of, much less expected to be conveyed thither aboard a British warship. Louis, the eighteenth of that name, had mounted the throne of his ancestors, having learned nothing from the events of the past quarter-century.

The Grand Alliance of armies that had driven Napoleon eventually to Elba had broken up, and only the Commanders were still to be reckoned with, since the Prince Regent had invited Czar Alexander of Russia and King Frederick of Prussia to England for a Victory Celebration.

As in large affairs—said a certain wise man in another century—so in small. The restricted world of London Society saw its own alliances, marriages sanctified by contract if not by undying passion.

Julia was not one of the ladies claimed as bride. She was relishing her days as a child might, loosed in a confectionery's. It was a marvel to Lord Charles that her zest for enjoyment never flagged.

It was true that at times there were dark smudges under her violet eyes, telling of sleepless nights, and sometimes she was pale from headache. Charles, at those moments, was half-inclined to make his next move. But he was possessed of unlimited patience, and found his reward in her swift restoration to glowing health.

Julia was not aware that Lord Charles paid particular heed to her state of mind. She had noticed that he seemed always to be in view, somewhere in what an artist might call Middle Distance, but since his grave expression altered only rarely, she was not privy to his thoughts.

That was not to say she was not curious. She had been born with a lively interest in her fellows of low and high degree, and it would have been demanding far too much of her to ignore even Charles. Besides, a distressing tendency to shortness of breath and a certain unsteadiness in her knees when he spoke to her caused her to be quiveringly aware of his proximity, even when, as was more and more frequently the case, Napier Wood was her devoted escort.

Julia was not the only one who was conscious of Charles's presence. Miss Maria Sutherland's light blue eyes missed little that had bearing on her own interests. She considered Lord Charles Langley, whom she once had expected almost daily to offer for her, as a prime concern.

Unused to what she could only consider shabby treatment, she was not sure how to deal. In the event, she lost her grip on diplomacy. Catching Lady Harriet alone for a moment at a supper at Devonshire House, she said with insincere sympathy, "How shocked you must be by that hoydenish Miss Edgeworth! I wonder you do not drop her!"

Stiffly Lady Harriet replied, "I find her delightfully unaffected."

Miss Sutherland next mentioned, in the most concerned way possible, to Lady Norland, "I can't think the Edgeworth child can be a good influence on a sweet girl like your dear Amelia."

With vigor, Lady Norland snapped, "Julia is a good girl. I couldn't be more pleased if she were my own!"

These rebuffs did nothing to improve Miss Sutherland's temper, already unsettled, by the realization that even after five Seasons she was no closer to snaring a husband than she was on her first day in London. She had a rather large fortune of her own, but she dreaded the epithet "ape-leader."

Lord Charles had been attentive. She enjoyed his company, for he could charm the birds when he chose. But even more, she had reveled in the prospect of sharing his titles and honors. How she would delight in being his hostess, a fabulous fortune at her command! It all had been within her grasp, she believed, and now . . .

Miss Sutherland saw clearly the cause of her disappointment—Miss Julia Edgeworth.

Rage grew within her. Ridicule had not served her purpose, for the minx had too many besotted friends. Sterner measures were in order.

She must think it all through. The opposition was formidable. But Langley was hers, hers, hers!

The shapes that had stirred before in her mind now came more clearly, and when she had reflected sufficiently, she sat down at her French desk and began to write.

At about the same hour that Maria Sutherland turned to her letters, Charles was sauntering across Grosvenor Square toward Minton House. Harriet was gratified to see him.

"My dear," she cried, reaching both hands to him. He kissed them and let her lead him to a chair. When they were comfortable, she said with a half-concealed laugh, "Have you come to tell me something?"

"I shouldn't presume to inform you of anything at all. You are always before me with news."

"Wretch! You know what I mean."

"Do I?"

"Of course you do. I do not mean to pry, Charles, but I cannot bear you to sit there with your eyebrows lifted quite into your hair, trying to appear innocent. You are perfectly aware that Miss Sutherland expected you to offer as soon as you returned from Oxford."

Indifferently he said, "She should be wide-awake on that score. If I haven't by now, I won't."

In a burst of relief, Harriet exclaimed, "I must say I'm not sorry. I *cannot* like her."

"Nor can I."

After a moment, Harriet inquired, "But you are back from Oxford. Was it dreary?"

"Beyond belief. The honored visitors were fêted in a most boring fashion."

Diverted, she demanded, "Tell me!"

"Nothing to tell. Gold plate, half the candles in England, and howling spectators in the gallery. I swear they watched every mouthful the Czar put into his elegant mouth. And Blücher so drunk he fell in his soup."

"Alexander is most attractive."

"But with an eye for what benefits Alexander," Charles pointed out. "I do not quite like his constant snubbing of our poor Prince."

"I agree. Charles, you won't credit this, but I heard that the Czar actually *lectured* Prinny—told him he must consider becoming more tolerant and liberal."

"Good God! That from a Czar of Russia!"

When they had digested this latest *on-dit*, Harriet broached the subject nearest her heart.

"Tell me, dear Charles, what is going on? I *loathe* being in the dark."

This time he made no pretense of not understanding her. "Julia?" Harriet nodded. "You do like her?"

"She is a *darling*, and much too good simply to be made use of."

"*Use* of? What do you take me for?"

"My own dear brother," she responded warmly.

He gave her his rare sweet smile. "She is well launched, thanks to you. I am beyond all grateful."

"I hope I have sufficient credit for that. But—"

"My dear, have you ever known me to play the rake?"

"N-no."

"Then trust me."

"Of course I do."

Whle Lady Harriet was assuring her brother of her trust, Becky Moray's thoughts ran along quite different lines.

Her exposure to the higher circles of society had had an odd effect on her. Her young years had been spent in the north, and she had escaped that austere life with Alfredo, a mistake she still regretted.

Now the past two months had borne in upon her the unyielding nature of Convention. The more she realized what the world expected, the shakier was the ground beneath her feet. What Julia might have called the Adventure of Green Street was well on its way to turning sour. Becky fretted.

Julia, not prone to inner reflection as a rule, kept her thoughts determinedly upon the necessities of the moment—invitations, gowns, flirting with Napier Wood and Aubrey Keniston, keeping each at arm's length. Her instinct served her well. Of the two, she considered Napier the greater threat. He was assiduous in his attentions, quite cutting out Aubrey. It was a relief when Lord Charles joined Sir Matthew in providing escort for the two ladies. Fortunately, Lord Charles, with a lift of an eyebrow, was able to discourage the most rash suitor.

Julia was not ready to consider an offer, even from the highly eligible Mr. Wood. Imperceptibly she began to favor Aubrey Keniston.

Her motive, straightforward as it was, somewhere went awry. While gossip linked her with Napier Wood, Aubrey entertained ambitions beyond his deserts.

At breakfast one day, Julia confided in her aunt, "Aubrey is going to call this morning. Oh, Becky, I think he is going to offer!"

"Are you sure?"

"As sure as may be. Lady Keniston watched me all evening."

"That means nothing. She always does, you know."

"But, upon leave-taking, she pressed my hand quite deliberately!"

Becky was dismayed. "Not so soon!"

Julia was in agreement. "Dare we put it off?" Surprisingly, she echoed her aunt's darker thoughts. "How long can this go on?"

Stoutly Becky said, "We'll know when the end of Mr. Clinton's money runs out before anyone else, my dear. Let's wait and see. Of course, if you love Aubrey . . . ?"

"Not in the least."

Curious, Becky ventured, "Is there someone you do?"

"N-no." Julia hesitated before adding, "How could there be?"

Becky's anxiety over how best to answer Aubrey's certain request for permission to speak to Julia was, in the end, for naught. When she learned that Aubrey had arrived, Julia was already descending the stairs, followed by her abigail. Both were dressed for the street, and Emma carried a small parcel.

"Oh, Aunt," cried Julia with exceptional cheerfulness.

"There you are! Aubrey has come, as you see, to take me to return my book. It will be quite all right, for Emma will be with me!"

Bemused, Becky saw them off. Julia had outfoxed Aubrey this time. But there would surely be a next time. And any suitor would expect more than Julia's hand—in fact, a dowry was certain to be demanded.

But from where? Surely the Family Friend could not be expected, after providing a lavish existence, also to support the additional expense of a dowry! But—just possibly—arrangements had already been made. In any event, since Becky had no instructions as to what to do with a marriage offer—her attention had heretofore been concentrated on repelling quite another kind of offer!—she was within her rights to beard Ralph Clinton once again.

He was delighted to see her, so he said.

"Thank you, Mr. Clinton. I should tell you how grateful we are for all the arrangements you made. All has gone quite smoothly."

The lawyer smiled sourly. "As well it might, since you have enticed my Miss Sparrow away."

Serenely Becky informed him, "You underrate her."

"Not at all. She is invaluable."

"I suspect that you have never thought it worthwhile to tell her so? No, I thought not. Appreciation means more than money."

Mr. Clinton turned thoughtful. "You did not come to talk about Miss Sparrow, I suppose?"

Her rejoinder was crisp. "You mentioned her first, I think."

He stared at her for a moment, wondering whether he had underrated her as well as Miss Sparrow. To gain time, he rubbed his hands together and said heartily, "Well, well, I am forgetting my manners. I haven't offered you tea." Raising his voice, he called, "Jonas!"

Jonas within a short time brought tea. Becky eyed him curiously. Was he as resentful of his employer as the sharp glance she had caught might indicate? She dismissed him from her mind. Mr. Clinton was a doughty opponent, and she must keep her wits about her.

"Now to the point," Becky began. "I have reason to believe that my niece may receive an offer soon."

Mr. Clinton raised an eyebrow. "And?"

"What shall I do?"

Since Mr. Clinton was equally at sea on the question, he drew out his answer. "An offer, you say. For Miss Edgeworth."

Too quickly Becky answered, "Of course!"

"My own information is that Miss Edgeworth is not alone in her triumph over the gentlemen."

Becky hewed to the line. "If a dowry is mentioned, I shall have to say there is none."

Mr. Clinton spread his hands wide. "I am sorry I cannot help you."

"Mr. Clinton, I did not expect you to furnish my niece with a dowry. I cannot think why you misunderstood me so completely. My query is only this. If the invalid lady who has been so generous toward us has already mentioned the subject of a dowry for Julia, I should like to be acquainted with the terms. Otherwise, of course, I should not presume to expect anything."

"I have no instructions on a dowry, Miss Moray, believe me. But I can see there could be a question—in your mind. I shall inquire."

Thinking only of Julia's needs, she said, "Pray do."

"Do not hold much hope for a positive answer."

Presently she commented, "I have been racking my wits to discover a means of postponing the inevitable, at least until I know what to do. I believe it would be best for me to take my niece to Bath for a few days. Perhaps her suitor will be less ardent on our return."

Mr. Clinton had instructions on this eventuality. "I must ask you to reconsider. My client—that is, the Family Friend—wishes you to remain in London."

Becky rose with consummate dignity. "I should pay the cost myself."

The lawyer rose too. "It is not a matter of cost, Miss Moray. It is simply a stated wish."

"Not a condition?" Becky was astringent.

"Not in the least. There is no intention of holding you captive, as it were. But simply a wish, which I know you will want to honor."

Well, of course he was right, she thought as she left his chambers and turned out of Chancery Lane onto Oxford Street and found a hackney. She could not go against the wishes of their most generous benefactor, whoever she was. By the time she alighted before the door of the house in Queen Anne Street, she was in need of sorting out her thoughts with an impartial listener.

"Dear Elsie!"

The door opened wider, and at once the foyer was crowded. Sally and Polly, and young Harry, and Mrs. Wilkes as well, joined Elsie in welcoming her.

She was filled with a warm rush of affection for these people she had known so well, who had gone through fat days and lean with her, and never faltered in their support.

Even the boarders were delighted. Mrs. Prince, even though it was the end of June, still huddled in her layers of shawls. "Wish it'd get summer," she complained.

Miss Rachel Owens displayed her new piece of embroidery, quite a handsome one of silver fish in green water. Miss Cooper, as befitted her past as a lady's maid "with a way with hair," was adorned with a fantastic new hair fashion, called, she told Becky, "*à la Tite*." The style bore little resemblance to those of that name she had seen elsewhere.

At last Elsie pulled Becky into the small room used as an office. "Did you come to look at the ledgers? They are ready, anytime you like."

"Not at all," said Becky. "I know without Julia and me to feed, you'll be making a profit."

Elsie said simply, "Yes."

"The work isn't too hard on you?"

"Not at all." In truth, Becky noticed, Elsie looked fine, with a sparkle in her eyes, and a lilt in her voice. "Becky, how is it going?"

"I don't know. Of course, we are on the go all the time. I truly do not understand, Elsie, how one can dance all night, and ride in the park in the morning, and picnic or shop all afternoon, and then dress for another ball that evening!"

"Is it possible!"

"I myself take a small nap in the afternoon, or I couldn't manage."

At length Elsie said softly, "But you're worried."

"Yes, I'm worried! Who wouldn't be? Who is she?"

"Julia's friend?"

"I'm not sure I believe in the Family Friend. Let me tell you . . ." She told Elsie the substance of her conversation an hour before with Mr. Clinton. "And we are not to leave London. Does this seem reasonable to you?"

"Maybe it is the expense?"

"No. I told him I would stand that. He simply said it was a Stated Wish of the Benefactor. I could almost see the capital letters when he spoke."

Elsie pondered. "But nothing havey-cavey so far?"

"Not one thing. Lady Harriet Minton has been very kind, and we are often with her. Her *cachet* is impeccable, of course."

Later, as Becky rose to leave, Elsie told her, "You're different, you know. You've changed a great deal. Meeting old friends does it, I should judge."

"I never had any here. I never came out, you know, except in Edinburgh."

Elsie, convinced that Becky had not told her the whole truth, gave her advice. "Something will turn up, always does. See how this whole affair showed up out of the blue to get our Julia a Season. Don't worry, you'll see your way clear in the end."

"It's what's between here and the end that concerns me." Becky laughed. "But at least we have Lady Harriet!"

11

If Becky could have seen Lady Harriet at that moment, she would have felt her confidence departing apace.

Without notice, before the Minton door on the south side of Grosvenor Square, appeared an enormous traveling coach, the Knebworth bearings evident on the door panels. This carriage was followed directly by another coach of the kind called a chariot, built for carrying freight, so to speak, and not humans. From this latter vehicle emerged two maids and a footman.

Yonge, Lady Harriet's butler, stood bemused for a full two minutes before his wits returned and he sent a footman galloping for their mistress.

"What is it, Yonge?" demanded Lady Harriet, hurrying to answer the agitated summons. Yonge, still more or less speechless, simply stood aside to afford her the better view.

She closed her eyes in disbelief. When she opened them, the spectacle had not disappeared. She breathed, "Good God!" and then descended with proper dignity to the pavement.

There was sufficient tumult already in town, thought Lady Harriet, without the unheralded and most unwelcome arrival of her elder brother and his wife. Privately, Lady Harriet thought that even the Czar could not have arrived with more consequence.

While Yonge was directing servants to the baggage, and Lady Harriet's coachman appeared, looking without favor upon the enormous vehicles he must find room for in the mews, none too large at best, the Duchess of Knebworth descended in full consciousness of her worth. Even her hat, plumed and ribboned, gave no sign of having traveled in a bouncing vehicle for the better part of five hours. The chapeau was set at a precise angle, and Lady Harriet had a swift mental picture of her sister-in-law sitting bolt upright for forty miles in order not to mar her costume. Such self-discipline was certainly typical of Eugenia Langley, Duchess of Knebworth.

But where was Edward? And even more urgent to Lady Harriet's peace of mind, where were her nieces, Olivia and Clarissa, quite the most unpleasant females she had ever met?

None of them appeared. Eugenia stood alone on the pavement, paying no heed to servants with portmanteaux, bandboxes, jewelry cases. She had long led a pampered life, being the oldest daughter of the Right Honorable the Lord Goode, now, to the gratitude of his family, deceased. He had a strong and ineradicable notion of right and wrong, based entirely upon his own consequence and what was due his station in life. Eugenia resembled him exactly.

Lady Harriet greeted her visitor and brought her inside to the small blue salon. At once furnished with tea and, in consideration of her extended journey, small sandwiches and cakes, Eugenia explained the absence of the rest of her family.

"Edward did not wish to come to London quite yet. Of course, he will be here for the Victory Celebration—whenever the Regent can manage to arrange it—but I am sure you know why I am here."

Lady Harriet, unworthily suspecting that Eugenia's motive was simply to cause the greatest annoyance possible, shook her head.

"I shall not be a bit of trouble to you," said Eugenia with that air of smug serenity that infuriated those who knew her best. "But I did not think it worth the trouble to open Knebworth House."

"Not at all," said Harriet vaguely.

"I shall send the coach home, you know. I shall manage with my maids and of course Palmer. I thought it best to bring my own footman, for I may have messages to send."

Lady Harriet murmured, "How thoughtful."

"Yes," said Eugenia matter-of-factly. "But, Harriet, I

must say that Edward is greatly disturbed about the rumors that have reached us."

Since Harriet was not really listening, she did not answer directly. Instead, the thought that gripped her mind found voice. "How long can you favor us with your company?"

Eugenia shot a sharp glance at her sister-in-law. If she knew Harriet at all, she knew that Harriet merely tolerated her, and would never in the world greet her with open arms. However, there was more going on in Harriet's mind than met first glance, and Eugenia, who, though narrow in intellect, was no fool, had a shrewd surmise as to what it was. Harriet had always been in Charles's pocket, and her strained expression now told Eugenia that the rumors had been quite right. Charles was about to kick over the traces.

Eugenia spoke aloud, quite kindly. "Not above a fortnight. I do not like to be away from dear Knebworth, you know."

"Then Edward is not expected?"

"Not at the moment, as I told you. I am perfectly capable, Harriet, of straightening out this small *contretemps* myself, you know. Knebworth was good enough to leave all in my discretion."

Harriet, who knew her elder brother well, translated Eugenia's remarks as meaning that Edward had simply given up trying to rule his strong-willed Duchess. A pity, for Harriet was quite sure, based upon Eugenia's past exploits, that she was sure to muddle everything.

Harriet was not quite certain what "everything" might be construed to mean, but she was altogether sure that Charles had a distinct *tendre* for Julia Edgeworth. If Julia were the person to make Charles happy, then she, Harriet, would see that all worked out for him. She believed that in the last weeks Charles had lost that cold, lost look in his eyes, and her gratitude to Julia—if she were the reason—was unbounded.

Now, in the guise of Eugenia, came disaster.

When Harriet paid heed to her guest again, Eugenia was saying, "Of course I know who Julia Edgeworth is. Her father had no strength of character, and her mother simply could not manage him." Having pronounced her judgment, Eugenia unbent enough to say, "But she was lovely."

"And so is Julia," said Harriet stoutly. "And a dear sweet child as well."

"That may be," said Eugenia crisply, "but hardly the stock we wish to see in the Langley family."

"Now, Eugenia—"

"Is it true that the chit let the animals in the Tower Menagerie out of the cages?"

Faintly Harriet said, "No."

"I heard differently."

"From whom?" demanded Harriet, bristling. "I was there myself, you know."

"At the Menagerie? I cannot believe such childish amusements would attract you."

"Well," confessed Harriet, "in the ordinary way . . ." Too late she saw the direction in which she was leading Eugenia.

"Ah, so it was Charles who dragged you along—simply, I must believe, to chaperone Miss Edgeworth." Harriet's silence was as good as a confession of guilt.

"But what of the Menagerie? If she did not loose the animals, and if you were present, then I must accept your word, but what *did* she do?"

"She only *mentioned* liberating them," said Harriet, beginning to be seriously irritated. "The lion came to the bars to look at her. Truly, Eugenia, he looked like a great kitten, so *dear*, and he just looked at Julia most intently." She reflected a moment. "It was quite odd."

Eugenia considered Harriet's information. This news did not quite square with certain word she had received from a cousin resident in London. "I wonder, Harriet," she resumed, moving along to the next item on her mind, "that you could stand by, quite calmly, and watch her being impertinent to the Prince."

Harriet was swiftly making a discovery. Behind favoring Julia for Charles's sake, she was realizing that she herself was excessively fond of her for her own sake. And Harriet, usually placid and kindhearted, was becoming angry.

"I wonder who can have so grossly misinformed you? If your correspondent should be—as I believe—your cousin Lady Pyatt, I beg you will endeavor to set her right. If her tongue must rattle like a bell-clapper, it can at least ring true."

Eugenia permitted herself a slight smile. "No matter," she said, clearly unpersuaded. "My purpose is not to clarify these small incidents."

"Then," said Harriet bluntly, "what *is* your purpose?"

The Duchess favored Harriet with a long, level look. "Surely you are not so blinded by affection for him that you cannot assess the real danger before us? I have come, with Edward's blessing, to save Charles from committing an irrevocable blunder."

Harriet, stung, was yet guiltily aware that she was dotingly fond of Charles. On the other hand, he was her dearest brother—her only brother, truly, for Edward had ceased to count, the moment Eugenia had by sheer weight of will taken charge of him.

"Now, Eugenia," she protested. "I fear you are not in full possession of the truth. Julia is completely eligible, I assure you. Her manners are impeccable, she has been well brought up, and she is accepted by Lady Cowper and even Princess Esterhazy. Surely their *cachet* counts for something? Besides, no offer has been made to her. I am sure I should know if Charles had spoken." She reflected upon her statement. Not too far from the truth as far as Charles was concerned, she decided, and eyed Eugenia hopefully.

Eugenia was unmoved. "It is precisely to forestall such an offer that Edward has sent me here to you."

Harriet's heart sank. If Edward were truly to interfere in Charles's plans, then, knowing her younger brother's fierce independence of mind, she feared the outcome.

"I shall send for Charles," resumed the Duchess. "I confess I shall be glad when this melancholy duty is done."

Harriet, rashly, burst out, "I wonder then that you do not leave Charles to do as he thinks best!"

Eugenia only looked reproachfully at her, and asked to be shown to her room.

Even the Duchess of Knebworth, as nobly as she conceived her duty, was forced to wait upon events.

London was preparing for the splendid Victory Celebration, and entertaining her famous guests. Napoleon Bonaparte was not, for the first time in more than ten years, disturbing the peace of Europe.

His invasion army had more than once waited for wind and tide on the opposite side of the Channel, poised for action.

England's signal fires were ready along the high cliffs, and anxiety was pervasive. Her armies had come to the aid of her ally Portugal in the Peninsula, and with great effort had only recently prevailed there.

The overwhelming rejoicing was a measure of their recent fears. Now London was showing its gratitude to its saviors.

The first welcoming banquets and fêtes were only a beginning. Daily parades and fireworks enlivened the scene. The Regent could not do enough to win favor with the conquerors. He commissioned Sir Thomas Lawrence to paint portraits of the Czar, King Frederick, and General Blücher, as a means of honoring his guests as well as detaining them in London.

The General, whose zest for living at times overcame him to the point of becoming lying-down drunk, was such a favorite with the crowds that they carried him on their shoulders wherever he went. The daily traffic snarls were incredible and insurmountable.

Harriet did her best to amuse her sister-in-law. *Distract* would have better described her motive. She introduced Eugenia to the Grand Duchess Catherine of Oldenbourg, the Czar's sister—platter-faced, as one peer described her, and as rude as Alexander himself. Eugenia was beguiled by tales of the Grand Duchess arrogantly stopping the music at a state banquet, simply because she had not a musical ear.

Alexander, coolly aware of his preeminence as leader of the Grand Alliance, made no secret of his disdain for his host, even refusing to attend the magnificent banquet arranged at Carlton House for the Czar's first evening in England. Instead, he dined with his sister in the small hotel where she had taken rooms.

"All in all," Eugenia summed up, "a far from edifying pair. Of course, one must be duly grateful for their victories over the Corsican, but I daresay when the dear Duke arrives, all will be put in their place."

Wellington was due shortly, it was rumored. The great Victory Celebration would be delayed until his arrival.

Harriet was tantalized by a fancy which took the form of Eugenia pointing out her clear duty to the Grand Duchess. Alas, the whimsy faded. But, to give Eugenia fair credit, she would not have shied away from the task, if it fell to her lot.

At length, Eugenia became restive. "I have been in London for two days," she pointed out at breakfast the third day. "Where *is* Charles? I expected him to call upon me at once, when he learned I was in town."

Lord Minton, concealing his dislike of Eugenia, told her, "I doubt he received your message. He has been in Paris these few days."

"Paris?" echoed the Duchess. "What is he doing there?"

Even though Lord Minton knew exactly the delicate errand Charles was carrying out at the Bourbon court—indeed, he had himself sent Charles thither—he replied blandly, "Everyone has gone to Paris this summer. As soon as Bony was on his way to Elba—so I'm told—Paris held more English than French. It's quite the thing."

"Not everyone has gone, Minton. I myself could not endure leaving the Castle for any length of time."

This pronouncement, promising a quick departure, caused the Lord Minton to appear more cheerful, and the thoughtful decision of his lady to carry off their guest that evening to the theater put him once more in an agreeable frame of mind.

Lord Minton escorted his ladies to the Theater Royal, but declined to join them in their box. He was quite sure that Charles would have returned to London in time for the theater and, knowing Charles, he would certainly make his appearance in public, especially if young Miss Edgeworth were expected to attend.

Lord Minton took up his unobtrusive stand near the theater entrance, and was rewarded almost at once. Charles, dressed in superlatively cut black, entered the foyer. Catching sight of his brother-in-law, he made his way through the thinning crowd to join him.

Minton, after listening to a murmured report on Charles's journey, informed him of the current threat to their joint felicity. "Eugenia's here."

106

"Good God!" said Charles with feeling. "Eugenia here? In London?"

"Not only in London," said George Minton dryly. "At Minton House." To Charles's incredulous stare, he added, "To be precise, she's here in the theater."

"Where's Edward?"

"At home, where he belongs. As I wish to God she was!"

"What's she doing?"

"Interfering," said Minton bitterly. "What else has she ever done? Poor Edward."

The two men observed a moment of silence in sympathy for the Duke of Knebworth. Minton resumed, "She's on your trail."

Charles tightened his lips. "I should have known. She objects to my behavior, George?"

Minton nodded. "As a matter of course, she would, you know. But, may I be frank, Charles?"

"You will be anyway," Charles commented without rancor.

"Hope you're not getting in deep water. She's quite a green girl, you know. None of my affair, but . . . too bad if she got her hopes up too high."

Secure in his own rectitude, Charles reassured the other. "Don't fret, George. I know exactly what I am doing." In this, however, he realized as he made his way to Lady Norland's box, he was wrong.

Lady Norland and Amelia were accompanied by Julia and Becky. The usual young men were in informal attendance at the rear of the box. Charles nodded to Napier Wood, the Keniston boy, young Poulteney. Then his glance, as though drawn by a magnet, fell upon Julia, and his heart began to pound most distractingly, a phenomenon hitherto foreign to him.

He took pleasure in watching her without her knowledge. Those raven curls lying gently upon her slender neck, the fetching rose-pink gauze, filmy on her lovely shoulders—Charles indulged himself in high-flown fancies.

She stirred. The play was proceeding on the stage below, but her attention was pulled away. Apparently without volition, she turned her head toward the rear of the box—and saw Charles. She smiled—with unassumed delight. If Charles thought he was happy before, just looking at her, what he felt now was as near ecstasy as made no difference.

Could he contain himself in patience till the end of the Season, when his careful plan called for his next step? He was not at all sure.

In his preoccupation with Julia, he had forgotten George Minton's warning. In a few moments, however, he was conscious of a prickly uneasiness, the sure sign that someone was watching him intently.

His gaze traveled till he found what he was looking for—his sister-in-law peering across the theater from the Minton box. He cursed silently. Julia, seeing the altered direction of his glance, also saw the haughty woman—whom she did not know—glaring at her through a *face-à-main*. Julia was not certain why the stranger should look so disapprovingly at her, but she felt distinctly lowered. She pulled her gauzy shawl close in a vain gesture of self-protection, and turned again to Charles, happiness fading from her face.

Charles now wore his forbidding mien. Angry with Eugenia, furious with himself for not guarding his expression more carefully when he had first looked at Julia just now, he deemed it wisest to withdraw, to draw Eugenia's strictures down upon his own head, and away from Julia.

Charles bowed distantly to Julia—let Eugenia make what she would of that!—and vanished. He did not know that he had just made a grave mistake.

By the time intermission came, Julia was in a sorry state of mind. The lady in Lady Harriet's company clearly disapproved of her—without any reason Julia knew. Charles had deserted her without so much as speaking a word. He had been much in her company recently, even though always with others, and she had grown accustomed to his quiet presence and unobtrusive attention. Now she felt quite alone.

Eugenia, satisfied that she had just now seen proof of her suspicions, turned to Harriet. "I have arrived barely in time. He is totally besotted."

"And why shouldn't he be?" demanded Harriet, exasperated. "He is a grown man, with much experience. Surely he is permitted to know what he wants?"

Eugenia said calmly, "Knebworth does not approve."

Rashly Harriet snapped, "You mean, *you* don't approve."

"My dear husband and I think alike," said the Duchess, closing the discussion.

Harriet simmered. Fortunately Charles was possessed of a nabob's wealth, and was not dependent upon his brother's favor. But Charles had a temper, however well he had it in hand in the ordinary way, and Harriet dreaded the storm she believed inevitable.

Besides, Harriet wanted Charles's happiness above all else, and if Eugenia were to attack Julia directly, who could then foretell the outcome? Harriet was conscious of an overpowering urge to throw herself bodily between Eugenia and the objects of her censure.

She was interrupted by Eugenia's pointing out certain activity in Lady Norland's box. "Isn't that Sir Vincent Fitzgerald? I thought he had long since been carried off to debtors' prison."

"I . . . I don't know."

"Of course it's Fitzgerald. You see what low standards the minx has."

"Eugenia, I vow I am out of patience at your speaking so ill of a young lady you are not even acquainted with."

"Nor do I intend to be."

"Unworthy of you, Eugenia. Look again—there with Lady Norland. Mr. Keniston. I believe that is young John Pirie—quite top of the trees, you know. And Lord Field." Harriet waxed sarcastic. "Surely they must meet your standards?"

"I have seen sufficient, Harriet."

But the pinnacle of Harriet's indignation was reached when, upon Eugenia's summons, Miss Sutherland appeared in the Minton box during the second intermission. Harriet heard little of the ensuing conversation. Quite accustomed to Eugenia's way of pursuing her own ends, quite as though lesser beings like her sister-in-law didn't exist, Harriet was, if not insulted by the low tones of their private conversation, to a degree disgusted. From the corner of her eye she took note of the air of complete understanding between the two. She would have wagered a handsome sum upon her belief that Eugenia had enlisted Miss Sutherland's active support.

Although, Harriet considered, not much encouragement would be needed, for Miss Sutherland's nose—to use George Minton's pithy phrase—was so out of joint over Charles's apparent defection as to be as good as broken!

12

It was at this time in her life that Lady Harriet Minton was convinced, totally and irrevocably, of the power of devout—and somewhat desperate—prayer.

The next day, Eugenia said, not caustically but with clear disapproval, "I suppose Minton is still abed. I should not be comfortable myself with such leisured town hours."

"I am sure you are right," said Harriet, adding hopefully, "I imagine you will soon be much more easy at Knebworth Castle."

Eugenia gave her a suspicious glance, but seeing nothing in her bland expression to take exception to, said merely, "I should like the use of the Gold Salon this morning, Harriet. I have sent for Charles, and I expect him at any moment."

"S-sent for?" Harriet quailed. She *knew* Eugenia would muddle all. "Oh, no, Eugenia, you *must* not—"

The Duchess raised her eyebrows. "*Must* not? Harriet, I do know my duty to the family. Or is it the Gold Salon I may not use?"

Even Eugenia ought to know that no one simply *sent for* Charles! Harriet had struggled the better part of a sleepless night to come upon a way of averting the head-on collision that Eugenia seemed bent on. How like Eugenia to come in like a ... like a *dreadnought*! And wreak the most fearful havoc!

Suddenly Harriet's resolve collapsed. Whatever happened, she could no nothing more. She drew herself up with dignity. "Of course you may use the Gold Salon."

"Then I shall tell Yonge to put Charles there when he comes."

Harriet, bereft of the power of speech, sought refuge upstairs with her husband.

Lord Minton was not still abed. He had had the forethought to order his breakfast served upstairs—a much more comfortable meal than one attended by the Duchess—and was finishing his second cup of coffee when Harriet burst in.

One glance told him she was distressed beyond the ordinary. Quickly he rose. "My dear Harriet!"

"What shall I do?" she wailed.

His answer was prompt. "Send her home."

"Oh, no, I can't."

"Quite right, my dear," he said thoughtfully. "If you did, next thing, we'd have Knebworth himself here."

This possibility had not occurred to Harriet. Her mouth formed a round O in horror. "You can't think—"

"No one could think—not with him prosing on and on, that is certain. But, my dear, you take it all too hard."

She wrung her hands pitifully. "Such a storm *distresses* me so!"

At once, Minton folded her to his brocade dressing gown and patted her shoulder. "There, there. Perhaps Charles won't appear this morning. Wouldn't myself."

Her voice was muffled against his shoulder. "He'll come. He is always ready to take on Eugenia."

"There you are, then. He will give as good as he gets, you can be sure of it."

Much restored by Minton's simple faith in Charles, Harriet came downstairs again. Yonge, clearly excited, informed her, "My lady, his lordship is here. I mean his lordship Lord Charles."

The voices emanating from behind the closed door of the Gold Salon bore proof that Lord Charles had indeed responded to Eugenia's summons, and, equally clearly, was not in the least intimidated. Harriet recognized the shrill tones revealing that Eugenia was losing her composure. Already in mid-argument, the Duchess cried, "You cannot mean to marry this Miss Edgeworth!"

"I cannot? Pray why not?"

"She is the daughter of a gambler, Charles!"

"What is that to the point?"

Eugenia appeared to take a long breath. "The entire point, Charles—and I wonder at your denseness—the

Langley name is old and honored, and I cannot abide the slightest stain on it!"

Harriet opened the door and then slipped, unseen by either of the combatants, into the room, closing the door firmly on Yonge's quivering curiosity.

Charles lifted his eyebrow. Referring apparently to a previous part of Eugenia's diatribe, he said, "Now the veil lifts. It is *you,* not Edward, who objects."

Eugenia was only slightly taken aback. "He has given me full authority to speak for him."

Harriet's eyes turned from one to another, and back, following the dialogue. Charles, judging from his suddenly pale complexion, was now thoroughly angry. "But I do not, my dear sister-in-law, give you authority to speak for me. You can have nothing to say to my concerns."

Harriet sank into a little chair near the door and closed her eyes. Without much hope, she sent up a petition to Providence for peace in her house.

The Duchess was as furious as Charles. "Who is behind this *nouvelle riche*? Surely she has no money of her own."

After a moment, Charles said, "Her aunt, doubtless, has a fortune. If it is a concern of yours, although I cannot see how it could be, I shall endeavor to ascertain." His voice dripped with scorn.

Harriet, listening in dread of what might come next, altered her petition. *Let Charles hold his temper.*

"Then, Charles, you persist in your defiance of the head of your family?"

"Is that the nub of all this sound and fury? Simply my brother's *amour-propre*? Edward doesn't care a fig for my defiance. And you've come to town about a mare's nest!" It occurred to him, belatedly, that Eugenia was perfectly capable of summoning Julia to her presence. That possibility must be scotched at once. With a casual air, Charles continued, "There is really nothing to all this, you know. Miss Edgeworth goes her own way, and I have nothing to say to it."

"I cannot believe that. I am told you are constantly with her."

"That is not true."

Eugenia ignored his protest. "And I have myself reason to believe you are not indifferent to her. Charles, I beg of you, remember your duty to your family."

Charles was now thoroughly alarmed, more on Julia's behalf than his own. Being alarmed, he lost his temper. "Speaking of duty to family, how are your *daughters*? Dear Olivia, and—what is it—Clarissa?"

This pertinent reminder that the Duchess failed in her own duty to provide the family with the required son and heir at last silenced her.

Harriet's eyes closed again. Her lips moved silently, praying for Eugenia's immediate departure. She heard the door open and close. She opened her eyes hopefully, but Eugenia was still there. Charles had gone. She could at least be thankful that he had not slammed the door off its hinges.

At last Harriet found her voice. "Well, Eugenia, I trust you are satisfied. You have doubtless thrown Charles's happiness out of the window."

"What nonsense, Harriet! What has happiness to do with anything?"

How true! thought Harriet. Eugenia was born without the capacity for happiness, and therefore seemed determined to stamp out felicity in the world. At least, she was making headway in that direction in her immediate surroundings: witness Harriet herself, Charles, dear Julia—even Minton, forced to breakfast in his room while Harriet provided courtesy to their uninvited guest.

"Happiness—"

Eugenia interrupted. "Fustian, Harriet."

Harriet gathered her wits. "Well, you certainly rang a peal over him. If he had not already made up his mind, I am sure you have made it up for him."

Eugenia missed the point. It would not have occurred to her that anyone would be so goaded by her well-meant instruction as to do the opposite. She merely said, in great good humor, "I should hope so."

It was at this very moment that Harriet became convinced of the power of prayer. Yonge, bursting with curiosity, entered, announcing, "The coach has come, your grace."

"Coach?" demanded Eugenia. "What nonsense, Yonge!"

"The coach from Knebworth Castle, your grace," he explained, with a harassed glance at his mistress. Yonge, in common with the Duchess's own servants, stood in marked awe of her.

Eugenia glared at him. Without a word he presented a letter with the ducal crest prominent on it. Eugenia scanned the contents quickly. "Fortunately, I have finished here," she said.

Harriet refused the evidence of her ears. "What do you mean?"

"The children are ill and my presence is required at home. They may be only girls," she said in rising anger, "as Charles indelicately pointed out, but they are dear to me and I am most anxious about them. I am sorry, Harriet, but you cannot persuade me to stay the entire fortnight. I shall leave at once."

So saying, she swept past Yonge, and her steps faded away. Harriet, who had risen to her feet to confront Eugenia after Charles's departure, now almost fell into a nearby chair. With promptitude, a small glass of brandy appeared, and she took it gratefully.

"Yonge," she said, feeling the first fiery sip stinging through her veins, "pray see that the Duchess's coachman has refreshment."

"Already done, my lady."

"And the horses cared for?"

"As well, my lady."

"Will she be able to depart by noon, Yonge?"

"I shall see to it, my lady."

Harriet closed her eyes. She had one more word for Providence. "Thank you," she breathed.

That same morning, Miss Maria Sutherland was in the grip of a mood best described as foul.

She had not slept, but she did not blame the excess of Gunther's Fine Sugar Plums she had eaten absentmindedly upon her return from the theater the night before. The food for thought that the Duchess had provided had, in fact, remained with her the night long.

The conversation that Lady Harriet had not heard in the play's intermission indicated that Miss Sutherland had the support of Charles's family in the question of his marriage. The Duchess had even suggested that the Duke would forbid the banns.

While, she reflected, this was all very well, she fancied she was better acquainted with Charles than his sister-in-law was. Charles would not be diverted, even by the Duke, from his goals, whatever they might be.

Just now, it was evident to all with eyes to see that Charles was pursuing the Edgeworth miss. In fact, Charles's courtship—contrary to his fixed belief in his own discretion—was already a nine-days' wonder to the *ton*.

The plain truth was that Miss Sutherland had lost out.

After her maid had been routed in a flood of tears, a footman bearing letters was so berated that he dropped his tray, and her butler was instructed not to bother her again to learn whether she would be at home for dinner, Miss Sutherland had left the house.

She had no destination, but she always thought better while walking, and she had much to think about this day. Charles might be besotted, as Eugenia said, but he must be drawn back to common sense.

She had already exhausted her own devices, however, and she could not think what next to do.

It was then that she saw Sir Vincent Fitzgerald coming toward her, and her plan sprang, like Athena, fully armed from her brow.

She greeted him like the old friend he was. Then she asked, "Any progress with your heiress?"

Sourly he retorted, "*My* heiress? You must know that Langley has the inside track there."

Deliberately she said, "I think not." He raised his eyebrows, and she added, "We cannot talk here. Stroll with me a bit. I am on my way . . . I think to Hatchard's bookshop."

Amused, he pointed out, "Piccadilly is not in this direction."

"No matter. I wish to tell you that Langley will not succeed with Julia Edgeworth."

"How do you know?"

"His family will not allow it. I have it on the best authority."

"I saw her," he said dryly, "last night. She glared at me like a boiled owl."

They walked slowly, turning back toward Miss Sutherland's town house. Sir Vincent soon voiced the objection already considered by his companion.

"Langley's not one to knuckle under, you know."

"I agree."

"I'd hate myself to have the taming of that one. He can be savage."

"The point, Sir Vincent—and I am surprised you have not seen it, is this—if the minx is not available, then Charles cannot succeed with her."

"Available," mused Sir Vincent, "or, perhaps, no longer eligible?"

They smiled at each other in perfect understanding, and talked of other things.

It was a measure of Sir Vincent's desperate situation that his scheme was conceived, revised, and put into motion within the space of forty-eight hours.

He arrived at Devonshire House in mid-evening. The environs of the great house were crowded as usual, with carriages and coachmen lined up on Piccadilly and around the corner into Berkeley Street. The gay Georgiana Ponsonby, now the Duchess of Devonshire, was lavish and tolerant in her entertaining, and Sir Vincent—while not invited—was not turned away.

Julia, as he had gathered from certain of his friends, was expected to be in attendance. When he caught sight of her in the throng, he took her presence as an omen that his scheme was sound. And Langley, as far as he could see, was not there.

So far, so good.

Julia's thought on the subject of Charles's absence was not as sanguine as Sir Vincent's. In fact, Charles had chosen quite deliberately not to join Matthew in escorting Julia and Becky this night. He was shaken by the revelation that his intentions had become—as witness Eugenia's knowledge—the subject of speculation among his acquaintance. While he considered Edward's proxy instructions to be beneath his notice, he was most concerned that Julia's reputation remain untarnished. But he arrived at Devonshire House—shortly after Sir Vincent—merely to catch a glimpse of her, even if he decided to remain at a distance. No more immune to the tender passion than a schoolboy, he told himself ruefully, but he could no more change than he could stop breathing.

He sought her face in the crowd, and found her dancing with—of *all* people!—Sir Vincent Fitzgerald. Impassive of expression, Charles moved unobtrusively closer to the dancers. Julia should know better than to encourage a man of that ilk!

Julia did, indeed. But Sir Vincent had persisted, and asked for a dance in such a deferential manner, and there were so many people around, that she saw no impropriety in dancing one set with him.

The impropriety came almost at once. "Such a charming young lady," he commented, "must have many offers?" When she frowned, he added quickly, "Truly I do not mean to pry, but I am fearful that my own suit might not prosper."

"Your own s-suit?" she stammered.

"You surely cannot mistake my feelings!" he said reproachfully.

She longed for an end to the set. But it would cause scandal to walk away without ceremony, even here in Devonshire House, where very little had the capacity to shock.

"I wonder . . . can you, my dear Miss Edgeworth, give me any encouragement?"

"You must know," she protested, "that this is improper. You should speak to my aunt." And my aunt, she thought, will send you on your way with a flea in your ear. An inelegant phrase, she knew, but that was due to the influence of Harry, the potboy!

Her partner's grasp tightened. She looked up, startled. "I wish you wouldn't—"

He said in an altered tone, "Don't be frightened. I simply want to talk to you."

Suddenly they were beside a door, and without warning he swung her away from the other dancers and through the door. Only one pair of eyes watched them go.

Those eyes had found Charles the moment he arrived. Making her way with determination toward him, Miss Sutherland promptly engaged him in conversation.

"Charles, I have missed you! Someone told me you had gone to Paris."

He bowed in agreement. It took an effort for her to bite back the chiding words that leaped to her tongue. There had been a time when she would have known where he was, at least most of the time.

Now, however, she spoke with purpose, for she had

seen Sir Vincent urging Julia through the door on the far side of the room. Although she did not know the details of his scheme, she doubted they included the attention of Lord Charles, so she seized the opportunity to aid in Julia's undoing by keeping Charles occupied.

"I wish I had known your plans, Charles, for I would have asked you to take note of the newest fashions. We are so removed from the French . . ."

Charles had heard it all before, if not from Maria, then from others so near like as to make no difference. No wonder, he mused, that his Julia had so beguiled his fancy! He would never tire of her, not so long as they both lived. His glance slid over the dancers—and Julia was gone!

He gave an involuntary start. She was nowhere in sight, nor was Sir Vincent. While Charles had stood captive to Miss Sutherland's prattle, he had failed to keep Julia in sight. Now, he realized, Maria had cast a few surreptitious glances toward a far door.

He said, "I am sure your friends find you quite up to the mark in fashion. Now, pray excuse me. I believe I am required elsewhere."

He made his way without apparent haste toward the door in question, leaving a vexed Miss Sutherland behind him. Swiftly reviewing the geography of Devonshire House as known to him, he remembered that a terrace lay just behind the door, and a garden beyond.

He reached the door and paused. He looked back. The expression of Maria's features confirmed his suspicions, and he went out onto the terrace. The shadows at the far end of the terrace moved, and Charles felt a chill descend upon him.

Julia's voice was muffled, but the words were intelligible. "How dare you speak so? Pray let us return at once."

Sir Vincent rasped, "Hanging out for Langley? Waste of time, I promise you. That cock won't fight."

Charles's eyes became accustomed to the lack of light. Now he could see Julia, her gown a blur of lightness against the dark. She moved convulsively. "Let me go!"

Sir Vincent suddenly bent his head. His mocking laugh came, searing Charles's ears. "That's not bad, is it? I've got a coach waiting, my dear. You'll learn to like my kisses before I'm finished."

The paralysis that held Charles rooted to the spot left as suddenly as it had come.

"You're finished now," he exclaimed, and strode forward.

Julia could never remember just what happened next. One moment she was struggling in panic against Sir Vincent's infamous embrace, feeling his hot wet lips on her cheek, and the next moment she was released so suddenly that she fell panting against the stone balustrade.

There was a confused milling, and a savage grunt. Sir Vincent appeared to be doubled over—and then he was gone.

"What . . . what happened?" She did not realize that she had spoken until Charles answered. "I trust you will exercise better judgment another time." He spoke with icy restraint, for his fear for her had been mountainous.

Her only answer was a muffled sob, but it galvanized him.

"Oh, Julia, my dearest love!" His arms opened and, drawn by a force she did not recognize, she moved into them and felt them close tightly around her.

She could not stop shivering. Even though she knew—with a certainty that would never change, her life long—that she had found the haven of her dreams, she could not leave off trembling.

Charles moved, and suddenly his coat—Weston's pride—encompassed her and she felt the warmth of his body against her. He held her close, so close she could feel his heart beating, hear his meaningless comforting words against her hair.

"I'm sorry," she said at last, in a wee voice that stirred him mightily.

He placed a finger beneath her chin and tilted her face to his. The look in his eyes shook her. "Oh . . ." she breathed, and he smiled.

"Now you know," he said. "Don't you?"

"I th-think so."

After a moment he said idiotically, "May I?"

"Oh, please!"

He kissed her.

A thunderbolt could have struck beside them, and neither would have heard it. Charles was far from inexperienced, and yet the sweetness of her lips on his, her wordless surrender to his embrace, which was rapidly becoming unchaste to their mutual satisfaction, was like the beginning of the world.

For her part, she felt as though the old Julia had stepped aside to let a stranger take over her quivering limbs, her reeling senses, her spontaneous submission to his myriad kisses.

At length, she drew back, reluctantly. Charles did not try to hold her. "I must go," she said.

He nodded. "Don't go far, love. I shall see you in the morning."

"In the morning?"

He recovered a bit of his usual aplomb.

"Will you be willing to receive my addresses?"

Her eyes, shining in the dim light from within the house, told him what he wanted to know. He lifted her hand to his lips and kissed each finger. "*À demain*," he said. "Now, my darling, go."

She slipped alone into the house. He stood with his hands on the cold marble balustrade, giving his fevered thoughts time to cool. Always rather proud of his unemotional bearing, his trust in reason and common sense, he was now thoroughly at sea.

A *tendre* was one thing, he reflected, but quite another was this wild passion that gripped him—and which, for a brief time, Julia had shared.

Quite another thing altogether.

13

Maria Sutherland, bursting with curiosity over the very odd events of the night before, considered, at breakfast, that she of all people had a right, even a duty, to be well-informed.

Sir Vincent had not made her privy, of course, to his scheme. This was as it should be. She had no wish to delve into the depths of his capacity for trickery.

But to see from a distance Julia Edgeworth entering, so unobtrusively as to appear stealthy, from the terrace, with an entranced look in her eyes obvious to Miss Sutherland from across the room, and not know precisely what had transpired, was more than she was prepared to accept.

Beyond that, she had seen Sir Vincent escort the girl through the outer door, at the first, and despite her own efforts, Charles had followed. But although she had waited for more than an hour, neither gentleman reappeared. Surely Charles had suffered a revelation as to the character of the mysterious Miss Edgeworth? Perhaps he had found her in Sir Vincent's arms!

With cheerfulness, Miss Sutherland waited for Charles to call. By now he certainly must see where his best interests lay.

A caller, indeed, was on his way to her door. Sir Vincent was in a savage mood. Nursing his wounds, both physical—Langley had an efficient right jab—and mental, he cast about for someone to blame for his failure. He turned his recriminations and his steps toward Berkeley Square.

Without preamble, Maria demanded, "What happened? Is the girl ruined?"

"You know better than that!"

"I thought you planned—"

Viciously he interrupted. "You don't know what I planned!"

"To mar her reputation, I should hope."

"Hope in vain, then. You told me Langley was out of it. He's not."

"But the Duchess—"

"The devil with the Duchess! She knows less than a babe in leading-strings about her precious Lord Charles. And I'm out the hire of the coach, too."

"Coach?" she echoed. "Just as well that I did not know your plans."

"You wouldn't have stopped me."

"Most likely I should. I truly do not wish the girl harm!"

"What do you take me for? All I wished was to take her a ride in a closed coach, letting her out where the right people could recognize her."

"And then see what Lord Charles would say!" she crowed.

"Not my worry. But her trustee, whoever he is, would find the girl dead on the marriage mart."

"Except for you."

"Exactly." He fingered his excessively sore jaw. "But it didn't work."

After a few moments she said, "Well, we must try something else. Since you cannot manage to accomplish anything, I had better take a hand myself."

Instantly resentful, he exclaimed, "It was not *my* fault that the scheme went awry. It was *you* who assured me—"

"Yes, yes," she broke in impatiently. "So I shall deal with the girl myself."

"What will you do?"

She shook her head. "I shall not make you privy to my efforts. This snare needs a fine feminine hand!"

While a gin was prepared for her feet, Julia was wrapped in her own dreams. She had told Becky nothing of the incident on the terrace. She was loath to confess that she had allowed Sir Vincent—a man of little reputation—to lead her from the floor and into a private *tête-à-tête*. She really could not have prevented him, except at the cost of a public scene. But Becky would have chided her just the same.

However, if she hadn't got into that scrape, then Lord Charles could not have rescued her, and . . . Her recollections lost clarity and dissolved abruptly into such rosy clouds and delightful vistas of an ecstatic future that she could no more have put words to them than she could walk across the Thames.

When at last she came down to breakfast, reluctant to meet Becky's sharp eyes, she found the breakfast room deserted. She rang the bell for the butler.

"Oh, Buell! I am quite late, I am afraid. Is there coffee? And where is my aunt?"

"I could not say, miss," said Buell, pouring coffee from the warmer on the buffet. "Miss Moray and Miss Sparrow left the house quite some time ago." Buell's active resentment of Miss Sparrow surfaced. "They did not inform me of their plans," he said stiffly. "Not even the hour when they may be expected to return."

Julia was disappointed. Suppose Lord Charles came, as he had promised, to call on her aunt, only to find she was not at home? Would he take that as proof that Becky frowned on his suit?

Diasater loomed before her.

Breakfast was over, and still Becky did not return. Nor did Lord Charles appear.

Fevered with impatience, Julia wandered from one room to another, expecting Charles any minute, longing to see him and dreading his arrival before Becky's return. What would she, Julia, say to him? Or he to her?

By this time, she had relived the moments on the terrace so many times that they had become as figments from a half-remembered dream. Had he said he would call? Had he truly called her his love? Set on her oath, Julia could not have sworn to the truth. He had called her "darling"—or had she dreamed it? She realized that Charles figured frequently in her dreams. And, now that he hadn't come by eleven o'clock, she was deep in doubt.

But if those kisses were only dreams, then she was shamed by their vividness. No well-brought-up young lady should have such deliciously wicked thoughts in her head!

By the time a visitor was announced, Julia's poise had

fled and her mind was a shambles. She rose, trembling, to face Lord Charles.

Miss Sutherland entered.

"Y-you!" breathed Julia, forgetting her manners.

Her visitor seemed quite at her ease. Without haste she closed the door behind her. Coming across the room, she broke into a shallow laugh. "I daresay you were not expecting *me*, Miss Edgeworth. Is it possible . . . ? No, no. I do not think you foolish enough to expect Lord Charles!"

"Foolish!" echoed Julia.

"Will you not invite me to sit down?" Automatically, Julia nodded. "Very well. This is much better. I have a good deal to say to you, and we shall be much more comfortable now."

Julia was far from being at her ease. To receive, without warning, a visit from the reigning belle of Society was distracting enough, without the added apprehension of the arrival at any moment of Lord Charles.

"I regret my aunt is from home, Miss Sutherland," said Julia, gathering together what poise she could.

"No matter. In truth, what I have to say is better kept between you and me."

Miss Sutherland hesitated. Her hostess was clearly expecting callers—or perhaps, more especially, one particular caller. Julia wore a green-and-silver-striped morning gown, which set off her raven curls to perfection, and complemented her startling violet eyes. How young she looked, thought Maria Sutherland, how . . . *pristine*! Even Maria herself in her first Season had not seemed so unspoiled.

"I cannot think," said Julia, "why you have honored us by this visit."

"Not *us*, dear Miss Edgeworth. *You*. I suspect you expect Lord Charles." Julia's start told her she had hit the mark. "I have come in time, then."

"In time?"

"My experience in the world, you must admit, is far superior to yours. And I think it a great pity that you should delude yourself."

Julia watched her visitor much as a coney eyes an approaching ferret.

"Surely you must know that your behavior last evening was quite scandalous?"

"I don't know what you mean."

"Of course you do," said Miss Sutherland in a bracing manner. "Slipping away for a *tryst* on the terrace, especially with a notorious rake—!"

"Miss Sutherland," said Julia, rallying her forces. "I cannot believe you take it on yourself to chide me for an incident which was not at all my fault."

"Not at all the *thing*, I should tell you."

"I quite fail to see how my behavior, whatever it might be, concerns you."

"Only my sympathy for you brings me here. I should have expected you would misunderstand me." Maria rolled her eyes in the direction of heaven, as though to demand patience. "You cannot believe that Lord Charles could condone what was, after all, quite *raffish* behavior!"

"It was not like that."

"Your denial, I must tell you, is not likely to weigh with Lord Charles. Nor with his family."

"His f-family?"

Miss Sutherland reconsidered. She had expected Julia to collapse like an empty sack at the outset. She had not, and indeed she appeared ready to defend herself. Miss Sutherland was not overly astute, but her instinct was strong, and it occurred forcefully to her that perhaps more had transpired on the terrace than she knew. Charles might even have *declared* himself!

It was clearly time to bring up her heavy weapons. The girl would never know that the ammunition was flawed.

"If Charles intervened last night to preserve your reputation—you see, I *do* know what occurred, and you may imagine who was my informant—it was only to save Sir Matthew from embarrassment. Everyone knows Sir Matthew is a frequent visitor to this house."

Julia endured Miss Sutherland's hammer blows without protest. She had a memory or two to cling to. His kisses—he had called her "darling."

Then Miss Sutherland delivered the *coup de grâce*. "I have seen Charles this morning..."

This morning? Julia's protest was silent.

"... and I can assure you his rescue last night meant

nothing—he did for you no more than he would have done for any green girl who played the fool."

Whatever else Miss Sutherland may have said that morning passed out of Julia's life as soon as it was spoken. Julia's pain suddenly was so intense as to exclude all else.

Miss Sutherland spoke with the confidence of the righteous. Whatever doubts Julia had held as to her opponent's veracity—buttressed by her memory of Charles's arms holding her tight, the dizzying words he had whispered—now dissipated like the clouds of a summer storm.

He had promised to call on her—with most serious intent!—and instead he had gone to Miss Sutherland. Worst betrayal of all, he had, so her visitor had just intimated, regaled her with the amusing tale of Julia's scrape.

"Believe me, my dear," Miss Sutherland, pleased with herself, said. "Every word *I* spoke is true."

Leaving her victim to struggle with the implication that the truth was not in Lord Charles, Miss Sutherland tiptoed out, and emerged at last on Green Street.

If Charles were indeed to call here this morning, as the Edgeworth miss seemed to think, it would be well, she thought, not to encounter him. She hastened on her way.

Let Charles explain away Miss Sutherland's accusations if he could! she reflected. He might swear up and down that he had not called on Maria Sutherland that morning. It was the simple truth. But also the truth was that she *had* seen him—walking on the far side of Berkeley Square, no doubt on his way to Carlton House. The Prince Regent had need of his friends often at odd hours, and did not brook refusal.

Julia was more than crushed. She was devastated. She had believed herself on the brink of unparalleled happiness, and her misery now was correspondingly intense.

Her thoughts were chaotic. Phrases swept through her mind: "Only to save Sir Matthew from embarrassment." "Raffish behavior." "I have seen Charles this morning . . . this morning . . . this morning . . ."

The delights she had clung to this morning, Charles's endearments, his arousing caresses, faded away like a child's vision of Christmas. Only this morning—while she dreamed in her fatuous hope—he was calling on Miss Sutherland!

Julia stumbled into the hall. Buell stifled a surprised exclamation. "I am not at home, Buell," she said through stiff lips.

"Miss . . . I beg your pardon. Are you ill?"

"Ill?" She seemed to consider the idea. "No, Buell. I do not *think* so. But I shall see no one else this morning."

She went slowly up the stairs. The butler watched her. "That's how she'll do it when she's ninety years old," he decided.

The rest of the day made strenuous demands on him. It seemed that the world and its brother came to call. Miss Moray was still from home, and Miss Edgeworth did not even answer Emma's rap on her door.

Buell was forced to turn away Lady Norland, Mr. Poulteney—no loss there, thought Buell—and Mr. Keniston. And—what was to the point—Lord Charles Langley, *twice.*

When Becky, apprised of the situation, penetrated Julia's retreat late that afternoon, she managed to hide her shock.

"Buell tells me you are ill?" she said. "Come, now, let's have some light." She jerked open the curtains. She peered at her niece, anxiously exclaiming, "Julia! You *are* ill!"

"No, Aunt. I don't think so."

"I shall call a doctor."

"No, please. I am only a little tired." Her voice seemed to come from a far place.

"I am so vexed with myself," Becky fretted. "I should have been here sooner. But Miss Sparrow and I were busy—on footling matters!"

"It doesn't matter."

"It does, but then, it's done. Now, my dear, you must make an effort. Matthew is coming to take us to Carlton House for the Prince's gala, and he expects to bring Lord Charles—"

Agitated, Julia stood up. "No, no, Becky, pray don't force me!"

"Of course not, child. I shall not force you." She was puzzled in the extreme. "But what will Lord Charles say?"

There was no answer.

"I shall stay at home myself," Becky announced.

But Julia refused to accept the sacrifice. "I shall be fine in the morning, and you shall tell me all about the party."

There was, in the morning, much to tell, even though Julia did not hear it. Miss Sparrow provided a satisfactory audience.

"A mad extravagance," Becky pronounced. "You would not credit it all. A special hall built for the occasion. Draped, I should think, in all the white muslin in London."

"Muslin? How odd."

"It was like sheltering under an enormous umbrella. I danced in fear it would collapse about our ears."

Artificial flowers concealing two bands, arcades to supper tents, all framing what were called "allegorical transparencies." "An orgy of bad taste," Becky finished, "and a crush fit to suffocate. Even with Sir Matthew and Lord Charles to protect me, I thought I might well not emerge alive."

" 'Orgy,' I should imagine, is the right word," laughed Miss Sparrow. "I was awakened by carriages returning home in the street after daylight!"

"No wonder Prinny looks so tired! The royal guests are running him off his feet." Becky allowed a moment for contemplation of the pitiful condition of the Regent. Then she said in a brisk manner, "I should like your opinion of Julia."

Miss Sparrow obliged. "I looked in several times on her. This morning she will not leave her bed. I believe she must be seriously ill."

When Charles, balked yesterday of his interview with Julia's aunt, presented himself in Green Street this morning, he was struck by the presence before their door of a tilbury bearing the unmistakable stamp of a physician he knew. "What's Dr. Temple doing here?" he muttered.

He was soon informed. Matthew waited in the salon. "What's amiss, Matthew? Is it . . . Miss Edgeworth?"

Matthew nodded. "Old Temple is upstairs now."

Charles dropped into a chair, his thoughts milling. Yesterday Julia had denied herself to him, and refused to attend the Carlton House gala. Something had gone awry, he suspected, between the time he had sent her inside at Devonshire House, and the next morning.

Had he moved too quickly? Had he frightened her by his caresses? He went back—not for the first time—over every moment he had held her in his arms. He tried to remember even the words he had spoken.

"Probably an excess of delicacies," pronounced Matthew. "Those small cakes at Devonshire House had gone off, I thought."

Charles's brow cleared. "That must be it. But here's Temple. He'll tell us."

The issue did not appear to be settled, judging from Becky's worried frown. Matthew went to stand by her. She looked up, bewildered. "Matthew, he doesn't *know*."

Dr. Temple cleared his throat for attention. "Miss Moray is like most of my patients, expecting miracles to happen the moment a doctor steps into the room."

"An expectation fostered," Matthew said dryly, "by doctors."

"That may be, Sir Matthew. But I see no cause for alarm here. The young lady is suffering, no doubt, from . . ." He cleared his throat again before delivering himself of a many-syllabled term.

"Which means?" demanded Charles, unable to keep silent. It was *Julia* lying upstairs in bed, not just any patient.

"In lay terms, an overexcitation of the nervous system, as is so prevalent in highly strung females."

Charles bit back the word "*Balderdash!*" Julia was as far from being highly strung as . . . as that table there. Aloud he inquired, "She will recover in a day or two?"

"In these cases," said Dr. Temple, "we must wait and see."

14

Julia had suffered the proddings and inquisition of Dr. Temple without protest. She knew the source of her quiet misery, and there was nothing Dr. Temple could do for her. Not even Becky, whose anxiety was almost palpable, nor Miss Sparrow, whose ministrations were above all practical, could ease her.

But time at last, if it did not provide a cure, at least began the process of healing over the deep wound. Miss Sparrow's wisdom, applied without fanfare, prevailed—after all, a girl healthy in body could not abide thin gruel and starch pudding for more than a week!

In the meantime, since he was not allowed to see Julia, of course, nor could he gain much comfort from Becky's worried reports, Charles moved in a constant state of consternation.

All his well-laid plans were going well, until now. He could not refrain from speculation. Something had gone awry, and he suspected that there was a deeper reason for Julia's illness than a simple cake that had gone off. A week, surely, would be sufficient time to recover from a digestive indiscretion?

In his unhappiness, he went to the greatest friend in his life—Lady Harriet.

After greeting him, she waited for him to tell her the reason for his visit. She could guess, for there was little that passed for truth in her world that she had not heard. The buzz of rumor had hovered around Charles's head, for a week now, and he had been missing from his usual haunts, thus adding fuel to the gossip.

"What am I to do, Harriet?"

She looked solemnly at him. "It is pointless for me to

pretend that I don't know what you mean, dear Charles. It is Julia, is it not?"

He nodded. "She is too ill to come downstairs. At least, so I am told. But old Temple talks fustian about nerves and exhaustion. I swear, Harriet, I have never seen a lady less prone to nervous attack than Julia!"

"I quite agree. But . . . I have heard it was poisoning? Food poisoning, of course."

"That's Matthew's idea. He says he had a twinge of it himself. But a week, Harriet!"

"That does make nonsense of it," she mused. She studied her brother for a few moments. At length she made up her mind. "Charles, you know more about all this than you have revealed."

"Of course I do. I should have known I couldn't deceive you."

With spirit she told him, "You didn't come here in order to deceive me, Charles."

"Are you sure you haven't heard about that affair at Devonshire House?"

"No, but I am not surprised. You know nothing that happens at dear Georgiana's would surprise anybody, and no one talks about it." She smiled wryly. "I suppose they themselves do not wish to be talked about. Whoever *they* are."

"I hadn't intended to go that evening," he said. "But . . . I went."

Couldn't help himself, Harriet judged shrewdly.

"And a good thing I did." He went on to tell her how he had missed her, gone onto the terrace, and routed Fitzgerald. He did not reveal Miss Sutherland's attempt to keep him occupied, because he had already forgotten her.

His audience was spellbound. "Fitzgerald! Why did Julia—?"

"A large crowd, I suppose, and Becky off with Matthew." With a pitiful attempt at humor, he added, "I vow the chaperone requires a duenna!"

"And now, poor child, she is ill."

"But, Harriet, that's the nub of it. I can't think she is really ill—with fever, or the plague for example."

"But what, then?" She gazed at him as the most surprising idea of the week presented itself. "You don't mean that she won't receive you? And feigns illness?"

132

"What else can I think?"

"My dear, there isn't a woman in the world who wouldn't leap at the opportunity to receive you!"

Simply, he told her, "There is Julia."

"But, my dear Charles, what on earth could you have said to her?"

"I don't know."

"There has to be a reason . . ." Her voice trailed off. Then, more briskly, she said, "Charles, I do not mean to pry into whatever you saw fit to say to dear Julia after you rescued her from that man. I shall rely upon my own experience to inform me of the general tenor of your conversation." She gathered her courage. She would not in the ordinary way dream of asking him anything of such a personal nature, but after all, he had come to her for encouragement if not actual assistance, and she regarded his presence now as permission to say what she would.

"Charles. Did you declare yourself?"

Charles had sat with his forearms resting on his knees, his eyes fixed upon a design in the Turkey carpet. Now he lifted his head and looked at his sister. She was shocked at the clear misery she saw. Never before had Charles looked so desolate!

"I might as well have done," he said. "I said . . . well, never mind what I said. But I told her I wished to call on her aunt the next morning."

"That's clear enough," said Harriet. "And did you?"

"I did. Julia refused to see me, and Miss Moray was not at home."

"Was she really?"

"I think so. At least, later I saw the carriage on Bond Street. I assume Miss Moray was within."

"Then it is only Julia who . . . is ill."

Charles abandoned his chair and began to pace. "Harriet, I know she was not indifferent to me. Why won't she see me?"

"She is ill, Charles," said Harriet. "That is all there is to it." She hoped she sounded convincing.

"No, Harriet. There's too much obfuscation—Temple, Miss Moray, even Matthew. There's another reason."

"Do sit down, Charles. I vow your striding back and forth will serve no purpose. Besides, I am sure you will give me a headache."

His sister's incipient ailment was ignored. But he stopped pacing and dropped again into his chair.

Harriet studied him surreptitiously. She knew him well, and she strongly suspected that his high self-esteem, even though warranted, might be the better for a setdown. A slight snag in his smooth life would do no harm, and might do a good deal of good. But this irruption into the smooth tenor of his days was more than slight. Indeed, her sisterly instinct told her, it was likely to be his ruin.

Charles had received his extravagant fortune from his mother at an unduly early age. The grace of his person, combined with faultless taste, a formidable mind, and impeccable manners, had made him far and away the most sought-after *parti* in London. He had been pampered, she knew. He had only to make his slightest wish known to have it fulfilled, either by his excessively well-paid servants or by some fawning mother with a marriageable daughter.

He was, to tell the bare truth, greatly spoiled.

But he was her dear brother, and beneath the veneer of elegance, there beat a basically modest heart and a sincere kindness.

"Perhaps it is not you at all," said Harriet. "Perhaps there is something in her past."

"Her past! Harriet, she is so innocent—"

"I did not mean something shameful, Charles. There is no need to rip up at me."

"Sorry."

"But her background is mysterious, you must admit. Suddenly, without any warning, so to speak, Julia and her aunt are in the midst of Society."

"You provided the entrée, Harriet, so she is not mysterious, after all."

"On your request, Charles. I know no more of her than anyone else does. Of course, I know of her family, and her breeding leaves naught to be desired." She broke off, for Charles was gazing at her, his eyes hard.

"Is this faint praise?"

"Not at all," she said with a rush. "She is a dear girl, and I am most fond of her. But, Charles—I merely say this—perhaps there *is* something we do not know. I daresay I am so fond of you that I cannot envision anyone turning away from you. But if she is not ill, depend upon it—it is most likely that we do not know all."

She congratulated herself. He had clearly been given food for thought. He was so abstracted as to hardly hear her when she said, "Charles, shall I call on her? Would you like me to?"

Abruptly returning to the present, he gave her his rare sweet smile. "I have a thought, Harriet, but . . . let me consider what is best."

Relieved, for Charles seemed at least to be moving in some direction, whether it was the right one or not, she said, "Pray let me know if I may help."

"I shall. As a matter of fact, I should like you to do this." He began to speak rapidly.

In Green Street, Becky had reached the end of her tether. Julia was refusing to accept any of the many invitations that still came into the house, and, as well, refused to say why.

"Only that I am tired, Becky dear," she would say.

"But, Julia . . ."

Julia would smile gently, and Becky's remonstrance died on her lips.

But Becky had more than Julia on her mind. Matthew had come back into her life in a fashion almost miraculous, and this time she was not going to be so foolish as to whistle him down the wind.

No Alfredo would interfere this time, and Becky's gratitude for a second chance was deep. But she could not give herself over to plans for a future with Matthew until she had arranged affairs for Julia.

And now the girl was refusing to go anywhere, to receive guests, no matter how importunely they asked. Lord Charles, for example, called every day, and Becky suspected that his interest ran deep. If she could arrange a marriage with Lord Charles . . .

She shook herself impatiently. Top-of-the-trees he was, and not likely to want to leg-shackle himself to a comparatively unknown like Julia.

There it was—the nub of the affair.

Becky and Julia, both, were neither fish nor fowl. Neither had a clear understanding of their resources, nor sufficient means to subsist after the Season. It was out of the question that the Family Friend, whoever she was, would continue to support them in this most lavish manner. Becky believed she could count on Sir Matthew, and neither she nor Julia would starve, but she was too proud to cling to him like a limpet on a sea-girt rock.

Becky could not rid herself of her fears about their backing. She spoke with confidence about the Family Friend, but in truth she did not believe in the Friend's existence. There was some reason for anonymity, she believed, and the reason must be shabby.

She knew what she must do. When Lady Harriet's invitation came for Julia to join her in her carriage to view the Victory Celebration, in comfort, Becky seized the opportunity.

"I do not wish to go," remarked Julia with quiet resignation.

"But this time, my child, I shall insist. This affair will never see its like in this century. You must attend. Lady Harriet has been more than kind from the very beginning, and you dare not insult her now by your refusal."

"I do not wish—"

"Nonsense," said Becky stoutly. "You will wear your yellow muslin. Now, Julia, I do not wish to hear another word."

Julia gave in, feeling it easier to accede to Becky's strong will than to insist on her own. And if Lady Harriet insisted upon bringing her brother along, then Julia could quite well ignore his presence. At least, she hoped she could.

Becky, seeing Julia at last seated in Lady Harriet's carriage, her only guest, breathed a sigh of relief. She had got Julia out of the house and into a social affair once more. And Becky herself had an errand to accomplish.

She was going to *find out* this time—the identity of the Family Friend, for one, and the Friend's intentions for their future, for another. And there would be no nonsense about asking the monkeylike Ralph Clinton to disgorge the truth, either. She had given up on the idea of questioning him again. The only way one could penetrate his secrets was to hold him up by the heels and shake them out of him. Becky was determined, but she doubted she had the strength for such drastic measures.

Halfway to Chancery Lane, she realized she had made

a mistake. There was no chance there would be anyone in Mr. Clinton's rooms, for the Victory Celebration was already under way. It was nearly inconceivable that at long last the Prince Regent had made up his mind and allowed the great event to be organized. So many delays had quite taken the edge off the celebration.

It was equally incredible that there was one soul left in his ordinary purlieus in London, for all the world seemed to be streaming toward one or another of the Royal Parks.

She almost turned back, convinced of the futility of her journey. But since she was not in a celebrating mood, she did not want to turn and travel with the crowds, either. She was rewarded by the sight of Mr. Clinton in his carriage bursting from Chancery Lane into the Strand at a speed which precluded his recognizing her.

Her way was clear, and she hurried on toward his rooms.

Lady Harriet saw her way clear, as well. Her barouche, the top laid back so as to provide a clear view of the festivities on the river, was drawn up on the Embankment. Other carriages stood close, but since all eyes were on the preparations for what was expected to be a Great Balloon Ascent to be followed by a mock naval battle, Harriet and Julia were comparatively private.

"My dear," Harriet, mindful of Charles's instructions, began, "pray forgive me if you feel I am impertinent. But I have such an affection for you."

Julia turned her gaze from the many-striped balloon at a distance—a safe distance, she hoped—to look in surprise at her hostess.

"And above all, I adore my brother. Perhaps I am wrong, but I think you are not entirely indifferent to him?"

Julia felt a tight band constricting her breathing. But she managed, as the silence threatened to extend immoderately, to whisper, "N-no."

"I thought as much."

Julia rallied. "No, no. I fear I have given you the wrong impression. I should have refined upon my answer."

Harriet's heart sank. She was bungling the entire affair. "But have you no feeling at all for him?"

"Very kind," whispered Julia. "I'm grateful."

At the mention of Charles, the place within her that had been frozen now began to stir again. No one could live in such a state of suspension for long, as Becky had pointed out. Julia believed she must henceforward lead a life—a short one, she hoped—without Charles. She thought she had over the past lonely days come to terms with bleakness. But now, at Harriet's gently probing questions, hope began to stir. She could say no more than she had already said, but the expression on her face, as though a light within began to shine, told Harriet what she needed to know.

Quite sure now that Julia's heart was entangled, Harriet gave way to optimism. "I suggest perhaps a little more than gratitude? That is, after all, a cold feeling." Her voice lowered into a coaxing tone. "Will you talk with Charles?"

"No. Lady Harriet, I cannot."

"He has been greatly disheartened since you refused to receive him." Julia began to study with great interest her fingers entwined in her lap.

"There will be no living with him unless you do at least see him. Pray have pity on me, even if you have none for him."

Harriet had to bend to hear Julia's response. "Most unsuitable. Pray don't ask me."

Harriet paused. Clearly Julia had not thought up that answer by herself. There was nothing at all unsuitable in a match between Charles and Julia. *Unless*—she realized—there was some impediment in Julia's life that no one else knew. She also knew that Julia would tell no one unless she confided in Charles. Certainly Harriet would get no more from her. Julia was now quite clearly engrossed in the process of inflating the gaudily striped gas bag.

In a firmer tone, Harriet told her, "You owe it to Charles, you know, to tell him yourself, if you do not wish to receive him."

"But . . . I did."

"A butler's excuse," said Harriet, feeling that she sounded like Eugenia on one of her worst days, "is no excuse at all."

Julia was silent a long time. Finally she said, "You cannot mean that he . . . that he . . . *likes* me?"

Harriet answered promptly. "More than that. But he will tell you himself."

Then Miss Sutherland must have been wrong! thought Julia, allowing her hopes to escape from their cage. Then it was possible—indeed, if Charles indeed liked her, then all things were possible!

Harriet, judging correctly that the moment was ripe, gave the prearranged signal to Charles, watching intently from a short distance. At once he strode toward Harriet's barouche. In a moment, he thought, he would *know*!

Even as he approached the barouche, his eyes fixed on Julia, his expectations came to naught. From his left, somewhere behind the booth where Jubilee Nuts and Regent Cakes were sold, came a voice that made him cringe.

"There is your sister, Knebworth. I told you we should find her here. If it were not for the dear girls, I should find this a most unlikely place to seek amusement."

Knebworth mumbled something Charles, rooted to the spot, did not hear, and his wife responded, "But then, I am sure I have never considered Harriet's taste in the least *elevated*!"

Charles, giving thanks that his brother and his family had not seen him, disappeared behind a pair of hogsheads labeled respectively "ALE" and "PORTER," and retreated from the field.

He could not pay suit to Julia right under the eyes of the Duchess of Knebworth!

15

While Charles's mission was balked by the arrival of the Duke and his Duchess, Becky's efforts prospered.

She watched Mr. Clinton's rig out of sight, and then resumed her progress toward his offices. She told herself there was little likelihood that the clerk, on a day when the most touted spectacle of the century was taking place, would remain in the fusty rooms of his employer. She would find the doors locked, and no one within, and her time would be totally wasted. There was no question in her mind as to the futility of her errand on this day, but nonetheless, prodded more by the lack of anything else to do than by expectations, she continued on her way.

To her great surprise, there was a figure on Mr. Clinton's doorstep, wielding a broom with vicious motions. It was the clerk.

He did not look up until she stood directly before him. He was muttering darkly, and his frown spoke volumes.

"If you want *him*, you're too late," he informed her sourly. "*He's* gone to see the sights, he has."

"And left you behind?"

"Not only that, miss. *With* strict orders not to leave."

Compassion warmed her voice. "Why not just go?"

"Be just like him to come back to spy on me," he said.

She nodded. Her opinion of Mr. Clinton, never very high, now sank even lower. "A cruel man," she agreed.

"Besides, miss," added the clerk, "he didn't give me my pay. So as I won't get *depraved* on Celebration Day. *He* says." He leaned on his broom. "Whatever that means. Can't get far on a shilling or two."

Becky was pleased. She had come to suborn the clerk, quite simply, and here he was ready to hand, and, she suspected, more than willing. She smiled sunnily on him. "How depraved could you get on a sovereign?"

His eyes grew round. He considered. Finally, the mathematics of it escaping him, he said, "Enough, miss."

She began to fish in her bag. He interrupted, "What is it I got to do, miss?" His eyes never left her hand. She judged that if the sovereign appeared, glinting gold in the sunlight, he might even give her the run of Mr. Clinton's rooms.

"Not very much," she said. "I only want a small piece of information. That's not much, is it?"

"Depends."

"Can you guess what I want to know?"

The clerk nodded. "He'll kill me."

She found the sovereign and held it above the open bag. "I shouldn't think he would know about this. I saw him leave, didn't I?"

The clerk considered. He was full of resentment, and a wish for vengeance of any kind shook him as though by a strong wind. "He left, all right."

Becky waited, and when the clerk said nothing more, she made as though to drop the coins back.

"I've a notion to . . ." the clerk said quickly.

"To what?"

"I don't owe him nothing anyway."

At length, Mr. Clinton's unfair denial of the clerk's clear rights to see what everyone else in London was seeing bore its bitter fruit. The clerk leaned forward, and whispered a name.

Seeing that Becky stood as though turned to stone, the clerk deftly removed the sovereign from her paralyzed fingers. "Don't tell him I told you nothing," he warned.

At length Becky was able to move. She looked down at her fingers, as though she had never seen them before. Empty—and she had thought to give the boy a sovereign. She found another in her bag and gave it to him.

Feeling somewhat guilty, the boy said, "Miss? Are you all right?"

She turned and walked away, without answering. The name was of such stupendous importance in her thoughts that she was aware of nothing else. She had only the wish to get away from even the neighborhood of Mr. Clinton's rooms. He had certainly done them no favor by tempting them with the Green Street establishment.

She did not know where she walked, nor how long. Eventually she found herself almost at Piccadilly, and the throngs milled around her, impeding her steps. She was forced to stop more than once, while recommendations to move or get out of the way assailed her ears. But all she could hear was The Name, drumming in her head. The name kept her company as she ran the gamut from shock, through disbelief—but the clerk could not have imagined the name!—to curiosity. What could their benefactor, no longer unknown, find of benefit in the most ramshackle scheme she had ever heard of?

The shock was wearing off, to be replaced by a steely determination to remove both Julia and herself from their establishment, built upon shifting sands, before their reputations were irretrievably damaged.

Shame was not somewhere around the corner, as she had felt instinctively all these four months. Shame now sat on the very doorstep of Green Street, brought thither by the web spun by Lord Charles Langley.

Becky stopped short. Julia was this moment, in all innocence, comfortably in the carriage of Lady Harriet. Becky's first duty was to remove her niece from her clutches. Reason might have told her that Lady Harriet was incapable of any action of questionable honesty. But Becky heard the voice of reason no more intelligibly than she listened to the cries in the street.

She was nearing the river. The crowds were impenetrable. She was dimly aware of a commotion in St. James's Park, where the tall replica of a Chinese pagoda, built astride the small bridge over the canal, exploded untimely, sending at least one bystander into the next world.

At length, Becky was so immured in the crowds—more than half a million persons stood shoulder to shoulder—that she gave up the idea of plucking Julia right away from Lady Harriet's barouche.

Eventually, reason came to her, along with the chill of the evening and the smell of gunpowder from the fireworks and the mock naval battle on the Serpentine in Hyde Park, and the aroma of roast ham and gingerbread. Her thoughts, set in motion by the festivity around her and the nostalgic smells, took her back to the Frost Fair, no more than six months before. Would that she were back there in time and the decisions were hers to make anew.

Green Street would never have received Becky and Julia, that was certain!

Becky, held captive in the press, began for the first time to think constructively. She was painfully aware of the need for their removal from the equivocal comforts of Green Street. But she had experienced before the very severe discomfort of being abroad in the world without funds. And their benefactor, she reflected, owed them at least a few days to settle their affairs.

Besides, she had an itch to tell Lord Charles exactly what her opinion of him was, in pithy and wounding terms.

She also realized that once again her future with dear Matthew was ruined. Her own fault before, deceived by the glittering Alfredo; this time, she was innocent, but nonetheless heartbroken. Sir Matthew would feel obliged to call out Lord Charles, who was an excellent shot— Becky could not abide the thought of Matthew wounded or even killed, especially on her behalf.

No, she must deal with their benefactor in her own way. Lord Charles could not have ruined them more thoroughly, had he tried.

She needed time to consider what was best to do. And in the meantime, she must keep her own counsel, make her plans, and above all, be vigilant on Julia's behalf.

Becky's thoughts, even the next morning, still moved as though on a treadmill, unceasingly active but getting nowhere.

Julia prattled to Miss Sparrow over her coffee. Even Becky could see that Julia was nearly restored to her cheerful vitality, after that inexplicable illness. Good, thought Becky—she will need her strength.

When Miss Sparrow left, and Julia turned her conversation toward her aunt, Becky realized that she had been paying insufficient attention to her. Now, as though hearing an echo, Becky listened, appalled.

"Coming here?"

"Yes, Becky. Did I not say that? Charles is coming here. And I do think that he is going to *offer*!" Julia's eyes shone.

Becky felt a pang of remorse. *What have I allowed to happen?*

"Julia, my dear, let me be sure I understand. You say Lord Charles Langley is coming here, to this house, to offer?"

"Lady Harriet said as much yesterday. She said that he was much attached to me. I had thought so, myself, but then . . ."

Her eyes focused vaguely on the silver coffeepot, while she remembered how dreadful had been those days when Miss Sutherland's scorn worked poisonously in her. But that was all past now, she remembered.

"Lady Harriet said—"

Becky broke in ruthlessly. "You will not see him."

Julia's mouth fell open. "Not see him? But why not? Becky, it is beyond everything what I want. He is so kind, so considerate . . . When I thought him indifferent to me, I wished I were dead, truly."

"You would be better dead, then."

Julia was appalled. "Becky! What on earth has come upon you? Surely you cannot fault Lord Charles? He is excessively eligible! He has, so I believe, sufficient money, and . . . and besides, I don't care whether he has a cent! Becky, I do so love him!"

Becky was riven by a wish to give her niece everything her heart clamored for, and yet, she knew it would be the girl's ruin.

"It is out of the question," said Becky in a voice rendered harsh by emotion.

"Becky!"

Becky hardened her heart. "Do you recall our benefactor?"

"Of course. But what has she to signify?"

"The invalid lady from the north?" Becky insisted. "Will you be surprised to learn that there is no invalid lady?"

Bewildered, Julia shook her head.

"In fact, our benefactor," Becky continued, hammering each word home as though she were driving nails in a coffin, "our *friend* who has furnished you with jewels, with gowns, a carriage, servants—in fact an entire elegant establishment, at no *apparent* cost to us—is no other than Lord Charles Langley."

144

An immeasurable time passed before Julia said, "Charles? But *why*? Why did he do this?"

"The reason must be clear. No gentleman provides such material benefits without expecting a return."

"But if he offers? Surely, Becky, if he *offers*?"

Becky's expression was grim. "Offers what?"

Julia seemed somehow diminished, as though her stature had shrunk inches. Finally she said without conviction, "I don't believe it."

"My dear, it is only that you don't wish to believe. You know we suspected at the first that there might be something quite out of the ordinary in this arrangement. We were right, my dear. I blame myself. I should never have agreed!"

Feebly Julia said, "Not Charles! He would never treat me so."

"He is the same man, you will recall, who drove off in his curricle, leaving us in sore distress."

Neither recalled that Becky had stoutly defended this action on the part of Lord Charles, pointing out that his help, sent from the next town, was vastly superior to any rendered on the spot.

At last Julia rallied. "I will not believe this, Becky. For some reason of your own, which I confess I cannot fathom, you are making this tale up."

Becky's retort did nothing to mollify her, and a few more words between them resulted in Becky's flouncing out of the breakfast room in a state of great irritation.

Absently Julia poured another cup of coffee, and sat down again. Her thoughts took her over the past four months, from April through yesterday, August the first. Nowhere had Lord Charles made any gesture of a questionable nature. Never had he so much as hinted that his interest was less than the honorable one she deserved.

But then, Becky did not lie. If Becky said that Lord Charles had provided what could be called almost a demimondaine arrangement, then Becky believed it to be truth. Even though their social engagements took them into the highest circles, the nub of the matter—thought Julia, who was no fool—was the question of whatever payment Lord Charles would expect.

Harriet had said that Charles would call this morning. Her clear intimation was that he would offer marriage.

But suppose Harriet herself was deceived by her brother? Surely Lady Harriet Minton would not be privy to a shameful deed.

Inevitably, Miss Sutherland's venom returned—Charles was too exalted for poor Julia. Surely Julia—scoffed Miss Sutherland—would not expect him to consider her?

But if not marriage, *then what?*

Before Julia had quite made up her mind, Buell announced the arrival of Lord Charles Langley.

"But, Buell, I can't . . ." Becky had said she must not see Charles. But Julia, suddenly coming to a decision, amended her answer. "I shall see him, Buell, in the small salon."

She hurried to greet him. Surely he would straighten all out! If he were able to mollify Becky, then all might yet come right.

Charles, as collected as any man in London, turned to face Julia. Her dark curls escaped fetchingly from the ribbon that held them in thrall, and her violet eyes looked larger than ever.

Suddenly Charles's aplomb fled incontinently, leaving him dry-mouthed and at sea.

He did not remember the first words he spoke. He had felt no need to rehearse his statement to her, nor would such a speech have stayed with him in this moment of crisis. The mere fact that his wits strayed was enough to appall him, and his tongue stumbled over the simplest sentence.

With growing horror he heard words he never planned emerge from his lips. "My sister tells me . . . It cannot come as a surprise to you . . . My feeling for you is out of the ordinary . . ."

He flung her a desperate look of appeal, and received nothing but an expression of interest. She made no move to help him from the morass of words into which he was sinking.

"I may not have a gift of easy conversation—well, of course you know that—but it doesn't, that is, without that gift, it doesn't signify . . ."

Had he had the strength to move, it is likely that he would have fled, his cheeks flaming, to lick his wounds and try again another time. But Julia's eyes were fixed on him with what he believed, correctly, to be an expression of hopeful encouragement.

His ineptness at that moment played him false. In order to assert his control over his tongue, he drew himself up in an attitude that appeared to be most arrogant. His stilted words came out in a haughty manner. While his attitude would not have been fatal to his suit, his offer, such as it was, fell short of the mark.

"I cannot contemplate a life without you nearby—I shall make it my prime purpose to care for you, meet your every wish . . ."

Struggling on against a paralyzing silence, he finally blurted out his heart's cry. "I *need* you, Julia!"

He could not have faulted her attention. She clung desperately to every word. "Care for you," he had said. "Meet your every wish," he had promised. "Need you," he had cried.

But nowhere did he say the one word that would have meant success for him—*marry*.

After his last heartfelt cry, he was struck by her lack of answer. Perhaps his little Julia was overcome, too shy to respond. He turned to meet her eyes—not, to his utter amazement, glowing with love, but, instead, quite blazing with fury.

Aghast, he could only stare at her. What had he done wrong? Harriet had encouraged him to think that Julia was more than willing to accept him.

"Julia?"

"I must tell you," said Julia icily, "that there is no way I would consider accepting your offer."

"But you told my sister that you were not indifferent to me!"

"And, Lord Charles, truly I am *not* indifferent. I am, quite simply, insulted beyond words!" She still had, however, a few words left that she favored him with. "I wonder you dare to bring your sister into your scheme!"

Charles was bewildered. "What has turned you against me?"

"If your conscience is clear, Lord Charles, I shall not attempt to instruct you. I am without much experience of the world, but I am quite wide-awake on *that* score."

Charles's own anger was rising. "I had not thought you

a flirt," he told her stiffly. "But I see I have been greatly mistaken."

"Indeed you are, although not, I must tell you, on the subject of flirting. Your mistake runs much deeper."

He felt his self-control cracking. He dared not stay, lest he say something that he would regret his life long. He strode to the door. But he could not leave her thus.

He paused. "Is there nothing I can say to alter your decision?"

Her answer was as though writ on stone. "My decision is irrevocable."

She heard the door close behind him. She buried her face in her hands. Her life was over, and there was nothing left but to mourn.

Becky found her thus. "My dear child!"

Julia's voice was muffled. "You were right, Becky. He did offer—but not a word of marriage."

"What did he say?"

Julia shook her head. Even as shameful as she conceived his proposal to be, yet it was her own, and all she would be likely to have from him. She could not share it, even with Becky.

"Let it go, Aunt. You were right."

Becky put her arm around her. "You should not have seen him. I would have sent him away."

"But then I wouldn't have known, would I?"

At length Julia sought the privacy of her room. She must plan, must keep active, must do *something*, else she become insane. She was caught in a trap, partly of her own making, but she must strive to find a way out. Her thoughts yielded her no comfort.

An hour later, Becky tapped on her door. "My dear, Lady Harriet is downstairs."

"Lady Harriet!"

"You do not need to see her. She is most insistent, but I can send her away."

Julia opened the door. "I shall see her myself. Then we shall be shut of the entire family."

With great dignity, she descended the stairs. Becky thought that Julia had aged ten years since that morning. *What have I done?* she demanded of herself. It was not surprising that she received no answer.

Lady Harriet was agitated. "My dear, what has happened?" she cried. "I had thought that all was settled! How could I have been so mistaken?"

"I cannot say, Lady Harriet."

"But what have you done to Charles?"

"Nothing at all. At least," Julia added scrupulously, "nothing that he should not have expected."

Lady Harriet searched Julia's face for a clue. Charles had come to Minton House not an hour since, alternating between seizures of savage anger and equally distressing bouts of depression. It had been a harrowing hour for Harriet.

"Nothing? But he is raging!"

"I simply refused his offer. I cannot see that he should be furious on that account. He will surely be able to find someone else, perhaps a dozen others, to serve his purpose!"

Julia's choice of words seemed odd to Harriet. "But I understood . . . Julia, my dear, my ears certainly did not deceive me yesterday when we spoke. You *do* like Charles more than a little!"

Julia's anguished eyes met Lady Harriet's. "Pray do not ask me more, Lady Harriet. We should not suit, and there's an end to it."

Lady Harriet left more bewildered than when she arrived. She would have made serious inquiry of Becky Moray, but that lady was not in sight when Buell showed her out.

It was the most puzzling affair that Lady Harriet had ever heard of, she told Minton later. "A pair of idiots!" she summed them up.

"I'm sure you're right, my dear," said he, "but unfortunately, there is no law against witlessness."

149

16

That same afternoon, Napier Wood paid a call on the Green Street ladies. He was more than a little smitten with Julia's vivid charms, but he had a most prosaic outlook on life—that is, his own life—and while his felicity might be assured were he to marry Julia, yet he believed that she was far from feeling a strong *tendre* for him.

Also, be it confessed, he was a bit anxious on the subject of a marriage settlement. He had sufficient income to live in comfort, but he must expect his bride to bring an equal sum to the marriage, in order to keep beforehand with the world. He had seen little in Julia's affairs to encourage him along this line.

He came this time opportunely. Julia's morning had been filled with turmoil, and the rack of her emotional storm had not disappeared. In truth, her plans, swiftly taking shape, were furthered by his appearance.

While Becky's first thought was to avoid scandal, Julia's was, quite simply, based on a powerful wish never to see or hear of Lord Charles Langley again.

She greeted Napier eagerly. "How glad I am you have come!" she told him. "I must go out for a half-hour, and I shrink from going alone. Could you, Napier, possibly spare me the time?"

"Of course," he agreed, adding gallantly, "Anything you like."

In a short time he found himself strolling along Bond Street, Julia at his side, and her maid Emma a few steps behind.

Napier was led to discuss the spectacle of the Grand Victory Celebration. "And do you know that the Regent himself selected all the fireworks? Such pains as he has taken to make sure that all went well!"

Dutifully Julia encouraged him. "I did not know that."

"All the Roman candles, the girandoles—those were the huge clusters of skyrockets, you know. And those like trees—I vow I have never seen anything quite so splendid!"

Engrossed in his conversation, he did not notice that, somewhere along their walk, Emma had disappeared. Julia, in furtherance of her purpose, now had only Napier's presence to do away with. She managed it without guile.

She stopped before the shop of Mr. Warble and Son, Jewelers.

"Shall you want to come in with me?" she asked prettily.

"In . . . into the jeweler's?" he protested, aghast. "What would . . . ? No, I thank you. I shall wait outside," he finished with dignity.

She entered the shop. Napier, uneasily on one foot and then the other, looked around furtively to see whether any of his acquaintance were within sight. Reassured that he saw no one he knew, he still thought it wiser to wait before the next shop. No matter what it was, whether a draper's or milliner's, at least he would not be seen near a jeweler's shop with Miss Edgeworth. In his world, to be noticed in that circumstance would give rise before nightfall to a certainty among his friends that he was well into parson's mousetrap.

In the meantime, Julia was ushered into Mr. Warble's small office at the rear of his shop.

"And now, Miss Edgeworth," said Mr. Warble, "how may I be of service?"

She took out a small parcel and laid it on his desk. "I wish to sell these," she told him.

"Sell? My dear Miss Edgeworth, *sell*? I cannot believe you wish . . . *truly* wish . . . surely . . . But Miss Moray?"

Julia was quite capable of dealing with Mr. Warble's scruples. "I think, Mr. Warble, these jewels are mine? You will recall, I am sure, that Miss Moray had nothing to do with choosing them."

Mr. Warble recalled all too well how these jewels had

been obtained. That redoubtable Miss Sparrow had come in, chosen the necklace and the bracelets as swiftly as though she were buying potatoes, and instructed him where to send the bill. In fact, since his charges had resulted in quite a nice profit for him, he was excessively reluctant to see the jewels back in his hands.

However, his sharp mind told him that there was more than one means of profiting from whatever came his way, and he fell in with Julia's wishes without more than a token protest.

When she left the shop, she had a larger sum of money in her hand than she had ever had before. Charles had indeed been generous. Her lips tightened, and tears stung the back of her eyelids. She would not take the money for herself. But she would take as much as she had brought with her to Green Street. Surely Charles owed her that?

"There you are, Napier," she exclaimed. "I simply left a bracelet with Mr. Warble. The stones seemed loose in their settings."

So far, she thought, so good. She had money enough now so that she was not destitute. She was no worse off than when she had accepted Mr. Clinton's proposal to move to Green Street.

No worse in pocket, but how much lower in her mind!

She would have been more uneasy had she been privileged to watch Mr. Warble's actions after she left his shop. His thoughts scurried like mice. Something was sadly amiss with that young lady. He did not know the details of Mr. Clinton's "arrangements," but he did know that his inflated bills had been paid promptly. Now, reflection informed him that the thing to do was to inform Mr. Clinton of this new development. While he had the jewels in his hands, he was not out of pocket. And there might be another bit of gold coming to him by way of Mr. Clinton's gratitude.

That miss had something up her sleeve besides her arm, or Mr. Warble was far off the mark!

Mr. Warble's note reached the lawyer late in the evening, too late to call at Green Street. Having spent a sleepless night, Mr. Clinton appeared at an unseemly hour on Julia's doorstep, in a mood that boded no good for anybody.

The lawyer, as well as Becky Moray, had experienced pangs of doubt in connection with the entire Green Street venture. An enormous amount of money had been placed at Clinton's disposal, on the express condition that his client's identity would be guarded like the Crown Jewels.

But something—Mr. Clinton did not yet know precisely what—had gone awry. Any reason that would cause young Miss Edgeworth to sell the jewels—which were not hers to sell—escaped him. Dealing as he did often with the seamier side of humanity, the one explanation that leaped to his mind bore a criminal taint.

He could deal with wrongdoers. What he could not face was the fear that his client might learn that the scheme had developed a snag of the first magnitude. The client, whose name he did not even breathe to himself, was not one to suffer mistakes tolerantly. He could easily place all blame for this *contretemps* on the lawyer's hunched shoulders.

Secrecy—that was the watchword!

And now that Miss Edgeworth had returned the jewels, all of London would be whispering scandal before nightfall unless he could in some way stop this pair. Not for the first time, he lamented the lapse of wisdom involved when Providence first fashioned *women*.

He was admitted by Buell.

Miss Sparrow, hearing a voice she recognized, slipped quickly through the baize door leading to the kitchen. If Clinton saw her, he might be unpleasant on the subject of her defection from his service to that of Miss Moray. She did not know that by this time he was so angry he would not have recognized her if she stood before him.

"I should like to see Miss Edgeworth," he told Buell.

Instead, he was received by Becky. He was too full of his own unjust position to notice that she was equally agitated.

"What do you wish to see my niece about?" Becky demanded directly.

"That is my business," he said. "That is, my client's business."

"Your client has nothing more to do with Julia."

Mr. Clinton stared. "What do you mean, nothing more? She is here in this house, which my client pays for—"

"Pray do not rehearse to me all these shameful truths. I

have had a sufficiency of being reminded exactly how much we owe your client."

"Reminded?" Mr. Clinton was suddenly wary. Clearly, he thought now, the affair of the jewels was only a part of what was ruffling the waters. "I do not quite understand."

"Your client," she said with scorn, "has as base a character as I have ever encountered. And that includes my late husband."

"Base?"

"Pray do not stand there like a parrot, repeating my every word, Mr. Clinton. I wonder you dare show your face here after the dastardly turn you have served us."

Mr. Clinton made a valiant effort to regain control of this discussion. He had planned his attack, but his adversary had routed him at once.

"Now, Miss Moray——"

"You see, Mr. Clinton, I have penetrated your little subterfuge. There is no invalid lady in Yorkshire, as you led my niece to believe."

"It was *her* suggestion——"

Becky, warming to her diatribe, swept on. "You see, I know who your client is. And I can see why he chose someone of little reputation like you for such a shabby affair."

Mr. Clinton winced. He had little defense against Miss Moray's shafts. But, belatedly remembering that the best defense is an aggressive offense, he struck out.

"Ah, then, I see your game."

She glared at him. "Game? Mr. Clinton, I don't think you quite understand me."

"Oh, yes, I do." His voice broke into a snarl. "It's not enough for you to have all this—house, servants, all the fancy gowns you women . . . excuse me, you *ladies* like. A carriage, and who knows what all else! The bills, I can tell you, were large enough. A good thing my client has sufficient dibs, else you would have bankrupted him. And now, it seems that's not enough!"

"Mr. Clinton, I do not know in the least what you are talking about. Surely our expenses were not exorbitant. You could have told us at any time . . ." She realized that he had succeeded in putting her in the wrong. She resumed, ice dripping from every word. "Surely your client expected to receive value from his . . . his investment. I cannot be sorry it is not to happen."

"No, I can see that," he sneered. "Not enough to live in luxury. You must have it all."

Becky was by this time truly angry. "I have had quite enough, Mr. Clinton. I shall ask Buell to show you to the door. Out."

"Buell! Who pays Buell, I should like to know? I do, that's who."

Buell was at that moment earning his wage. He had overheard every word from the salon, and, far from being grateful to Mr. Clinton for his position, he had developed a marked sympathy for the ladies of the house. Mr. Clinton, he considered, was behaving very badly.

When Sir Matthew Morrison appeared on the doorstep, as was his daily habit, Buell welcomed him.

Matthew was about to speak, when Buell's clear air of secrecy stopped him. Buell's finger lay on his lips, and a nod toward the salon gave Matthew the information he needed. To Matthew's horror, the raised voices were shocking.

"Don't try to gammon me, my girl!"

Buell was relieved to see a frown creasing Sir Matthew's brow. Here was a rescuer, he thought, in time to save Miss Moray.

Buell would be more than happy to throw the lawyer out, but Sir Matthew could well save him the trouble.

Matthew moved toward the salon door.

Becky's voice, seeming harassed, was shrill. "How dare you speak so to me?"

"Don't play the innocent! Your game is to take everything, and don't think you can come the innocent with me. Everything in this house, I suppose, you think is yours? Have you tried to sell the furniture yet?"

"This is nonsense!" cried Becky. "You have quite lost your wits. I do not know what has brought you here, but I can tell you you are not welcome."

When Matthew opened the door and slipped through, he saw the unprepossessing figure of Ralph Clinton for the first time. Ugly little monkey, was his first thought. His second was a powerful urge to shake him until his teeth rattled.

"I suppose you know nothing about the jewels," said Mr. Clinton, oblivious of Matthew's entrance.

"Jewels?" Becky was bewildered.

"Yes, jewels. You sent that niece of yours—your accomplice, I may say—to sell the jewels. And you claim to know nothing of it."

"I certainly do know nothing about it. You have become the victim of lies." Becky seethed. "As you might well, since you have told us sufficient untruths!"

"Well, then, let us just have Miss Edgeworth down. We'll see what kind of story she tells."

"All right," said Becky promptly. "She will put your fancies to rout, I believe."

She turned to ring for Buell, and saw Matthew. "H-how much did you hear?" she breathed.

"Enough," he said, coming to her. "Who is this rascal?"

"No matter," said Becky quickly. She hoped to keep Matthew ignorant of the ramshackle venture that had brought them together again.

"Now, m'dear," he said firmly. He turned to Mr. Clinton. "I cannot believe you are quite sane. I heard what seemed to me—and you must correct me if I misunderstood—a clear accusation. Surely you do not intend to call Miss Moray a thief?"

Mr. Clinton felt the ground quaking beneath his feet. He had expected to deal with two women who were particularly in debt to him, and here was a quite formidable gentleman taking their part, and examining him as though he were a particularly unpleasant specimen of insect.

"Wh-who might you be?"

Matthew said, "It is not your affair who I am. It is your own presence here which needs to be explained. At once."

Mr. Clinton's alarm betrayed him. "Quite right, sir. You are not my affair. But Miss Moray's actions certainly are."

Matthew's mild manner concealed an atavistic longing—to have a claymore in his hand, the pipes skirling at his back.

"Miss Moray no longer has aught to do with such as you. I suggest you take your departure, before I become seriously displeased."

156

Mr. Clinton hesitated. When Matthew set Becky to one side, and was clearly ready to put action to word, the lawyer found wings on his feet. He said one last word. "I'll be back. With the bailiff!"

Matthew and Becky stood together in silence, hearing the outer door close behind the caller, and Buell's steps coming to the salon. "Begging your pardon, miss," he said, and closed the salon door, leaving them in welcome privacy.

Matthew put his arm around Becky's shoulders and drew her to sit on a sofa. "Now, m'dear, what's all this about?"

"Matthew, I would weep if I had not used all my tears last night."

"Now, m'dear. What is this about the bailiff? Are you pockets to let?"

"No. That is, yes. That is, I truly don't know, Matthew."

"This is not really helpful. Best tell me."

"I didn't want to. I hoped you would never learn about all this . . ." She waved her hands vaguely in the direction of the elegant furnishings. "Not now, at any rate."

Matthew forbore to question her, but his very presence, his arm comfortingly around her, and the strength of his integrity drew her as no words could.

"Matthew, it's a long story."

"I have time."

"Well . . . I don't know what you'll say."

"Neither do I, until I hear it."

"Well, in the beginning, Julia received a letter . . ."

Matthew didn't say a word until she had finished narrating the events of the letter and the aftermath of moving to Green Street.

"Didn't it occur to you that such a proposal was, to say the least, out of the ordinary?"

"Well, Matthew, of course it did! But it was an opportunity for Julia. You must see that." He nodded. "And besides, she asked him . . . however it was, he led her to assume that the family friend was a very old woman in the north of England, who could not come to London."

"Knew he was a rogue, when I first saw him."

"Matthew, you do see why?"

"Of course. I see you had to give Julia her chance. But

157

had you no thought as to the outcome? Suppose someone offered for her?"

"Someone did," she said flatly.

"Well, then?"

She moved away from him. It would not do to claim his affection while she told him the dreadful aftermath. "You see, the offer was not one of marriage."

"What! You don't tell me! Who was it? Keniston? I'll break his head!"

"Now, Matthew, don't be so Scottish!"

"But . . . I gather that the family friend was not an old woman?"

"No. A very presentable gentleman. It was he who made the offer, you know."

At length Matthew was led to understand the whole. The gentleman who had provided the establishment for Julia and Becky was also the man who had made the shameful offer.

Matthew reflected that a claymore was hardly sufficient to inflict the damage the unknown rake deserved. However, it might do for a start.

"Who is he, Becky? I insist on knowing. You've told me this much. I must have it all."

She told him.

"Charles!"

Matthew rose in agitation. He paced back and forth in such anger that the small room seemed unable to hold it. "He wouldn't!" He threw out his hands and glared at Becky. "You're mistaken, Charles couldn't be so cynical! The girl's a lady."

But then, Matthew recalled, Charles had seen her that day at the Frost Fair, a hoyden in a snowbank, and perhaps his wits were addled at the onset. "Becky, Charles is an honorable man," he pleaded.

Her silence spoke volumes.

At last he stood before her. "What do you want me to do, call him out?"

"Oh, no!" She tugged at his hands, and he sat again beside her. "Dear Matthew, no!"

"There must be an explanation."

"I cannot think of one. He came to offer for Julia, and she told me he didn't mean marriage."

"Well, there's nothing for it but to get at the truth. Let's send for Charles."

"Send for him? Oh, no, Matthew. I mean, he wouldn't come, would he? How can he explain such an infamous act?"

"We must give him the opportunity, m'dear. Now, then, pray send for him."

"*You* must, Matthew. I cannot bear the sight of him."

"It is your house." He was firm, and despite her dislike of the proceedings, she had to admit that Matthew's suggestion was fair.

"Not *quite* my house," she said wryly, going to her desk.

Charles believed that Becky's summons meant that Julia had given way to second thoughts. He had suffered the unlikely experience of facing an angry young lady who held back nothing of her unadulterated scorn. Now, his pride told him that she deserved no more of him than a polite refusal to return, but he was on his way to Green Street before his thoughts settled. He thought wryly that his Julia would always be able to draw him to her, no matter how merry a dance she led him!

But Julia was nowhere in sight when he was shown into the small salon. Only Becky and Matthew greeted him, and to his surprise, there was a noticeable lack of friendliness in their greeting.

"I think," said Matthew soberly, "that you have something to tell us."

"Oh," said Charles, surprised, "I can't think in what way I am accountable to you, Matthew."

"Not to me, Charles. To Miss Moray."

Charles hesitated. There were undercurrents. He could feel them swirling about him, but he could not recognize them. He mused, to gain time, "Miss Moray, is it? Not Becky, then?"

With spirit, Becky said, "Not to you, Lord Charles. I should tell you that your minion Mr. Clinton has been here."

"Ah, so that is the nub of it. I feared the fool might have a loose tongue."

"He is not at fault," Becky said. "But I now know the shameful device you have snared us with."

Charles was irritated. Still smarting from Julia's scorn, he was not prepared to accept strictures from anyone else. "Not quite snared, Miss Moray," he informed her. "Miss Edgeworth has rejected me out of hand."

Matthew interrupted. "Then you did offer?"

Charles swung on him. "What do you take me for? Of course I offered."

"The question is—" Becky was silenced by a frown from Matthew.

Charles, feeling responsible for his agent, said, "I can see that Clinton has bungled everything. Pray tell me, so that I can deal with him."

Becky burst out, "He called me a thief!"

Charles was aghast.

Matthew muttered, "Blackguard!" and whether he meant Charles or the lawyer was not clear, even to him.

A strangled sob escaped Becky. "He said I was s-selling the furniture!"

Matthew had had time to contemplate the entire outrageous situation. Now he said, "It occurs to me that something brought all this on. Why did Clinton show up with such accusations? Not out of the blue, that's certain."

Charles said slowly, "Perhaps Miss Edgeworth has somehow precipitated this crisis. Matthew, may I leave it to you to straighten this out? I . . . I cannot."

Matthew became aware of a deep emotion stirring in Charles. A certain sympathy grew in him. He too knew what it was to be thwarted in his suit, and while his own intentions had been honorable, he could not believe that Charles had stooped to dishonor.

"Charles," he said, "*why* did you arrange such a ramshackle scheme?"

Charles, unused to explaining his reasons for anything, let alone disclosing his deeper feelings, could not now help himself. He had been disappointed in his offer, he had been ripped up by his dear Julia, he had had time to face a future entirely unpalatable to him. His defenses had been breached, his aplomb shattered, his reserve melted.

"I'm almost thirty," he said in an anguished tone. "I owe it to my family to marry, for you know that Edward has only daughters. I had no choice, so it seemed to me. Undesirable, but yet my duty. You see?"

Matthew was dubious. "Far afield, Charles. Not to the point."

"And then I saw Julia. On the road to Brighton, you know. She stood up to me, scolded me—not in the least in awe of my so-called consequence. I couldn't get her out of my mind."

Becky, feminine to the core, relented. "You fell in love, at first sight?"

He shook his head. "Not quite then."

Unexpectedly, Matthew burst out, "At the Frost Fair!"

Charles nodded. "But how could I simply offer for a young miss who didn't know me—just out of the schoolroom, as she appeared, without knowledge of the world? You must see it was not fair to her."

Whether it was Charles's explanation, or the misery that was clear in his eyes, the result was that Becky was near to being reconciled to him. "Then you truly did want her to have a Season!"

Charles nodded.

"That rogue Clinton was right!"

"Exactly," said Charles. "To let her see a little of the world." His lips twisted. "Well, she's seen it, and she finds me wanting!"

Becky hastened to encourage him. "We can explain to her. She knows that you have provided this establishment. But . . . you did offer marriage?"

"Of course!"

She shook her head. "She didn't understand that. You can see how it would look to her!" She ignored her own part in convincing Julia of Charles's villainy. "But at least she must listen now."

"Do you think she will?"

"Of course!" said Becky stoutly. "I shall see to it!"

Becky's relief was almost palpable. The scandal she felt breathing down her neck, so to speak, was routed by Charles's clear determination to set all right. An announcement of a forthcoming marriage in the *Gazette* would stifle all derogatory rumors.

Becky's sense of duty led her to be sure that Julia's affairs were straightened out at once, but she would have been less than human if her spirits had not lifted at the thought that her way with Matthew was as good as cleared.

She sent for Julia. It seemed a long time before Buell returned.

"I am sorry to say, Miss Moray, that Miss Edgeworth is not at home."

"When will she return?"

"I could not say, madam. Her maid tells me Miss Edgeworth went out shortly after breakfast. Without saying where she was going."

17

Becky was not yet alarmed.

Julia had come and gone many times in their sojourn in Green Street, and had not always felt it a duty to inform the household.

Besides, Becky had sufficient to think about just now, without speculating on Julia's whereabouts. She had run the gamut from anger to sympathy, from indignation to partisanship, all on account of Charles.

His device had been a shabby ploy to gain his own way. There was no question of trying to gloss over his methods. Such an air of secrecy, of mystery, was fit for one of Mrs. Radcliffe's novels, and it was small wonder—Becky had pointed out forcefully to Charles—that his motive could be questioned.

But he meant well—a diagnosis that would have mortified Charles had he known. Charles was not accustomed to be damned by faint praise, but he was wise enough in the ways of women not to be surprised by whatever queer notion took possession of them.

His own motive was sterling enough. To give Julia some experience of the world, and then to marry her—who could take exception to such a scheme?

Apparently, he thought now, almost everybody could.

He sat uncomfortably on the edge of a chair in Becky's salon. Across from him lounged Matthew, much more at home in this establishment than Charles, who had provided it.

"Charles," said Matthew, "I wish you had taken me into your confidence."

Becky agreed. "I should not have flown up into the boughs, had I known—"

"But you must admit, it's not an ordinary way of going about it," pronounced Matthew.

He could not refrain from chiding Charles. Matthew was of all people the most bound by convention. But he had a simple primitive admiration for a man who burst the shackles of society to get what he wanted. Had he himself followed such a high-handed way when dear Becky was smitten by that dancing master, would he now have behind him ten years of marital felicity? He shot a sidelong glance at Becky.

He sighed. Becky was cut from different cloth. Young Julia was far more biddable than Becky had ever been. Anyway, it was too late now to think of what might have been. It was more than enough to consider what was best to do at this moment.

Besides, he reflected in wry amusement, young Julia wasn't nobbled yet—far from it.

Charles was accustomed to calmness, even serenity, in his life. He was patient, so he thought, but his patience was of a man who had but to speak in order to obtain. His emotions were well under control, since he had formed the habit of having none. His affection was lavished on Harriet, since he had found no one else to command his interest.

Now, having allowed Julia to penetrate his reserve, he was aware of a great flood of passion that shook him to his roots. Once open, as it were, to love, he was constantly surprised to find that Pandora's box, as well as passionate yearning, contained rage, and resentment, and remorse, as well as a strong desire to shake the girl till her teeth rattled.

Where was she? Why didn't she come into the room this very moment so he need no longer worry about her?

The door opened, and all eyes swiveled toward it. But the intruder was only Miss Sparrow. She stood looking one to the other, aware vaguely of untoward emotion in the room, but unable to identify its nature.

"Julia?" asked Becky, leaning forward in her chair.

"No, Miss Moray. She is not in the house. I have questioned Emma, and together we have made an examination of her wardrobe."

"What for?" demanded Matthew.

But Becky understood, and color drained from her face. "What is missing?"

"As far as we can tell," said Miss Sparrow carefully, "not much. Only her yellow muslin."

"No wrap?"

"None." Miss Sparrow considered. "Well, perhaps that is not quite true. There was a cloak, the one she wore when she first arrived, Miss Moray. Green, with a hood. Do you recall it?"

Becky nodded. "Didn't she discard it?"

"Emma thinks not. But we are not of course quite positive on that head. At any rate, it is not in her wardrobe."

Charles grew impatient. "All of this tells us nothing."

Becky protested. "On the contrary, it tells us a great deal."

"Such as?"

"She has gone out, but not shopping, for she would not wear a yellow muslin gown on the street."

"If she is out, then she is obviously walking somewhere on a street," pointed out Matthew.

"But not shopping," said Becky. "Nor, if she took her cloak, does she expect to meet anyone she knows."

Charles rose. "You will forgive me, Miss Moray, if I tell you that I cannot make sense of all this." He glanced significantly at Miss Sparrow. "Surely Julia is simply out shopping."

"You are wide of the mark," said Becky, "if you think that Julia would spend one shilling of your money. You need not be particular about Miss Sparrow. She is privy to all."

Charles scowled. "Clinton, I suppose."

"Mr. Clinton employed me on *your* behalf, Lord Charles," said Miss Sparrow with spirit.

"We could not have done without her," said Becky loyally. "But none of this is to the point. Julia is gone, and there's no question about it. Besides, if Emma is still in the house, then Julia is not on an ordinary errand, for she would not have gone without her abigail."

Miss Sparrow had spent four months in the same household as Julia. Not only had her stay been most enjoyable, but it had, thanks to her young friend, fostered the rapid growth of her sense of the dramatic.

Now, with secret relish, she held out her hand. "I cannot think she would have gone far," she announced, "for she left all her money behind."

On Miss Sparrow's palm lay a handful of guineas. Enough, so thought Becky, to take Julia to the Antipodes, had she wished. Surely she would not have scorned such an asset.

Matthew echoed her thoughts. "She'll be back, mark my words."

Charles's thoughts were savage. The girl simply wanted to worry him, wanted a chance to rip up at him again, he decided. It did not occur to him that she might have no intention of seeing him again. She surely couldn't mean to turn him down irrevocably!

Since there seemed to be no clear-cut reason for Julia's absence, the four persons mulling over the question in the small salon reached out into realms of unreason. "Napier Wood!" exclaimed Becky.

To the three pairs of eyes fixed on her, she added, "Julia went somewhere with him yesterday. Perhaps he knows something."

Napier Wood, summoned peremptorily by Becky, appeared ill-at-ease. His conscience was clear, but common sense pointed out to him that one or two points about the expedition the day before could best be forgotten.

He entered the small salon, prepared to brave Becky's wrath, if, for some reason, Julia had kindled it. The tone of Becky's note had sounded ominous.

But besides Becky, there was Sir Matthew Morrison, a high stickler for convention, and Miss Sparrow. But the cold eye that transfixed Napier as a pin through a butterfly belonged to Lord Charles Langley. The voice that addressed him was equally frosty.

"Have you seen Miss Edgeworth?"

"N-not today."

"Then when? I warn you—"

Matthew intervened. "Just a minute, Charles. Wood, it's only that we wish to talk to her, and she seems to have gone off on an errand. Can you help us?"

Napier addressed himself to the friendlier Matthew. "I thought something was amiss. Pray tell me, she's really missing?"

Matthew said "No!" at the same moment Charles said "Yes!"

Napier looked from one to the other. Even Miss Moray seemed breathless. "Well," he said, "I suppose I'd best tell you."

Charles said savagely, "A very good idea!"

Matthew warned, "Charles!"

Napier explained. "Miss Edgeworth asked me to accompany her on an errand. All seemed all right, her maid was with her, and we strolled quite without haste. What I mean is, she didn't seem anxious. Nothing on her mind. But when we got to Bond Street, I noticed her maid wasn't in sight."

"And you thought nothing of it?"

"Not then. After all, maids get caught up in traffic, linger here and there. You know how they are."

"No," said Charles, "I do not know."

"Well, it's like this. I'm glad enough to see the back of some maids, when you want a little talk with the lady." He stopped, reflecting that perhaps he had not placed himself in the best light.

"So," said Matthew, "the maid disappeared. And did you then have a little talk with the lady?"

"Thank God, no. She went into the *jeweler's*. You know, Warble's?"

Becky was startled. "Jeweler's? Then that's what he meant."

Napier glanced at her curiously, but she shook her head. He finished the story quickly. "Prongs were loose, she said. And then we came home. And that was all."

At length they were satisfied that he had nothing more to tell them. After he had promised not to set this tale running through the streets, he left.

By this time, it was early afternoon. All thought of luncheon was abandoned. There seemed no place to look for Julia. But Charles was unable simply to wait until she chose to return. With a word of apology, he left.

When he appeared in Sir Vincent's reception room, his involuntary host backed away into a corner.

"L-Langley?"

"I have no desire to continue our conversation of the other evening, Fitzgerald."

"I must confess I am gratified."

"At the moment," continued Charles at his smoothest, "Miss Moray is in some distress, since her niece seems to have gone out without informing her when she would return." Suddenly, sharply, he demanded, "Do you know where she is?"

Vincent relaxed. His conscience was clear on this head. "No, I truly don't. You should have hung on to her the other night." He could not refrain from adding maliciously, "As you seemed to be doing the other night after I left!"

Charles eyed him with speculation. "You know, I am not at all sure I believe you."

Absently he took a step toward Vincent. "Now, wait a minute," cried Vincent. "Search the place if you want to. I don't know anything about her!"

There was a ring of sincerity in his voice that, despite his reluctance, Charles had to believe. He paused, however, in the doorway before taking his departure. "You know, if I were you, I should not mention this to anyone."

Sir Vincent, having lost the power of speech under Langley's cold eye, and recalling only too well the right jab of which he had intimate knowledge, nodded.

When Charles returned to Green Street, it was late in the day. Although Julia had not returned, there had been word of her.

"A note," said Becky tragically. "She's gone."

This was not news, thought Charles, but obediently he read the note: " 'Dearest Becky: I'm going away. I'm safe, and no one knows where I am. Pray do not try to find me. No one can tell you. Love . . .' Signed, 'Julia.' Well, we must find her."

"But no one knows where she is?" said Matthew.

"Nonsense. Someone knows. Look at this—she tells us twice that no one knows. That means, of course, that someone does."

Buell was able to tell them only that the boy who brought the message was graced with red hair and freckles. But surprisingly Becky did not share with the men her sudden certainty as to where Julia had taken refuge. This, now that she had something to go on, was her own business. Julia was sorely distressed—surely that blot on the letter was a tear?—and it would be best for Becky to talk to Julia alone, to convince her of Charles's honorable intentions, and bring her back to Green Street. There they would work out the final stages of this rocky court-ship of Charles's, and all would be well.

It was late in the day. Charles and Matthew left together, but separated at the end of the street. An ordinary man would have gone home to his dinner and made his plans for the next day. A search would have to be mounted for Julia, since the note surely meant that Julia was still in London. Did the girl think that all she had to do was say she was going away, and that would be the end of it?

Fustian! She had no idea what kind of trouble she might run into, and since Charles was the cause of it, then Charles would rescue her. Besides, without Julia, there was nothing left for him.

Charles was not an ordinary man. Even before his dinner, a heavy-booted man stood, hat in hand, in Charles's library, waiting to be told why he was there.

"I wish you to find a young lady," said Charles. "I have certain particulars written here, for your use. Description, clothes she is wearing."

"A young person, my lord?"

"A lady, I think I said?"

"I should wonder why, my lord? Only so that I have some kind of idea where she might have gone to?"

"I cannot tell you why," said Charles, holding back his anguish. "She has been away from home only today, so she cannot have gone far."

The inquiry agent forbore to mention what came to the top of his mind at once. My lord's fancy, now bedded down with someone else putting up the dibs, and my lord can't face it!

But since my lord's orders were clear, and the assignment could prove lucrative supposing it stretched out for some weeks, the inquiry agent bowed submissively and agreed to accept my lord's sovereigns.

Not much chance of finding a certain lass in all of London, he thought. Aloud he said, "Do my best, my lord."

On Buell's description of a red-haired messenger, Becky went alone to Queen Anne Street. Elsie was not at all suprised to see her.

Once furnished with tea, Becky looked around at the small office. "You've changed it."

Elsie with some reluctance admitted, "It can go right back the way it was, if you come home again."

Becky nodded. "I like it this way, though."

"You're coming home?"

"We'll see. Right now I wish to know where my niece is."

"I can't tell you."

"Don't tell me you don't know, Elsie. I should find it hard to believe that, when young Harry brought that note."

"I didn't say I didn't know. I said I couldn't tell you."

"Then you do know."

"She said she was safe. Isn't that enough?"

"You know it's not enough, Elsie. I wish to know *where* she is safe. Is she upstairs?"

"I can tell you that. She is not."

"Not in this house?"

Elsie shook her head. "Let the child alone for a bit," she advised. "She wants to get right away from That Man and his dastardly plot. I wonder you aren't running away yourself."

"It isn't quite what we thought," said Becky.

Elsie sniffed. "What else could it be? She said he made an outrageous proposal. Best she get out of his reach, I say."

Becky gathered her dignity. "I say, I wish to know where she is. Elsie, you have no right . . ."

Elsie was giddy with the excitement of conspiracy. She might be of a lower social class than Miss Moray and Miss Edgeworth, but she was the one that Julia had turned to in distress. She, Elsie Hastings, was the one who had provided comfort, counsel, and arranged a clear road for escape. She repeated, "I promised her I would not tell you."

Becky glared at her. "You tell me, her own aunt, that I am not to know where she is?"

Elsie busied herself with pouring another cup of tea.

Becky tried another tack. "What is she doing? She has no money!"

Elsie pointed out, "It was That Man's money, anyway. She wanted to get away from all that reminded her, so she said. I think she feels a bit of a fool."

"Why didn't she tell *me* what she wanted to do? I would have helped her!"

"It did seem to me she thought you were angry with her." In a burst of honesty, she said, "Truly, Becky, I didn't intend to interfere."

"I could, I suppose, have done a better job of telling her what a fix we were in."

Before Becky left, she felt more in charity with Elsie, but she still could not convince Elsie to confide in her. "I promised Julia, you see," said Elsie.

That promise was the last word Elsie had spoken to Julia before she walked away from Queen Anne Street, Harry, the potboy, beside her carrying a small basket in which were all of Julia's possessions.

To be accurate, the possessions in the basket, as well as the clothes on Julia's back, were hers only by right of recent gift. When Julia had fled to the haven of Elsie's comforting arms, she had brought only the yellow muslin morning gown and the bottle-green duffel cloak, as well as three sovereigns in her pocket.

"I had three sovereigns when I went to Green Street," she explained, "so I sold the jewels and took just what I had to begin with."

She had spent the sovereigns that Fanny's French lessons had brought her on a pair of long white kid gloves trimmed with gold lace. "Things are shockingly expensive, Elsie!"

"He owes me that much," she finished.

One of the sovereigns went to Sally, whose few garments had been commandeered by Elsie on Julia's behalf. They had to be taken in at the waist, a task that took the hours while Charles was explaining himself to Becky, and making increasingly anxious inquiries.

Late in that day, Elsie had bundled up Sally's three dresses and shawl, searched out a small basket to carry necessities in, and sent Julia on her way.

Harry escorted her to Lad Lane, where Julia took an overnight room at the Swan with Two Necks, a hotel and commercial inn, from whence in the morning a coach would take her on the next step of her flight from Charles.

There was no way anyone would be able to find her. The duffel cloak and the yellow muslin were now in Sally's hands, and Julia felt herself another being entirely.

Julia Norton was this new being—Elsie had christened her. "Best keep your own first name. Saves trouble sometimes when it's a familiar name they call you. Julia . . . Norton, that's it."

Julia, most of that night, sat at the window of her room looking out onto the yard of the Swan. Her future was clouded, but her past was beyond thinking of. Elsie had set her on this path, and she tried to remember all that she had been told.

Take a ticket to Tring, she checked off her mental list. Done.

There'll be a welcome at the back of the house, if not at the front, promised Elsie. The Gough family, where Elsie had served as housekeeper-companion to Mrs. Gough, would welcome anybody that Elsie recommended—so said Elsie.

"It's a big house, with a real park," Elsie had told her. "They are regular tradesmen, you know, not gentry. But that's all to the good. You'll not find anybody who knows you in *that* house. Now, what you should do is go to the back of the house. Tell Ferguson—he's the butler—that I sent you. *Butler!* When I first went there, a housekeeper was good enough. But the madam, you know, had such a high-flown idea that she had to have a butler, so there he is. And his wife is the cook, and they'll take you in."

"But what shall I do there?" said Julia pitifully. It was as though she had spent all her vitality in simply leaving Green Street and making her way to Elsie. Now she sat, misery-filled and wretched, and waited to be told what to do next.

"Whatever they tell you," said Elsie briskly. "You're no stranger to housework. You did plenty here. Remember, there's no better disguise than doing something they don't expect to see you doing. You could be a crossing-sweep, I'll be bound, and clear a way for Lord Charles himself, and he wouldn't know you. He wouldn't *expect* to see you doing that, don't you see."

The night coaches, toward dawn, began to arrive in the Swan's yard. Passengers, having ridden for bone-breaking hours, stumbled stiffly out of the vehicles, rubbing their eyes, and vanishing toward the inn itself, or out of the yard onto the still-dark city streets. What else had Elsie told her?

Oh, yes. The family Gough. "There's children—young Mr. Arnold must be most grown by now. Little Sarah Jane—and the other, bless me if I can remember!—oh, yes. Isabella. The little girls, they are."

Elsie prattled on. She had no compunction about sending Julia out into the wilderness of Hertfordshire alone. In the first place, the Goughs—or at least the Fergusons—would welcome her for Elsie's sake.

In the second place, Elsie knew very little if she did not know that Julia would be back in London within the month. Not that she had insufficient courage to turn her hand to domestic tasks—not at all—but Julia was quite clearly so deeply in love that she could not live apart from That Man.

Elsie, who had a low opinion of men, was also a realist. If love had, in such an intense form, come her way—and she was conscious of great loss that it had not—she knew that marriage or not, she would have followed where it led. And Julia was more kin to Becky in that regard than either would have allowed. Dancing master or lord—love was blind, in any event.

Julia, chin in hand, looking into the torch-lit yard below, was far from analyzing her own motives. Her hurt was deep, so deep as to be mortal, she had thought at first. Now she knew she would survive, but that knowledge gave her no comfort. It was not living to be suspended as she was, without hope, without regret, without aught but the need to put one foot before the other simply because there was nothing else to do.

Morning came at last, and she had not slept. Near dawn, the yard below began to stir again, as passengers and luggage, coaches and horses, and the smart, fast mail coaches came and made ready to depart again.

Julia picked up her basket and came down from the second-floor gallery, onto which her room opened. She could smell food that was provided for early breakfasters. Not even the aroma of hot buttered toast could tempt her.

The Swan with Two Necks was an establishment to

rock the mind. It was said that Chaplin, the owner, was possessed of eighteen hundred horses to draw his coaches. He hired coachmen and horsekeepers, ostlers and guards, chambermaids and cooks—rumor said over two thousand persons were on his payroll, not alone at the Swan, but at the Spread Eagle and Cross Keys, the White Horse, and certain other pieces of real estate.

Julia mounted into a distinctive black-and-red Chaplin coach, and scarcely knew when the vehicle left the yard for Lad Lane, to turn shortly into Gresham Street, and then on toward Elstree.

By the time they reached Elstree, they were already in Hertfordshire. They flew down the road past Hunton Bridge, and through King's Langley, the name of which aroused Julia to fresh pain. There was no sense of time, though, and she was surprised when the coach drew to a stop and the door opened.

"Here you are, miss," said a cheery guard. "Northchurch Halt. Come along, now, miss, no luggage? All right, then, there'll be someone to meet you, happen. Tring's just a step that way."

Her descent from the coach, as though from a tumbril, was swift and unwelcome. As long as she had been wrapped in the safe cocoon of Chaplin's best, she was safe, without need to think or to plan.

Now, watching the black-and-red vehicle vanish along the road to the northwest, she felt bereft of her last friend.

She swallowed a lump of self-pity that rose in her throat. No one knew where she was. No one would even miss her!

Becky might, but she had Sir Matthew to take care of her, and soon she would simply let Julia fade in her mind like a bit of lavender set to dry between pages of a book.

As for Charles—he would soon find another Paphian to take her place. It did him good, she thought darkly, to find that there was one girl who was not subject to such lavish bribes! It did her no good, though, to remember that he believed she was such a one.

It was already midafternoon, as she stood beside the road at Northchurch Halt. Tring lay not far away. Reluctant though she was to stir, yet she could not stand there forever. Besides, it looked as though it might start to rain any moment.

She squared her shoulders, and set out toward her destination, just as the first raindrops fell.

18

Although Julia had found sanctuary of a kind in Tring with Elsie's friends at what was called, grandly, Gough Park, Charles found neither ease nor comfort in London.

While Tring was remote, it was not quite off the face of the earth. Yet it might as well have been, as far as Charles was concerned.

Julia had vanished.

While his mind understood that he had bungled the entire affair from beginning to end, nonetheless he was aggrieved at the recurring realization that Julia preferred any fate rather than a life with him.

"Any fate" was literal.

His inquiry agents scoured London, so they told him, and he had no reason to doubt their efforts. Efforts in diligent plenty, but so far they reported no results.

For a week Charles haunted the house on Green Street. He was at times surprisingly humble. Becky wished Julia could see her ravaged suitor at this moment. She would likely not have recognized him as the same gentleman sitting above them all on the Brighton Road, not troubling himself to leave his curricle to assist the lowly.

"Can you think of nothing that your friend said, not the slightest clue?"

Charles was moving aimlessly around the small salon, picking up a figurine and setting it down, adjusting a vase of flowers more precisely in the center of a small table.

"Do you think I haven't tried?" she cried. "Charles, you shall simply have to move some of the furniture out of this room, if you keep pacing the floor."

"I?" He looked at her blankly.

"It is your house," she reminded him.

Not without Julia in it, he thought. Aloud he said, "Where could she be?"

Matthew, who had entered just behind him, said, "Maybe she's not in London."

"But where? She has no home anymore," cried Becky. "Brightoaks surely is not open to her."

Charles dismissed Brightoaks. "I've sent men to inquire in that neighborhood, in case she took refuge with an old servant. But they had no success. Your Miss Hastings cannot be bribed, you say?"

"She promised," said Becky simply.

"But she does say she is safe?"

"I don't want her safe," wailed Becky, suddenly giving way. "I want her *here*."

Matthew sat beside her and patted her hand. "Now, m'dear, she will come back. Charles will find her, never fear."

Charles was not nearly so optimistic. He wished he could believe that Julia was safe. He had no confidence at all in the assurances of a woman he considered stupid, although he had never set eyes on her. How could she countenance Julia's absence from her friends?

How could she know Julia was safe?

"I think, Charles," Becky interrupted his thoughts, "that I must not impose on your generosity further."

"What can you mean?"

"This house. Even the servants' wages are a charge on you that I do not like above half."

"Nonsense," said Matthew firmly. "You're not thinking of moving back to Queen Anne Street? If so, I recommend that you forget it at once. I shall not allow it."

"Allow?"

"When you leave here, you'll be Lady Morrison," he informed her, "and I shall see to the removal."

Charles brushed aside what was in fact a proposal of marriage taking place before him. "What if Julia came back and found the house closed? No, I cannot allow it."

Becky, accustomed for some years to make her own decisions, however hard, however distasteful, was struck into silence. To have her affairs taken out of her hands went against her—but not for long. At once she felt as though a load were physically removed from her shoulders. She had nothing more to say to anything. Matthew would take care of all, and even more surprising, Charles abetted him. Becky felt tears stinging the back of her eyelids. How sweet it was, just for once, to be taken care of!

Charles came to a stop before her. "You talked to Miss Whatever. But what about the servants? Did you get anything from them?"

Becky looked up at him, her jaw dropping. "The servants. No, I quite forgot them. Elsie would never confide in them, if there was a confidence involved. Mrs. Wilkes . . ." She thought a moment, then added with decision, "No, they would know nothing."

Charles left without further discussion. If Becky were so certain that the servants could tell them nothing, he must in a way accept her superior knowledge. However, he could not forget the ragamuffin who had brought Elsie's note to Becky. He had the strongest suspicion that the boy might be a valuable source of information.

Realizing his own consequence might well stop the boy's tongue, he sent Crouch, well armed with questions and a supply of shillings, with instructions to waylay a red-haired, freckled boy.

From his meeting with young Harry, Crouch went to the Swan with Two Necks, from whence he returned to his master with no success. "If she did take a stage," he finished his report, "then it's one in a thousand that ary one will call her to mind."

Charles considered. "Perhaps a louder jingle of coin would bring their memory back?"

Crouch shook his head. "Begging your pardon, my lord, but coins bring back more than memory at times. I say, we don't need no pigments of imagination. Just facts, my lord, else there's wild goose chasing for sure."

Charles made his way easily, through long experience, through Crouch's conversation. He was right, of course, thought Charles. Give a certain type of man sufficient blunt, and he'd recall angels with wings.

Another dead end.

Charles's overwhelming wish was to shake everyone concerned in Julia's disappearance until information rolled from them like coins from an emptied pocket. But he could not forget that his was the worst fault of all.

He had been so full of his own consequence, he ruminated bitterly, that he thought he had only to arrange affairs for her, and she would fall into his arms, at the time he thought best.

But he had not reckoned with Julia.

Even as he fulminated against her waywardness, he realized that it was her very independence that was a large part of her charm for him. No missish lass was she, nor yet an overbearing female who would take the reins of his houschold in hand and run it so efficiently that he must needs take refuge in his club.

Julia was—in fact—simply, Julia, and that was all she needed to be.

August moved on, and still there was no trace of Julia. The royal guests had left, and London Society settled down to its usual routs, drums, picnics, outings, galas, balls.

Charles began to appear again in his usual haunts. Harriet had all but forcibly dragged him to Lady Reading's party.

It was there that Miss Sutherland set eyes on him for the first time since that evening at Devonshire House. She hesitated only a moment before placing her hand on his sleeve and pulling him away from the others.

"You are quite a stranger, Charles!" she said. "I have expected you to call on me this long time."

Charles was long past a point where he wished to guard his tongue. He was not in the least fond of Maria Sutherland. At one time her obvious penchant for his society had been tolerable, but now, his feelings for Julia so poignant that they were like a toothache, he was aware of how much he truly disliked Maria.

"I did not wish," he said deliberately, "to intrude upon Fitzgerald's attendance."

She flushed. "Sir Vincent, as you would know, were you to inquire, has gone to Vienna."

"I had no wish to know," Charles murmured.

"I am thinking myself about traveling to Vienna. The entire world will be there in November, you know."

The whole world—except Julia! Without her, there was nothing.

"Charles? Are you listening? I said I should like to find a house there before the great rush. Unless . . ." She looked up at him. "Unless, Charles, you think it best if I do not go?"

She was quite clearly demanding from him more than he had ever been willing to give. "What you do, my dear Maria, can have little to do with me."

She gasped as though he had struck her.

"Can you deny, Charles, that you have led me to think—"

"Maria," he interrupted wearily, "have done with this. It is not the slightest use. We should not at all suit, you know."

She regarded him with eyes glittering in anger. Unfortunately, her disappointment led her into indiscretion. "I suppose you are still hanging after that chit of a girl. Miss Edgeworth, indeed. I must congratulate myself that I set her straight on her ambitions."

Charles was still. Only his eyes moved, watching Maria with acute attention. "Set her straight?" His voice was a whisper.

She faltered momentarily. She recognized a force in Charles that she had not known was there. She had considered him as elegant, wealthy, with impeccable manners, a suitable foil to her own splendor. But now she felt a quiver through her. She had somehow misjudged him, and she would be fortunate indeed if she emerged from this tête-à-tête without ruin.

But no one could fault Maria for lack of courage. She lifted her chin. "A climber, no less. Ambitious beyond belief. Imagine one whose father was a bankrupt, expecting to finish one Season with a brilliant marriage! I told her how foolish she was to expect success along that line!"

"Do I understand you, Maria? You *told her* she was not to expect an offer from me?"

She would have moved away, but to her surprise, his fingers closed tightly around her wrist and she could not escape. She answered at a tangent. "What if I did? It was clear to everybody that you were making a cake of yourself. You should thank me, Charles. Certainly no one else in London could see her for what she was!"

"And what was she?"

"She has disappeared, has she not? Why do you think a young lady would drop completely out of sight? I should be most surprised if she appears again before eight months at the least." She was now so angry and so frightened that she cared nothing for what she said. To wound this man was worth anything! "Sir Vincent, you must know, was most attentive."

Charles flung her wrist away as though it burned him. "Maria, I swear if you spew this filth again to anyone, you shall have cause to regret it!"

Blindly he turned and headed for the door. He was unaware of the uneasy glances that followed him, of other guests who scurried out of his way just in time. He would not have swerved had a coach-and-four been before him.

Now, as though his own need for Julia had not been sufficient prod for him, Maria's ugly hints made her return in the highest degree urgent. Charles cared nothing for his own reputation, for it mattered little to him what people thought. But he must protect Julia's good name at all costs, since it was problematical whether she would ever bear his.

But he had exhausted every avenue he knew.

The next day after the *contretemps* at Lady Reading's, Lady Harriet decided it was time to take a hand in her brother's affairs.

She made her way to Mount Street, and met an unprepossessing character on the doorstep. Just emerging, the man nearly ran into her.

"Apology, my lady," he said, "didn't see yer."

"No matter," she responded, seizing opportunity. "Are you the inquiry agent my brother has engaged?"

"The same, my lady. And what good it's doing is . . . naught, I can tell you that. A big naught."

"No trace of the girl?"

"Nary a track. I'd say, if you was to ask me, one out of two things is it." He waited, glancing sidelong at her.

"Shall I ask you, then?"

"Good enough, my lady. It's one—the girl don't want to be found." He raised a second sausage-finger. "And what I really think is—she's dead. Drownded in the river, more 'n likely. Lots of 'em do."

Faintly she thanked him and sent him on his way. She was looking after him, in sore distress of mind, when she saw a welcome sight. Dear George had come after her.

Lord Minton stepped down from his curricle and waved it away. "Thought you might be here, Harriet.

This came for you." He flourished a letter, with the familiar crest of her brother the Duke showing clearly.

"How could Eugenia hear so quickly? That dreadful scene with Maria Sutherland only took place last night! I vow if Maria had had a lance, she would have run Charles through!"

"An Amazon," Minton agreed. "But are we to stand out here on the pavement all day?"

The interview with the agent had not raised Charles's spirits. He was sunk in a leather chair behind the desk in his library. He didn't look up when Harriet, followed closely by her husband, entered.

"My dear Charles!" Harriet cried.

"Do you know what she said?" he asked. "I'll tell you, Harriet. There you are, George. That woman . . . !"

He told them briefly the poisonous hints Maria had dropped. Harriet said, quite simply, "She shall never enter my house again. Charles, how dreadful if you had married her!"

George remonstrated. "Never thought he would, you know. Now, Charles, what can we do?"

"I just don't know, George. I've done everything."

"Not quite," said Minton. "Or you'd have found her. Stands to reason."

Charles looked at his brother-in-law, startled. Was there something he had overlooked—was there hope? "What more?"

"Can't say. Something, though."

Harriet had sunk into a chair, digesting the dreadful information that Charles had provided. She was still holding the letter Minton had brought, and without thinking, she opened it and scanned the contents.

Involuntarily she cried, "Oh, dear! Now Eugenia's at it!"

She had the attention of both men. "Eugenia says that Edward is beside himself with—what is this word? looks like *fancy*—no, no, I see. Beside himself with *fury*."

"Edward was never angry in his life," observed Minton.

"She says, '. . . remove Charles from London . . .' "

"How will she do that?" Minton wondered irrepressibly. "A regiment couldn't budge Charles."

" 'Charles should *rusticate* until he comes to a sense of his duty . . .' Oh, Charles!"

Charles was savage. "Another word from the dear Duchess about duty and I shall take the greatest pleasure in strangling her. Her *duty*—the only purpose she has on this earth is to produce sons—"

Minton interposed, "Can't blame Edward, you know."

He exchanged a masculine glance with Charles, a glance that Harriet chose not to see.

But Minton had been thinking along his own lines. "You know, Charles, there's one thing. May not mean much, but there it is. None of these fellows that go around asking questions would know the child if she snapped her fingers under their nose. I'm not a wagering man, but I'd give ten to one that she's changed her name, and all this running around asking questions is moonbeams."

"But a description? Miss Moray has given them a full list of the clothes she was wearing, what she looks like—"

Harriet interrupted. "George is right. She's not wearing those clothes now, you know. Nor is she that distinctive . . . Oh, Charles, don't glare at me. I know she is of incomparable beauty and sweetness and all the rest of it, but she's not a hunchback or ugly, and believe me, to men most women look alike."

At length, he agreed. "That boy told Crouch she went to the Swan with Two Necks. Chaplin's place on Lad Lane. Crouch asked questions, but nobody could tell him anything. Now, I'm going to send Crouch, he knows her, and the other servants who have seen her—"

"Our servants, too . . ." Harriet glanced at her husband and saw his full approval.

"They'll go out along the stage lines," planned Charles, already reaching for the bell pull, "and stop at every town . . ."

Harriet and George left Charles to draw up his plans and send his minions out into the English countryside. The search would be long and tedious, but at least they could believe that the missing girl had gone toward the northwest, and not south, nor to the northeast into Essex or beyond. The Swan lay closer to Hertfordshire and Buckinghamshire, so it was most appropriate to look in that direction.

"Still a lot of ground to cover," mused Minton. "It

183

won't work. I know, it gives Charles a place to start again. But he needs some place special to look."

"But where, George? I vow the girl might as well be Morgan le Fay for all the trace there is of her."

"Wasn't there someplace they looked at first? The boy with the message? Miss Moray was on the track of somebody?"

"You're right. But Miss Moray seemed to me to be not quite so determined as she might be to go after the girl. Let me try to remember."

They regained Minton House in silence. Harriet set herself to serious thought. Miss Moray had clearly accepted the assurance from her friend that Julia was safe. And while Miss Moray was naturally anxious, and longed to have her niece home again, Harriet believed that Charles's need was far more desperate.

Even Miss Moray might well be agitated were she to hear the ugliness that Maria Sutherland had suggested. Harriet toyed with the idea of going directly to Miss Moray and informing her of the smear to Julia's reputation which would be augmented by the girl's continued absence.

But Harriet balked at the prospect of attempting to convince the very Scottish Miss Moray to make further inquiries. Besides, this avenue would take time, and Harriet was quite strongly anxious about Charles's state of mind. To her sisterly eye he had lost weight to the amount of as much as two stone, and she had never seen him so totally wretched.

Besides, she thought impishly, I cannot endure another letter from Eugenia!

Thus it was that Harriet, having remembered Miss Hastings' name, was in Queen Anne Street that very afternoon.

Elsie Hastings was quite overawed, as Harriet had intended. The barouche stood outside, with coachman and footman, waiting for their mistress.

"Miss Hastings? I am Lady Harriet Minton. Is there a place we can talk privately?"

"Of course, my lady." Elsie led her to the same small sitting room where Becky had unburdened herself after her visit to Mr. Clinton, and where Julia had broken down into wrenching sobs six weeks before.

"You are very comfortable here," commented Lady Harriet, glancing around with approval. "I don't wonder that dear Julia came to you. I should myself."

Elsie was gratified. She was, in spite of her sturdy middle-class independence, susceptible to the *cachet* of the upper classes. She knew quite well who Lady Harriet was, the sister of the present Duke of Knebworth, married to Lord Minton. But more than that, Lady Harriet was the sister of That Man.

Nonetheless, Elsie expanded under Lady Harriet's sunny smile, and even Lord Charles looked less villainous in her eyes.

"I have taken the liberty, Miss Hastings, to call upon you this afternoon, for I long to make the acquaintance of Julia's loyal friend. How fortunate the girl is to have someone like you who will help her, in such a tangible way, don't you know."

Elsie preened herself. "I am fond of Julia, you know."

"Of course. Anyone who knows her must dote on her excessively. I do, and I am most anxious to know that she is well."

"She is," said Elsie, pleased to be able to inform her. "I can tell you she is with friends."

"Oh? Then it is true she is not in London?"

"No," said Elsie. "But I must ask you, my lady, not to press me. For I promised Julia, you know, that I would not tell even Miss Moray where she is at present."

"I should not dream of piercing her privacy," said Lady Harriet untruthfully. "But I did wish to learn from you myself just how she is. For you know my poor brother is frantic with anxiety. He has half of London looking for her, you know."

Judging quite accurately the impact of Charles's concern on her hostess, Harriet gave details of Charles's search. Inquiry agents, servants, everyone who had the slightest knowledge had been questioned exhaustively. Now Charles was sending out men on every coach line from London to inquire minutely as to strangers newly arrived in the various vicinities.

"I had not thought Lord Charles to be so interested," mused Elsie. Clearly there was something to be said for a man who spared no expense, and no efforts, to find a girl whom he had insulted.

"You know, I think dear Julia misunderstood my brother. I should never wish to urge her to undertake a commitment she did not like, but I should rest much more easily if I were sure that she had not taken a wrong impression. It would be excessively tragic if she had made a mistake, and . . . and did not know it."

Elsie had been thinking along the same lines, in a vague fashion, ever since Julia, in Sally's clothes, had walked down Queen Anne Street and out of sight.

Caught up in Julia's near-hysterical distress, Elsie had thought only of how to calm her and help her escape. But Becky's visit had stirred up the doubts that common sense fostered. How would a man of Lord Charles's breeding convince his sister—who had provided them the first invitations upon their removal to Green Street—to abet a nefarious scheme of making young Julia his mistress?

Lady Harriet, now that Elsie had seen and talked with her, could not be suspected of anything in the least shabby. Elsie knew it in her bones.

Nor would any man of sense concoct such an elaborate plot to ensnare a young lady, especially one with any breeding at all.

Truly, none of it made sense. Unless, she reflected, all was aboveboard and honorable. In that case, it might be best for young Julia to come home and straighten all out.

"But I did promise Julia," said Elsie, a note of regret in her voice, "that I would not tell even her aunt where she was. I will confess to you, my lady, that I did not think Julia would stay away long." Anxious to appear in the best light before her guest, Elsie embroidered on her own actions. "I thought that she needed a bit of her own time, so to speak. She's been rushed here and there, never time to think, and being so young, she doesn't have the slant on things that you and I have, begging your pardon. But I cannot break my promise to her, and that's an end of it."

Lady Harriet, wisely, said, "Of course you can't. And I would not ask you to forswear your word. It was only that my poor brother . . ." She allowed a yearning look to appear on her features for a moment, and then smiled at Elsie, and talked of other things.

Elsie was pleased at Lady Harriet's interest in her boardinghouse—"I think of it as mine, you know, though

186

I shouldn't. But I shall be surprised if Miss Moray returns."

"So should I," said Lady Harriet, fully aware of Sir Matthew's plans.

Lady Harriet at last, having sipped her second cup of tea, adjusted her lacy shawl and prepared to leave. Elsie expressed her gratification at meeting Lady Harriet—"a lady I've heard much of"—and saw her to the door.

Whether it was the elegance of the shiny black barouche, or whether Lady Harriet's obvious affection for Julia, or, quite possibly, Elsie's own conscience, could not be told, but Elsie had quite clearly swung over to the opposite side.

"I should not venture to advise you, my lady," said Elsie, making her words heavy with significance, "but I find my thoughts turning to Hertfordshire. It is rising autumn, you know, and . . . it is very lovely this time of year, in *Tring.*"

Lady Harriet looked levelly at Elsie. The message was received. "Let us hope," said Lady Harriet, "that autumn will soon be delightful in London."

19

Mr. Ferguson, Mrs. Gough's butler, was by virtue of his position the chief of the domestic staff at Gough Park. He was a man of lugubrious appearance and pessimistic disposition, and for the most part ignored by his colleagues. Mrs. Ferguson, a dumpling of a woman, cheerful and breezy, ran both her husband and the kitchen with a minimum of fuss.

Ferguson might not have welcomed Julia that August evening in the rain, but the magic name of Elsie Hastings was invoked, and Julia was settled by the fire and provided with supper at once.

"She was a one," said Mrs. Ferguson, "Elsie was. She knew how to stand up to the mistress, which is more than I can say for some." She shot a dark glance toward her hovering husband. "Now, then, dearie, you're welcome to stay as long as you want. Though I don't know how you'll like it. It's not what you're used to, I'll gamble on it."

"Thank you," Julia said with a shy smile. There was nothing more to say. What Julia had recently been used to was not what she could look forward to, but it was all too complicated to explain. Besides, she might as well consider that she had reached the level of her future, a place—as the days wore on—in the kitchen of a large house, peeling potatoes, scrubbing vegetables, making beds.

But not serving at table, as it turned out. Ferguson was adamant on that. "One look at you by Mr. Arnold," he warned, "and the fat's in the fire for good."

"Mr. Arnold? Is he the master?"

"Only because he can wind the mistress around his finger," Ferguson said sourly. "Never can keep a parlor-maid. Except for Agnes."

Agnes leaned her elbows on the table in the servants' dining room. "What does that mean, Mr. Ferguson?"

"You know well what it means," retorted the butler. "I doubt if young Julia will be so agreeable. Young Mr. Arnold's a caution, and only sixteen."

His wife intervened. "Agnes is not a green girl."

Agnes tossed her head. "That I'm not. And what Mr. Arnold gets from me, he pays for. And, Mr. Ferguson, as I've said before, no need to get Vicar to ring a peal over me. Mr. Arnold hasn't got everything he wants, not yet."

Ferguson sighed. His women were too much for him, and he retired into his comfortably gloomy thoughts. They'd all go to the devil, and no one could blame him for it—he'd warned 'em!

Julia was grateful for the undemanding kindness that asked no questions, required no explanations. Four weeks came and went since her arrival at Gough Park, and she began to realize that she had indeed entered another world. Since Mr. Gough was merely a tradesman, although a very wealthy one, the world of the upper classes did not intrude upon their lives. The Duchess of Devonshire and the Prince Regent were simply faraway names in Gough Park.

Conversation at the Gough dinner table circled around Tring, its vicar, and the squire and his lady, who lived at Tring Hall, beyond the village. As above-, so belowstairs, and the servants' hall rang with spicier gossip about local personages.

At last Julia had given up looking down the drive, hoping to see a certain curricle dashing up to rescue her. If Charles knew where she was, he would come. But then she recalled her last words to him, and knew that no man could swallow such scalding insults and not suffer harm—and a revulsion of feeling.

She had wanted to be out of the world, away from Charles, and she had succeeded in her desire. She had not expected to be so wretched.

It was beyond expectation that Arnold Gough would not be curious about the new maid in the kitchen. He was inordinately proud of his prowess with the lower orders,

189

and considered himself a gay rake, the equal of any Corinthian to be found in London.

At sixteen, he was adored by his mother, despised by the butler, and ignored by his father, who in fact found his pleasure in his business, and in certain low establishments of which his wife was ignorant.

Arnold set out to hunt in earnest. Stalking Julia as cat with mouse, he followed her into the kitchen garden. Julia, wrapped in her own misery as by a waterproof cloak, did not know she was followed until arms came around her from the back and his lips kissed the air near her left ear.

"Oh! Stop it, stop it at once!" she cried, struggling like a bird in a snare.

"Now, lass, you know you've been wanting me to come along! What's the use— Ah, you vixen!"

The last term was jolted from him by a well-placed heel on his ankle, and he released her abruptly. "Don't look so pleased!" he told her, anguish edging his voice. "I'll get you for this!"

"For what?" she said, standing away and watching him warily. "Simply because I do not care to be mauled by an oaf like you?"

He stopped short. The maid had an unusual way of speaking, and if he didn't know she was employed in his mother's kitchen, he might expect her to be akin to Sir Lawrence Talbot, the baronet whose manor lay beyond Tring. Surely no kitchen maid could look at the scion of the house with such scorn.

"Who . . . who are you?"

"I am not a plaything for you," she warned him, "and that is all you need to know. Now, let me pass."

Struck with awe, and a kindling regard that went deeper than a tumble with a maidservant, he stood stiffly aside and watched her return to the house.

Arnold stared. Surely this kitchen maid spoke as though she were Queen Guinevere giving orders to a page? In that moment, Arnold succumbed. His romantic soul carried the day.

From that time on, Arnold was prey to a species of worship that had little to do with the small church on the green at Tring. He had, as had many another, fallen victim of the spell of flashing violet eyes, and he behaved much like a fledgling knight at King Arthur's table, anxious to prove himself in the eyes of his lady.

His opportunity came almost at once.

It was one of September's better days, clear and bright, the sky a blue so deep that one could fancy eternity was made of such a color.

Julia set out after lunch through the parkland surrounding the house, on a shortcut which she was assured would deposit her on the very doorstep of Tring. She was charged with errands. Miss Chase, the girls' governess, deigned to ask Julia to match some ribbon for her. Mrs. Ferguson had run quite out of ginger. "The girls been at me this long time to make them some gingerbread men."

Julia's spirits at last began to stir, and even give an indication that they might in due course rise. On the fact of it, it was unlikely that anyone could live forever in forlorn sadness. She considered that Charles had already forgotten her. Well . . . she would forget him!

Already the absence cure was working, she decided. There had been almost an hour after breakfast during which she had thought of him only once.

Her way through the park lay down a small slope, among some trees, over stones set in lieu of a bridge across a rill. She did not look back.

Behind her, in a highly clandestine manner, came Arnold. He was not sure of his intentions. Whether it were better to dog her footsteps in silence, or to approach her boldly, and with masculine persistence walk with her, he could not decide.

By the time she reached the outskirts of the village, he was in the powerful grip of shyness, lagging far behind.

Since all inhabitants of Tring were unknown to Julia, she took no particular notice of a man just emerging from the Rose and Crown. However, the stranger stopped short upon catching sight of the raven-haired girl stepping along the street.

The villagers of Tring would never know the stranger's name, but they would never forget the man himself. He had already made unwelcome inquiries in the inn, requesting the names and descriptions of any female newcomers in the area.

The landlord never wavered in his rhythmical wiping of

the counter. "Nay, naught I know on. What might ye want to know for?"

"That's my business," retorted the visitor unwisely. "But there's a bit of gold in it for the one who can tell me what I want to know." He winked broadly.

It was unfortunate for the stranger that he looked like what he was—a pugnacious Londoner with only contempt for those he termed "right rubes."

"Bit o' gold, is it?" The landlord straightened and tossed his bar rag aside. "I reckon it's not hard to figure on what your game is. And we'll have none o' that here."

The landlord's wife, attracted by the raised voice of her husband, appeared in time to hear his last remark. She joined battle.

"Ain't there enough women in London for ye? Let me tell you, none of our girls is fool enough to let you diddle 'em."

Bolstered by his belligerent partner, the landlord shouted. "My house is no place for the likes of you. We're respectable folk, we are, and I'll thank you to take yourself right out that door."

Belatedly the Londoner saw his mistake. He had been sent out by a certain inquiry agent in London to inquire as to the whereabouts of Miss Julia Edgeworth, description furnished.

While his employer held little hope for the girl's recovery, yet the nob that hired him was flush enough—and just maybe, if the girl were found, there would be guineas to spare for all.

Invited now to take his speedy departure, the private agent stepped onto the street, and immediately spotted the object of his search.

Black hair, long eyelashes so that he could not see the color of her eyes—but he'd be a monkey if they weren't violet!

Besides, there was something about the way she walked that looked out of place in these rural surroundings.

She must be the girl!

The sound of possible guineas clinked in his head. He didn't give a thought as to how to convince Miss Edgeworth to return to London with him, were she to be reluctant. Nor did he fully consider the temper of those villagers he had already met.

Foremost in his mind was to get a glimpse of that young lady's eyes. If they were indeed violet, he was already a rich man! He stepped down from the threshold of the Rose and Crown.

Julia, intent on her errands, was first made aware of his interest when he stood directly in her path.

"Good afternoon, miss." She looked up, startled. Violet they were, indeed!

The landlord was watching from the inn door. His wife peered around him and said, "What's he want?"

"Up to no good, I'll be bound. For one of them *places* in London, like as not."

Eagerly the stranger smiled. "Miss Edgeworth, isn't it?" If he had not been sure of her before, the stricken look on her face would have convinced him.

"N-no," she said, managing a frosty glare. "You are mistaken!"

"I don't think so," he said. "You're not fooling me, young lady. I know who you are!"

He had no clear idea of why his quarry had fled London to begin with. He strongly suspected that she was some lord's light-o'-love, no better than she should be. It was this mistaken conviction that led him into disaster.

"How dare you speak so to me!" Julia fulminated, fear spurring her indignation. "Pray remove yourself from my way."

"Or else?" he sneered. It was the last coherent statement he made.

Arnold, aware of the many eyes of Tring, had been loath to reveal his presence, lest all know him to be a moonling following a kitchen maid. His dignity, to say nothing of his carefully cultivated reputation as a *right one*, required that he maintain his distance until Julia was on her way home again.

He was not close enough to hear the exchange between Julia and the lout just leaving the inn, clearly foxed, judging from his outrageous behavior.

Julia was in distress.

The stranger was suddenly assailed from behind. Arnold's strong arm, painful against the intruder's windpipe, effectively cut off further conversation.

"Bother a lady, will you!" shouted Arnold. "You coward, you yellow-stripe! See how you face up to a man!"

193

The Londoner growled in his throat. No stranger to street fighting, he slipped out of Arnold's grip and faced his adversary.

The light of battle blazed in Arnold's eyes. Not for naught had he studied the methods of the great pugilists—Tom Cribb, the terrible Randall, even Gully and the Chicken.

One jab at the jaw, then weave—feint, jab again—that's how it was done. Arnold fought a good fight. But his opponent, while acquainted with the heroes of the ring, had learned his style in the streets of London.

Arnold fared badly. One eye was closed almost at once. Julia longed for a weapon. She wished it had been raining, for then she would at least have had an umbrella.

In the event, Arnold did not fight alone. Two bony-ribbed dogs, strolling in the sunshine, took exception to the unseemly racket, and sank their teeth into the nearest legs. Fortunately for Arnold, the dogs bit his opponent.

The landlord joined the fray, shouting, "He's trying to steal our women!" His wife jumped up and down in the street, screeching, "Shame! Shame!"

Julia, thunderstruck at the twin revelations—that, whoever he was, the stranger knew her name, and also that Arnold was quite likely to be killed on her behalf—had only her reticule to hand. She advanced on the pair.

Suddenly the fight was over. Arnold stood gasping for breath. The second eye was fast swelling, there were bruises reddening along his jaw, promising purple smudges by next day. But he was proudly, victoriously erect. And his recent adversary lay supine on the dirt.

20

Julia could never remember how it was that within moments, so it seemed, after her accoster had been leveled, she found herself in the vicar's pony cart, trotting along the road to Gough Park.

She had a quick memory of Arnold, both eyes swollen, dancing around his fallen opponent, jabbing blindly at the air. "Let me at 'im!" was his constant cry, until some kindly soul took him in hand and informed him of his victory.

She glanced now at the vicar, seated beside her, handling the reins with ease. "I must th-thank you," she ventured.

"We must be grateful," he told her, "that all has ended well. This time."

The vicar was filled with a pleasurable sense of a deed well done. George Melton found himself at times out of tune with his necessarily restricted life. Before he took orders, he had been quite a dasher. Of a powerful build, he had enjoyed what he called the "manly arts," and had even gone a few rounds with the Gas-Man and Bill Neate at Jackson's.

With regret he had put aside violent ways, but just now, his greater resentment was that he had arrived at the scene of the fight too late to enjoy it. In keeping with his present calling, it had fallen to his lot to disperse the crowds, send Arnold to the doctor, and prevail upon the landlord to convey the defeated and unconscious stranger to the Rose and Crown, to be cosseted in an upstairs room.

"But, Vicar, yon foreigner's trying to kidnap girls for"—the landlord's voice fell— "you-know-what!"

Melton, without tact, said reassuringly, "Well, I am sure your good wife stands in no peril. The man is out of his head, you know."

The landlord's wife was not best pleased. Vicar meant well, but what he as good as said was that no man would want her, for any purpose, moral or immoral. An obscure wish to retaliate came upon her, and she promised herself that the foreigner would receive the best of care. And when he came to himself, well . . . that was another tale.

So, having made his instructions clear to all within sound of his powerful voice, the vicar placed Julia on the seat of his pony cart, and they tooled out of town, toward home.

"All has ended well," he repeated now, "and we must all thank Providence that once again a brand has been snatched from the burning."

"What they said, you know, that he was trying to kidnap me, wasn't at all true," she said.

"No? Then what, pray, would a man from a lower class in London want with a servant clear the far side of Hertfordshire?"

She had no answer for him. The stranger knew her name. There was only one explanation—that someone who cared for her had sent him to find her. It was only bad luck that he had been ill-advised enough to seize her, to keep her from escaping again.

"You see, my child," said the vicar, comfortably sure of his own logic, "you have no knowledge of the evil there is in the world. As innocent as you are, how could you know of the Jezebels, the . . . painted women . . . the . . ." He broke off, belatedly realizing that it did not do to put such wicked notions into the girl's head. First thing one might expect was that the bright lights, instead of warning, might well allure such a greenling into the snare of sin.

He stole a glance at her. To his relief, she seemed not to have heard him. A good girl, not like that Agnes who was in service at Gough Park too. Agnes would have quite boldly asked him how she might meet the Jezebels of the world.

He frowned. He was not quite comfortable in his mind about Agnes. He feared he was a most inept shepherd.

But at least he had done well with young Julia here at his side.

"I trust you are not overset by this little to-do," he resumed. "A young female cannot be too careful. As Scripture says, a good name is rather to be chosen than great riches, and loving favor rather than silver and gold."

Her reaction was all he could have wished. She turned to look at him as though he were the Delphic oracle. "Loving favor?" she whispered.

"The love of a good man," he expounded on his text, "keeps a woman safe from temptation, wraps her in a cloak of virtue, and brings her to the very throne of God, safe from all evil."

"The love of a man," she paraphrased, traveling her own mental road.

"Thorns and snares are in the way," continued the vicar. If he were to tell the truth, he would have realized that his exhortations were directed more at the wayward Agnes than the poor serving-wench beside him. "But a virtuous woman's price is far above rubies."

The price of this virtuous woman, thought Julia, had not been measured in rubies, but in beautiful gowns, luxurious furnishings, the glittering temptation of Society, a house in Green Street.

Suddenly Julia drew in her breath. There was a great change taking place in her that very instant, and if she sat still, held her breath, she could watch the alteration, and understand it.

While the vicar had intoned certain admonitions from Scripture, as was his duty, yet in her memory echoed another verse from another sermon, another time.

"Better is a dinner of herbs," she recalled, "where love is . . ."

And she understood what was happening to her.

She was in love, totally and irrevocably, with Charles, and, as another remembered verse told her, "all her days are sorrows, her heart taketh not rest in the night."

A true word, if ever there was one.

She would fly back to Charles, and beg him to make his offer to her again. Even if all he offered was protection, he had said he needed her. She would go with him wherever he led, and she would be alive once more.

A jumbled, chaotic line of reasoning, perhaps, but she

knew that from the ravelings of logic she had found her own truth.

The pony cart turned through the big stone pillars that framed the drive leading up to the front of Gough Park. The vicar, careful to preserve the decencies, drove to the kitchen wing.

"Well, now, miss, I shall just see that Mrs. Ferguson does not blame you."

How could she? thought Julia, but said nothing. She let Mr. Melton lead her into the house. There were explanations to be made, he thought, and while she was wrapped in the exigencies of her decision to return to Charles, she left the field to the vicar.

His recital of the day's events wrung exclamations from Mrs. Ferguson and an interested response from Agnes. Just as Mr. Melton expected, Agnes sought the location of the flame that promised to burn her wings.

"Did the stranger leave town?" she demanded.

"No, he was unconscious, the poor man. Mr. Arnold has quite a right jab, so I suspect." He concluded wistfully, "I did not myself see the fight."

"Who is to tell the mistress?" demanded Ferguson harshly. "If Mr. Arnold is to come home on a hurdle, I won't want to be nearby."

"Quite right," said Mrs. Ferguson, on her husband's side for once. "She'll have a screaming fit, mark my words." She closed her eyes in shuddering anticipation.

"Well, then," said the vicar, "I suppose I shall. After all, it is my duty to comfort my sheep."

Agnes, who had heard the vicar on the subject of sheep, lost and found, more than once before, gave a snort of laughter. Mrs. Ferguson glared at her. But it was the vicar himself who chose to give the girl a setdown.

"Watch," he said sternly, "lest the Bridegroom cometh upon you unaware."

Agnes took him literally. "No bridegroom takes *me* unaware!"

Mrs. Ferguson jeered. "More 'n likely you'll pounce on *him* from the bushes!"

"And what is it to you, if I do?" demanded Agnes shrilly. "You can't have any fun out of it anymore." She shot a significant glance at the butler. "Don't tell *me* what to do!"

The vicar, held in spite of himself by the altercation erupting before him, attempted the pouring of oil on the waters. "Now, Agnes—"

"Now nothing!" said Agnes, all at once angered. "You're so set on getting me wed, Vicar—are you in the running yourself?"

The vicar's jaw dropped in genuine horror. "M-me?"

Mrs. Ferguson moved toward Agnes, her hand raised with clear intent. Agnes, suddenly aware of the outrageous nature of her remarks, clapped a hand over her open mouth and looked fearfully toward Cook.

Mrs. Ferguson was appalled. "Agnes! You . . ."

The vicar, who had flushed at Agnes' pert remark, now was pale as a sheeted ghost. How had he ever thought he could serve the Lord by counseling the sheep of his parish? An unworthy suspicion came to him that if this particular lamb had got lost, he for one would find it hard to make a search lest she contaminate the ninety-nine he had left.

He shook away the temptation to flee. "Agnes . . ." he began sternly. But his admonition would never be heard.

Mrs. Ferguson was in full cry. "No way to talk to Vicar! I'm shamed to have you in my kitchen! If you were mine—*which*, thank the Lord, you are not!—I'd wash out your mouth with laundry soap. And I'll do it yet!"

"You'll have a job on that!" retorted Agnes, with bravado.

"Your ma should have done it long since," shouted Cook. "*Or* took a strap to you."

The argument rose in intensity and pitch, and Julia watched as though from a far distance. She cradled her new decision as though it were a priceless treasure, and waited to tell Mrs. Ferguson that she had decided to return to London.

The happiness that surrounded her tinged all with a glow of the most perfect rose color, and she scarcely heard a word.

Suddenly the argument reached feverish dimensions. Agnes eyed Cook with a mixture of fear and daring. But Cook had reached her limit. She raised her hand again, and started toward Agnes.

Agnes, realizing that she had strained Mrs. Ferguson's

199

patience too far, and retribution was about to be exacted, backed quickly away from the oncoming threat.

She did not see the stool behind her. She gave a short screech as she felt herself falling, and then a wavering scream as she felt pain slice through her leg.

Mrs. Ferguson, bent on punishment, had too much momentum to stop. She put out her hands to catch the table, but in vain. She fell with all her twelve stone on the hapless maid.

The vicar's words were clearly a prayer. Julia darted to help, tugging at the entangled arms and legs. Ferguson gave advice, largely unheeded.

In the event, Julia never found the opportunity to inform the staff of her imminent departure. The doctor had come and gone before she had leisure to think. "Never been so busy since old Bradford blew up the malt kiln," said the surgeon.

Mrs. Ferguson's arm was not fractured, but excessively painful, and to pare a potato was quite beyond her. Agnes' left leg was broken. Ferguson had offered to have her put to bed right here in the house, but Agnes refused.

"Better off at home with my ma," she said, looking darkly at Cook. She jerked her head. "She'll let me starve."

Seeing mystification on the faces of her audience, Agnes explained, "Not me ma. *Her.*"

The vicar remembered his plain duty. "Now, Agnes, I am sure Mrs. Ferguson will forgive you—"

"Say what you will, Vicar," said Mrs. Ferguson, resting her arm in her lap, "it will be a cold day afore I do. A bad girl she is, and I'll not have her in my kitchen."

Since Ferguson's offer had nothing to do with the kitchen, an argument might have been mounted. But common sense clearly was on the side of removing Agnes at once.

Mrs. Ferguson was given a heavy draught of laudanum to kill the pain—"It'll take some killing, that it will!" —and Julia and the butler were left alone in the kitchen.

With all the combatants off the field, the kitchen seemed twice as large as before. "What will we do for supper?" grumbled Ferguson. With a heavy sigh he got up and headed for the baize door into the foyer. "I'll just have to tell the mistress."

He was gone a long time. Julia, brought down from her rosy clouds with a thud, set about the next thing to do.

She surely could not return to London now. She put on Cook's enormous apron, and felt at once more competent. By the time Ferguson returned, supper was in a pot on the stove, sending up a delicious fragrance.

"She's a one," he reported gloomily. "Mr. Arnold came home with naught but two black eyes, and she's as crazy over it as though he was dead."

Between them, they were able to put a kind of meal on the table. Julia sank into a chair when the kitchen was clean again, and Ferguson had gone to minister to his wife.

Julia could not desert the ones who had been kind to her. Even a week would not be long, if there was happiness waiting for her.

Besides, now that she had made her decision, it was as though an enormous load was removed. Charles had not forgotten her! The very existence of the stranger who knew her name told her that she was the object of inquiry. And who else would look for her?

She would have preferred to return at once to London, to the house on Green Street. It was possible, she thought, trying to be fair, that Charles was searching for her only because he felt responsible, since he had provided the establishment that had led, in devious ways, to her headlong flight. It was equally possible that Charles was by now betrothed to someone else, and Julia's return would be too late.

But she was too tired to consider seriously either of those possibilities. Surely life could not be so cruel!

Besides, a week more or less would make no difference. Nothing much could happen, she thought as she wearily prepared for bed, in only seven days!

21

However, much can happen even in a day.

While the hours went by much as they had before at Gough Park, marked only by Mrs. Ferguson's recovery the next day to the point of sitting in her kitchen as a captain sits on his deck, those same moments in London were far from uneventful.

At the same time that the agent was accosting Julia on the street in Tring, Harriet was seeking out Elsie Hastings. She had gained the information she had gone for, and now was being conveyed from Queen Anne Street to Mount Street. She instructed her coachman to wait for her, and she hastened up the steps to Charles's town house.

Charles was not at home. Leaving word for him to call upon her, she hurried home. There was little time to dress before she and Minton were to attend a dinner. She hoped that Charles would call before she must leave again.

Elsie had certainly given her Julia's direction, as surely as though she had written it down. Hertfordshire, it was, at a town called Tring. How had Julia ever found such a place? Impossible, of course, except for Miss Hastings' help.

Harriet was much pleased with her success. She had learned what all of Charles's inquiry agents had not, nor had Miss Moray been able to coax Miss Hastings into revelation. If Harriet knew her brother, he would like as not set horse to curricle this very evening!

Harriet ascended her own front steps. Yonge opened to her, his face a delineation of disaster. Her exclamation was cut short, when he announced, "Her grace the Duchess is in the Gold Salon, my lady."

"Good God, Yonge! What is she about?"

Since there was no pertinent answer—at least one that Yonge felt privileged to make to his mistress—she swept past him and into the salon.

"Well, Eugenia," she greeted her. "I wish you had told me you were coming."

"I did not know myself," she replied pleasantly. "I am sure you are engaged this evening, so pray do not change your plans. I am expected at my cousin's, so you need not bother about me."

"Would you not be more comfortable at Knebworth House?" wondered Harriet.

"Most likely. But I shall be here for only a few days. Hardly time to take the holland covers from the furniture, you know."

Harriet was hastily reviewing her own social schedule again. She had even toyed with the idea of traveling with Charles to Tring, and with reluctance decided it would not do. Now she must consider how best to entertain Eugenia.

"Pray don't wonder," said Eugenia, as if on cue, "how to entertain me, for I have come on business. As soon as I have finished with Charles, I shall return to the Castle."

"Not Charles! Eugenia, what now?"

"We have given much thought to Charles," said the Duchess regally.

Harriet was indignant. "Eugenia, he is not your charge. Nor Edward's, if it comes to that."

"Pity." Eugenia continued, "He has taken leave of his senses, you know, insulting his oldest friends, gaining a reputation for irascibility that reflects sadly on the family."

"You are wrong."

Eugenia swept on as though Harriet had said nothing. "Even poor Maria. I had not thought Charles cruel. Thoughtless, perhaps, but not deliberately malicious."

Harriet was stung. "He is never malicious! Eugenia, you cannot pretend to believe whatever Miss Sutherland chooses to say."

"I shall simply endeavor to smooth the ruffled waters between Charles and the woman he should offer for."

Harriet took a firm stand. "Eugenia, I do not know precisely what you have in mind. Smoothing the waters for Charles! I assure you he is perfectly capable of managing his own affairs. Take warning, Eugenia, he will not suffer your interference."

"Indeed?"

Harriet, once started, could not stop. "If you have the slightest intention of bringing Maria Sutherland here, I fear you will be embarrassed. Miss Sutherland will not be received in my house!"

Eugenia raised an eyebrow and looked at her sister-in-law speculatively, as though studying a strange zoological specimen. "Very well. I see you are beyond reason. Edward feared that you would lose your head over Charles."

"Eugenia!"

"I must see Charles. Edward wishes me to lose no time in putting our plan before him."

Clearly, thought Harriet, Eugenia was next to lunatic. Speaking of Edward's plan, of Charles's waywardness, of Harriet's own recalcitrance, Eugenia gave an impression of minor royalty. Indeed, Harriet was not sure whether Eugenia's "we" meant the Duke and Duchess, or simply a very royal "we."

Edward was the head of the Langley family. However, his position was not one of divine right, nor did its prerogatives include ordering the lives of his brother and sister, as well as a few cousins who relied on the Duke's bounty.

Besides, as Charles would be the first to say, Edward could not order his own household.

"Edward thinks," continued Eugenia, "that it is best for Charles to rusticate."

"Rusticate!"

"I must tell you, Harriet, that it is most uncomfortable to live in dread that sooner or later Charles will perpetrate some monstrous deed that will bring contumely upon our heads."

A voice spoke from the door. "Fustian!" said Charles, stepping into the room and closing the door behind him. "If you have regard for the servants, Eugenia, I am sure that Minton will not appreciate having your affairs common gossip among the servants."

"Common gossip, I must assure you, Charles, is the least of our concerns just now. You have made our name the subject of the rumor mill for too long. Edward is irritated."

Charles gave his detested sister-in-law a long contemptuous look, a look which she sustained with fortitude. Nothing Charles could say, was her attitude, could swerve her from her clear duty.

"Harriet, my dear," said Charles turning to his sister, "you wanted to see me, I gather?"

She nodded, bereft for the moment of speech.

"I wish I had been at home," he continued. "I was called out to look at another unfortunate woman, dragged from the river at Westminster Bridge." He glanced at the Duchess before turning again to Harriet. "It is a constant wonder to me to observe the workings of Providence. To take some and leave others! The reason behind such selections is unfathomable."

Eugenia smiled tolerantly. "I don't understand what you are talking of, but it does not greatly matter. Charles, I am greatly disturbed."

Charles was not in a kindly mood. He had been asked to view another body of a desperate young woman whose trials were over. He alternated daily between hopes that Julia was safe and fears that she might at any moment be looking down into the swift-flowing waters of the Thames, desperate and lonely, and he unknowing.

In the odd moments when he could think more clearly, he realized that—supposing she were safe—she was deliberately staying away from him. Either, he reflected, she could not abide him, or considered him of so little account that she did not even think of him anymore.

He glared at the Duchess. "I warn you, Eugenia, I shall not listen to whatever maggot you've got in your head."

Eugenia pursed her thin lips. She had always had a low opinion of her husband's younger brother, not least because he was beyond her control. "Your brother's position, Charles, demands that you pay heed to his wishes."

"Edward? The day I allow him to dictate to me will be a day to mark down on your calendar, Eugenia, for the world will turn upside down at that moment."

"He is the head of your family."

Deliberately Charles turned away. To Harriet he said with an appearance of calm, "My dear, you came to Mount Street. May I know why?"

Harriet was torn between allaying Charles's fears and not wishing to lay her information before Eugenia. She trod a middle path. "Nothing."

Charles lifted an eyebrow. "Nothing? Forgive me if I do not quite believe you."

Eugenia interrupted. "If you have quite finished? Edward believes it best for you, Charles—"

Charles said, "Eugenia, pray give my compliments to the Duke. Inform him from me, if you will, that *I* believe it best for *him* to deal with his own concerns, to the exclusion of mine. Now, Eugenia, I *have* finished!"

Seizing Harriet's wrist, he pulled her out of the Gold Salon with him, and shut the door with vigor behind them. In the foyer, he said, "Now, Harriet, what is it? Best tell me quickly, for I shall not be seen again in Minton House until that she-wolf leaves."

Quickly she relayed Elsie Hastings' final words. He frowned. "You mean that's all she said?"

"Charles, dear, don't you see? She could not tell me precisely where Julia is, for she promised. But I know she had a reason for mentioning that place."

"Tring?" he mused. "What on earth is there?"

Practical always, Harriet said, "Julia, without a doubt."

"Perhaps you are right. At any rate, I must go."

"I wish I could go with you," she said wistfully. "But I suppose you must take Miss Moray."

"Miss Moray! I tell you, Harriet, had I known just what Miss Moray was like, I should never have embarked upon this scheme. I should have brought Julia directly to you," he said with heat, "and married her out of hand."

"Charles! I should have been glad to have Julia, of course. But—"

"Miss Moray has become so smitten with Matthew Morrison that she lost her head when it came to Julia. She sent her up in the boughs when she learned of my scheme, and let her hare off to—where is it, Tring?—and now she simply bleats that dear Julia will come back when she is ready."

"Poor Miss Moray. I am sure she is worried far more than she tells you."

"She has Matthew to support her," said Charles harshly. He lifted Harriet's hand and kissed it. "Thank you, my dear. I shall be off at once."

"Not tonight!"

"No, I think at first light will be time enough." He hesitated on the threshold. "Harriet? May I bring her here?"

"Of course, you may." Guiltily she looked over her shoulder at the closed salon door. "Eugenia cannot stay long."

Pleasantly he said, "I shall have to think of more deadly insults to speed her on her way."

Harriet giggled.

Back in Mount Street, Charles gave himself over to thought. He had little faith in Miss Hastings and her promises. Surely any woman of sense would realize that Julia's safety was in question, and that a promise was not meant to be kept under those circumstances.

Now that at last Miss Hastings' bulwarks seemed to have been breached, in spirit if not in letter, he gave more serious consideration to the possibility that he had at last one end of a thread in his hands. If the thread truly led to Julia, he was prepared to think more charitably of Miss Hastings, and even of Miss Moray, whose Scottish stubbornness had not yielded to his pleas for information.

He sent for Crouch.

"My lord?"

"I wish the curricle ready at first light."

"Tomorrow, my lord? I'll be ready."

"Not you, Crouch."

The groom was wounded. "But, my lord, you'll want the chestnuts?"

"I was not aware there was a choice?"

"No, of course not, my lord. But the one I'm not easy about. You wouldn't want it to go lame, my lord?"

"If any of my cattle go lame, Crouch, you know whose head I'll have," said Charles equably. "I shall take Diggs, I think."

Crouch left Charles with no doubt as to his resentment. Ten to one, nay, a hundred to one, judging from his lordship's altered mood, Miss Edgeworth's whereabouts was now known. Crouch, who had been with Lord Charles when he first laid eyes on the lady, wanted desperately to be present when she was found.

Diggs! Crouch snorted. Sorely tempted to disguise himself and follow the curricle, he took his wrath out on Diggs.

But at first light, Crouch was on hand to see his lordship on his way. Charles pulled on his driving gloves as he stepped down from his house. Diggs was holding the chestnuts, aware of the high honor and yet frightened out of his wits lest he make some horrible error that would bring down his lordship's scorn.

"Ah, Crouch," said Charles. "I should have known you would see me off." He gave his head groom the sweet smile that his servants cherished. "I must have Diggs, you know, for Miss Edgeworth does not know him."

"Then the lady is found, my lord?"

"Perhaps, Crouch." He hesitated. Crouch was an old friend, and deserved better than to think he was not wanted. "I cannot take a chance on tipping my hand too soon. If she sees you, then . . ."

"I see, my lord." Crouch was mollified, even to the point of saying, "Good luck, my lord."

Charles nodded thanks. He gathered up the reins. Diggs swung up beside him, and the curricle was quickly out of sight.

Crouch scratched his head. The master had a scheme, all right, but Crouch had a healthy respect for Miss Edgeworth's wits. If she didn't want his lordship, then naught he could do would entangle her.

Suddenly he laughed. Just as true, if the lass wanted Lord Charles, then she'd have him.

For Lord Charles was as head-over-heels as ever man was!

22

Since the first separation of Chaos into day and night, sunrise has touched the spirit of man with new hope, a new beginning, a conviction that this fresh day will see no trouble.

Charles was not so hardened as to be impervious to such a lifting of spirits. Indeed, he was near to light-headedness.

He guided his fast-stepping chestnuts to the northwest out of London. Hertfordshire was not unknown to him. Several of his manors lay beyond Dunstable, but he had paid little heed to the smaller villages that lay between London and his various destinations.

Now he was bound for Tring. All he knew was that the town was in Hertfordshire, always supposing that the stubborn Miss Hastings had a firm grip on geography.

But since Julia had gone at the outset to the Swan with Two Necks, it followed that she had taken a Chaplin stage. Diggs had been dispatched, the night before, to inquire of the stage office the directions to various towns, including Tring, and now Charles was in fair understanding of his direction.

The swift clop-clop of hooves on road, the bracing fresh air as soon as they left the outskirts of London, even the birds singing in the fence-rows, combined to set Charles near to singing.

They passed Elstree, where the roads divided. Diggs directed him to the left fork, in front of the Old Holly Bush, and they moved out toward the middle of Hertfordshire.

Julia had come this way, mused Charles. Would she be glad to see him, or would she once again flee into the unknown? He realized that he truly did not know what she thought. He had believed, judging from certain vivid, heart-tugging memories, that she reciprocated his passion in full.

But she had scorned him, raked him with deadly contempt, and vanished. It was all his fault, and he must make amends. Not only did he know that she alone of all women in England was the one he cherished, but he was beginning to realize that she was not simply an attractive, piquant, mischievous delight to him. She was Julia, an individual with her own ideas, her own will—her own right to shape her life as she wanted it.

Charles was well on his way to becoming humble.

The morning was well advanced before they stopped at Hunton Bridge to bait the horses. Diggs found sustenance in a mug of ale, but Charles stretched his legs along the street.

A signpost, rubbed over with dirt and hardly decipherable, directed him to the right, down an overgrown lane, trees laced together to form a roof.

The lane, so he was led to believe, would take him to the mansion of Langleybury. Surely there must be a family connection, even though it might be tenuous as a spider's thread.

He hesitated at the mouth of the lane. Was this what all Langley possessions might come to? He shook his head. He had a strong sense of family, even though Edward was turning out to be such a dolt Charles hardly wished to claim acquaintance with him. It was, of course, his devotion to the concept of continuing the family line that had brought him to fall into this plight. Had he not traveled to Brighton in order to set his thoughts straight on the need for marriage, he would not have come upon Julia.

He turned quickly. Every moment spent in reflection was a moment delaying him in his quest for Julia.

The larger village of King's Langley failed to beguile him. Even though a queen had owned the manor, even though Richard the Second was reputed to have been buried in the priory, only Tring now had power to draw Charles.

"History is all very fine," he said to Diggs. "History keeps a man's perspective in order, you know."

"Yes, my lord," said Diggs obediently. His father had been a minor curate in a parish, the gift of which lay in Langley hands.

"King Richard was buried here, but now there's no trace of either him or the priory. And I will wager that neither one of us will be longer remembered than he was."

"No, my lord."

"Well, Diggs, we shall just wait and see. How far is it, do you think, to Tring?"

Diggs was informed. "First there's Berhamstead, and then Northchurch, and then Tring, my lord."

"Well enough, Diggs. Now, when we get to Tring, I wish you to do this."

The rest of the journey passed in instructions from master to man, and in increasing bewilderment, not expressed, from man to master.

At last, in midafternoon, Charles was driving down the main street of Tring. He had spent the journey profitably, planning his approach to Julia, wherever she was. He was suddenly made aware of the essential flaw in all his scheming. He did not know precisely where Julia was.

Tring was a sufficient destination, considering it against the background of the entire British Isles. But now, passing the small church and vicarage, and seeing various roads leading away from the main road, he realized that he had not the slightest idea of which direction to take.

He drew up before the only inn, the Rose and Crown. "Diggs, see what you can find out."

He walked his horses to the end of the street and turned them. He regarded the chestnuts with satisfaction. Neither had gone lame, in spite of Crouch's devious excuse to accompany him. They had made much faster time than a coach and six would have, and they seemed scarcely tired. They could have gone a double stage without faltering, he was sure.

When he pulled up again before the Rose and Crown, a startling sight met his eyes. Diggs fairly flew out of the door, followed by a small round fury in the person of the landlord's wife, brandishing a broom and raining blows effectively on Digg's hunched shoulders.

"My lord," cried Diggs. "They're all crazy in there!"

The woman stood on the threshold, hands on hips,

clearly victorious. She faltered, though, when her eyes took in the elegant black curricle and the splendid cattle which drew it. Besides, the nob at the reins was top-of-the-trees, even she knew that. And what her husband would say if she turned away custom such as this, went past all saying.

But she stood her ground.

Diggs scrabbled up to the seat of the vehicle.

Charles regarded him with some amusement. "I know you are not entertained, Diggs, but I should like to know what you said to elicit such a vigorous response!"

"My lord, I did just what you said. Asked for any new young ladies in the vicinity, said I should like her direction. And then that hag just yelled and grabbed up that broom!"

Charles observed, "I cannot think this is the best way to welcome custom." He spoke directly to the woman in the doorway. "Am I to judge, then, that you discourage strangers in Tring?"

"Aye, that I do. Particularly them that come asking for women to take off for their evil ways!"

Charles lifted a haughty eyebrow. "Indeed!" After a moment he added, "Perhaps it is not against your principles to direct me to your vicar?"

A new voice was heard. The landlord appeared behind his wife. He took an appraising look at the nob and his rig, and said aloud, "My lord, there must be a mistake somewhere."

"There certainly is," said Charles with relief. He was averse to dealing as directly with a woman as she deserved, but he had no compunction about putting a man in his place. The landlord's arrival was opportune.

"Would your lordship please to enter? I fancy I can furnish a little brandy that ain't too bad."

Charles's need to find Julia overcame his impulse to chastise the landlord. Handing the reins to Diggs, he stepped down from the curricle and entered the dim taproom of the Rose and Crown.

The landlord, scraping favor, hovered while Charles tasted the brandy. Then, seeing all was satisfactory, he deemed it wise to make some explanations.

"Wife tells me," he said confidentially, "that your man

asked about young ladies. I fancy you're wondering why wife took such a dislike."

"I confess the question crossed my mind. I can vouch for my man."

"Ah, that's just it! The other man—well, *he's* the one. Wife was upset, seems like."

With infinite and unaccustomed patience, Charles drew out the story of the stranger who had accosted Julia. That same stranger, it seemed, this very minute lay upstairs, weak as a cat. "And who's to pay the shot, I'd like to know?" Landlord looked slyly at his patron.

"Since I do not know, landlord," said Charles crisply, "I am unable to inform you. But I should like to see the man."

When Charles entered the bedroom under the eaves, he saw the victim of Arnold Gough's jab lying in a narrow cot.

Charles recognized him. "I've seen you before, haven't I?"

"Aye, my lord. Leastways I've seen you."

"You came with Mangus, the inquiry agent, one night."

"Aye, that I did. My lord, I think I found the . . . the one you're looking for!"

"*Did* you! Then, I shall like to hear about it."

The man struggled to sit up. Charles shoved pillows behind him, and waited till he was comfortable.

"Where is she?"

"Now, that I can't tell you, my lord. I'm wondering, though, how it is you came here? I couldn't send word."

"I am glad that I did. How badly are you hurt?"

"Not much. But that witch won't let me out of bed until I show her some blunt, and I can't send for any till I get out of bed. I wouldn't be much surprised, my lord, if they didn't turn out my pockets at the start."

Charles considered the landlord and his wife. "Nor would I."

Urged by Charles, the agent told everything he knew.

"So you do not know quite where Miss Edgeworth is."

"No, my lord. But I got an idea or two."

"Let's hear them."

The agent, under ordinary circumstances, would have withheld his ideas, to divulge them in trade for a good word to his employer. But this nob was different, he thought. Suddenly, with complete trust, he confided, "She's got another moniker. Don't know what it is. But the name I had given to me didn't strike so much as a spark here."

"But you did see her."

"Right as rain I saw her. No mistake about her. I've kept my eyes open here, my lord, while having 'em shut, so to speak. Nothing wrong with my ears, barring a little ringing there at the first. But Landlord spouts off when he thinks I'm out of it, don't you see, and there's a name or so I get."

At length, armed with the names of Arnold Gough and the vicar, Charles professed himself satisfied. "Now, then, how soon can you ride the stage?"

"To Lunnon? I'd do it right now!"

"I believe a night stage comes through here. I shall see that you have a seat—an inside seat. And I'll pay your shot here."

The stranger nearly wept in relief and weakness.

Charles paused in the doorway. "Tell Mangus when you get back that I shall send for him when I return to London. Tell him"—he hesitated, then smiled—"tell him you should receive battle pay for this job!"

"Thank ye, my lord," said the agent, choked by emotion. "I don't think I coulda stood much more of 'em here."

Charles descended to the lower floor, where the landlord waited. Charles gave instructions to him. "And you will make sure that the man is on the stage, and comfortable, won't you?" He shot the landlord a penetrating glance, and added casually, "You should know that I will not be leaving this vicinity for a few days, but when I return to London I shall learn whether you have followed instructions. Or not."

The landlord, promising everything he could think of, bowed Lord Charles off the premises.

Diggs, watching the door with great apprehension lest it disgorge that dreadful broom-woman, was relieved to see Lord Charles emerge, unscathed.

"Did you think she had nobbled me?" said Lord Charles, amused. "Now, then, we'll just move along here to the vicarage."

"I was wondering, my lord, maybe we should have

214

spoke for rooms back at that Crooked Billet. In Northchurch. Just down the road, there, we came through."

"Oh, yes. Never fear, Diggs. If all goes well, we will find a bed for the night."

Diggs glanced behind him, but forbore to make any comment. Besides, Lord Charles was already out of earshot, walking quickly toward the vicarage.

Diggs walked the horses. For the first time, he wondered whether it had been such an honor to accompany his lordship as he had thought. Crouch had been sore as a tooth when he didn't go, but Diggs, hungry and tired, would have exchanged places with Crouch now in the bat of an eye.

Who knew what scheme his lordship had up his sleeve? Diggs was quite new in Lord Charles's employ, but he knew already that his lordship was prone to sudden impulses. Most of this last month had been occupied by the search for this Miss Edgeworth. Diggs had never seen her, but those who had were united in their praise of her. Just the lady for his lordship! they said, and she was nowhere to be found. A havey-cavey deal, if ever there was one, thought Diggs.

It was dawning on Diggs that his lordship had suffered a sea change in the last day. Talking of schemes, saying if all goes well—it gave a timid man like Diggs a strong wish to be elsewhere. He had turned the horses for the fourth time, wretched with apprehension, before Lord Charles emerged from the vicarage.

"It's getting dark," offered Diggs, once they had left the village behind and were traveling on a rutted road toward the west.

"So it is, Diggs. All the better," said Lord Charles cheerfully.

For what? wondered Diggs, not really wishing to know.

After traveling for perhaps a quarter of an hour, Lord Charles pulled up at the side of the road. "Now, Diggs, here's what we'll do." He tied the reins to a bush, and rubbed his hand softly down the chestnuts' noses. "Come, Diggs, help me with this wheel."

Charles had already taken off his coat and rolled up the fine linen sleeves of his shirt. "Here, loosen this . . ."

Diggs was filled with wild surmise. His lordship had

215

quite clearly gone around the bend. It was more than lunacy that caused Charles to loosen one wheel of the elegant curricle. It was the work of a criminal madman.

"We'll be killed!" moaned Diggs.

Charles straightened. "Diggs, I had thought better of you. Crouch assured me that you had bottom. Now I must think he was mistaken."

"N-no, my lord." The undergroom drew himself up. "I'm game for aught you are." He heard the impossible words coming from his own lips. He too was lunatic.

"Very good, Diggs. But there is still time to change your mind."

"What will you do, my lord?"

"I shall continue as I planned. But I am willing to send you back to the Rose and Crown in Tring, to spend the night."

Diggs recovered his courage. "I'll do anything rather than that, my lord."

Together they loosened the wheel to a point Charles judged would take them safely another ten minutes before the curricle must collapse in a heap of kindling wood.

Charles professed himself satisfied. He rolled down his sleeves and reached for his coat folded neatly on the seat.

"Now, Diggs, you sit there. Be ready to jump off when I give the word."

Diggs mounted, sitting on the edge of the seat, gripping it with both hands. He swallowed hard.

Charles flicked the horses. They moved ahead, held gently by the reins, putting their chests into the yoke. "Gently does it," Charles said to them, "gently ahead."

The loose wheel wobbled uncertainly. Charles watched his handiwork critically, until he was satisfied it would hold. The horses were kept to a walking pace.

Charles soon was able to give his attention to looking for certain landmarks given him by George Melton. The vicar had confirmed that the young lady nearly seized by the blackguard from the city lived now in the neighborhood. "As a matter of fact," he said, "in Gough Park."

The vicar was no more proof against Charles's charm and obvious prestige than any other. Charles was now armed with names, directions, and an injunction to watch for the split elm and the beginning of the fence. He noted them as he passed.

Peering into the growing darkness, Charles made out the specified square concrete pillars that marked the entrance to the drive into Gough Park. "Get ready, Diggs," he warned.

Diggs tensed. When Charles said sharply, "Now!" he leaped into the darkness. After he rolled over twice and stopped, he looked ahead. The horses were moving faster. Charles had put the whip to them, after making sure that Diggs was safely away.

But the horses, spirited and nervy, took exception to the unequal pull caused by the wobbling wheel. Wishing at once to be done with it, they broke into a fast trot.

The wheel, turning eccentrically, gave up the struggle and rolled away from the vehicle into the ditch.

The equipage had not quite reached the concrete pillars. The horses clattered away, breaking their harness and dashing up the drive. The pole stuck into the ground, serving as an impromptu brake, and the wood splintered, the seat of the curricle itself rose abruptly into the air, and tossed Lord Charles, still holding the remains of the reins in his hand, into a grassy sward beside the road.

Diggs, panting up in horror, gasped, "Another foot or so and your head'd a been smashed in the middle of the post." Then, recalling himself, he added, "My lord."

The breath was knocked out of Lord Charles. He lay on the ground, stunned out of his wits, and heard Diggs as from a distance. When at last he was able to sit up, with his servant's help, he shook his head to clear it.

"Diggs, I should have listened to you."

"A lunatic scheme," agreed Diggs. "Are you hurt, my lord?"

"I think not. But help me up, can you?"

Charles tested his limbs. All was well except for his right ankle, excessively painful to put his weight on, but decidedly no broken bones. "Diggs, you were right. I should have tested my scheme before I put it into action."

Diggs stifled a moan. The only thing he could think of that might be worse than the current debacle was a previous test of the same—and two such was more than he wished to think on.

23

The runaway horses arrived, snorting and plunging in their harness remnants, before the front door of the Gough manor, spreading alarm.

When Ferguson, Mr. Gough, who was for once at home, and Arnold reached the scene of the accident, they found Charles standing apparently unharmed beside the shards of his curricle. Diggs, an extremely worried look on his features, stood by, watching his master.

Mr. Gough took charge of the affair. "Hurt? Anybody hurt? What happened? That rig's not going to be use to anybody again. I wouldn't travel through the country in one of them. Give me a nice brougham any day!"

"I fear I must impose upon your kindness," said Charles, "to give us shelter until I may send Diggs for my own people."

"Here, of course," said Mr. Gough expansively. He was quite aware that his involuntary guest was a cut above the ordinary. "You'll stay here at Gough Park. I'm Gough."

Charles managed without limping too obviously to walk up the drive to the house. By the time he had been shown to a velvet-and-brocade guest room, his ankle shot pains that threatened to explode.

"Diggs, I am waiting for you to tell me I should have taken your advice. But first, help me into this chair, if you will."

"My lord, I should not, I hope, venture to criticize."

"But . . .?" Charles's smile was one-sided.

"I fancy your ankle is all the remonstrance you will require, my lord."

"How right you are."

He had ruined all, he thought, lying back in the chair

with his eyes closed. He had not caught even a glimpse of Julia. She was clearly a servant in this household, to his great indignation. The vicar had informed him that the young person who had attracted the stranger's attention was, he thought, a kitchen maid. Charles did not enlighten Mr. Melton as to Julia's identity. But now here he was, an ankle paining badly, tucked away in a guest room, without means to announce himself to Julia.

He felt hands busy about his pantaloon leg, and opened his eyes. Diggs had bared the offending ankle, and prodded it with delicate fingers.

"Not broken, that's sure, my lord. As I said out yonder."

"Can you fix it up?"

Diggs leaned back on his heels and thought. "Don't see why not, my lord," he said at last. "Shouldn't be any different from a horse that's sprung a fetlock."

Charles managed to get downstairs for dinner without too much trouble. Diggs had done wonders, binding up the ankle so as to ease the pain. Charles was determined to catch a glimpse of Julia, even if he had to pretend to lose his way and blunder into the kitchen.

In the event, such a machination was not required.

The dinner table was small, counting only Mr. Gough and his wife, young Arnold, whose bruises were now turning an unpleasant saffron shade, and Miss Chase, the middle-aged governess for the Gough misses.

Mr. Gough was full of advice. While he realized that Charles was quite likely as toplofty as they come, yet he was no wiser than young Arnold there when it came to the ordinary affairs of life.

"I can't understand, Lord Charles," said Gough, not for the first time, "how it is that your man didn't know the wheel was loose."

With entire truth, Charles said, "When we left London, a loose wheel was the most remote of contingencies on Diggs's mind."

"I should not dream of giving you advice, Lord Charles," said Mr. Gough, proceeding to give it, "but I daresay I've got the reputation around here of being as right as they come. Not many can get between me and daylight, ask anybody."

Charles listened with only half his mind. He assessed Ferguson—a gloomy man who might be bribed. But he would not wish to count on him in a pinch. There must be a way to make sure that Julia was indeed resident in this house. Perhaps the vicar had leaped to wrong conclusions? He might be mistaken as to Julia's exact whereabouts. Or, the clergyman might have mistaken Charles's motives, and brought him out into the wilds to gain time to engineer Julia's escape.

If the latter were the case, then George Melton might look to his own safety, for Charles was prepared to deal harshly with him.

"If I were you," Gough was saying, worrying the subject like a puppy with a root, simply because he was in awe of his guest. What did one talk about with such a haughty aristocrat? "I'd sack your man."

"Gough, be quiet," said his wife. "Lord Charles doesn't need any advice from you."

Gough, who clearly thought that any idiot who smashed up a curricle needed advice from *somebody*, subsided.

"I'm grateful for your interest," said Charles smoothly, one eye on the door through which Ferguson came and went. "But I must take the blame."

"There, you see, Gough? Lord Charles knows the right thing. He won't pass out the blame to them who didn't do it." Her speech was unclear, but her meaning was not. More than once, Charles divined, his hostess had been accused falsely.

But where was Julia? He was weary of his hosts, painful of ankle, and suddenly desperately sure he had made a fool of himself. Had he spoken, he would have sworn vengeance upon Miss Hastings, the vicar, Becky Moray, and the entire Chaplin stagecoach line for failing to note where their passenger had gone. He held his tongue.

In the meantime, Julia was serving Diggs in the kitchen. She was greatly relieved to see him, for he was a complete stranger to her. Therefore, she reasoned, his master would be equally unknown to her.

Ferguson hurried into the kitchen. "Julia, time to remove the soup."

Blithely she followed in the butler's wake, and moved

220

directly to Mrs. Gough's right. She reached for the soup plate, and looked up at the stranger.

Charles!

Her hand shook on the plate. She did not know what she did next, but apparently she committed no *gaffe*. Charles, Charles! She had not expected to see him here. She was going to London, she was going to accept Charles, whatever he offered her, and she would be deliriously happy.

But now, to see him again, so unexpectedly, to see the hungry fire in his eyes, overset her so that tears sprang to her eyes.

By the time she finished her traffic in soup plates, and was again in the kitchen, she groped for a chair.

"What is it?" cried Mrs. Ferguson. "Did Mistress scold? What on earth happened?"

Julia could not tell her. She put up her hands to hide her face, and shook with the force of her shock. "It's him!" she finally managed to say.

"Him!" cried Ferguson. "I knew there was something ramshackle about him. Whoever heard of a nob smashing his rig, I'd like to know. The gall of him!"

Julia shook her head. "No, no!"

But Ferguson believed she meant she could not face the haughty gent who had come after her. Ferguson saw the whole scheme as though laid out in a picture. The hoity-toity gent, stooping down to snare a pretty maidservant, and then, when he was tired of her, tossing her aside like a broken toy. Ferguson grew indignant.

"Maggie," he said to his wife. "The lass better stay here. His servant's gone, has he? All to the good. He might snatch her away to do his lord's bidding. Now, Maggie, do you help with the serving."

They left Julia alone. Charles was here, and she did not misinterpret his presence. The need in his eyes matched her own, and she knew she would be happy. But she could not run to him now. Since he did not speak in the dining room, then she must wait for him to send for her.

He would manage all, she knew, feeling a kind of peace sweep over her. She did not consider how far a road she had traveled since she had met him on the Brighton road. He had managed all then, too.

221

Dinner was at last over. Julia plunged into the task of washing up. She had nearly finished when Diggs reappeared in the kitchen. When he left, he was possessed of a note of assignation for the rose arbor in an hour.

He was also, to his surprise, given a glass of milk. "For his lordship," said Mrs. Ferguson. "Hot milk's a wonder for helping sleep. And the poor man looked in such pain."

"Just the milk?" said Diggs dubiously.

"That's all there is in there," said Mrs. Ferguson indignantly. "You think I put some witching herbs in it? Nonsense."

When Diggs returned to the overly ornate guest room, he set the milk down on the table next to the chair.

"What is that?" demanded Charles sourly.

"A glass of milk to make you sleep," explained Diggs.

"I'll sleep when this is done with," said Charles.

He had spent a rueful hour waiting for Diggs's return from his errand to the kitchen. He had feared, in London, that if Julia were to have warning of his arrival, she might well flee again, and then he would have no way of finding her.

He had devised a scheme whereby she would be taken unaware. He would then talk to her, explain all, and carry her back with him. His plan had seemed impeccable in London.

Now, some ten miles from the nearest village, he realized he had overreached himself with his stupid ploy.

He should just simply have arrived and taken her away.

Reason demurred. At night? And where could he take her? To drive all night to London, even with Diggs at hand, was not to be considered. He boggled at the notion that he might drive up to Green Street in broad light, to the edification of all the neighbors.

Now he eyed Diggs. "Will she meet me?"

"Aye," said Diggs, and gave him directions. "One hour from now," he finished.

Sometime later, Charles emerged from the guest bedroom into the silent, shadowed hall. Diggs had furnished him with exact directions as to how to descend the servants' stairs and locate the door to the kitchen garden.

Charles was not one for intrigue. Never had he been required to contrive deceitful arrangements. Judging from his fiasco before the front gates earlier this day, it was as well that he need not depend upon his machinations for a livelihood.

He did not even attempt to understand why Julia had made the tryst for somewhere in the dark grounds. Another time, he would ask her reasons. Now his wish was simply to hold her once again in his arms.

The chill fresh air shocked him. He found the rose arbor without difficulty. But there was no Julia.

He waited. She did not come.

He convinced himself that she was paying him off for his bad judgment in arranging her residence in Green Street.

His ankle began to throb with the recent exercise. He leaned against the side of the pergola and put his weight on his good leg.

He had not thought her capable of malice. She scorned him on a previous occasion, but then she was direct, forceful, and honest. To send him out on a chill night to wait in vain for her . . . Well, he had not expected this kind of shabby treatment.

A figure approached, a shadow darker in the shadows.

At last. "Julia! My love!" he said in a muted voice.

"I'll Julia you!" came the rough answer. "You dirty . . ." A series of inchoate grunts followed, for Arnold's vocabulary was not extensive. "I heard about you. Ferguson told me everything!"

Charles rallied. "Ferguson? Your butler, I think? He could tell you nothing about me."

"He knows you're another one trying to find girls for your fancy place. Julia's all in a tempest over it!"

"You're castaway!" accused Charles. "You can't hold your drink!"

A thought struck Arnold. "How come you're not sound asleep?"

"Why should I be?" demanded Charles tightly. He glanced toward the house, but Julia was not coming.

"Because that milk—Ferguson put something in it."

"I should have known," said Charles bitterly. "Trust a house like this one to come up with a device fit only for the stews." He added in an altered tone, "What have you done with Julia?"

"She's better off," said Arnold cryptically. "Now, then, are you ready? I'll plant you a leveler—"

Charles stood up. "Much as I detest instructing the young . . ." he began.

Arnold did not wait. Drunk with the success he and the dogs had won in town the other day, he now felt himself invincible. He jabbed before Charles could balance himself, favoring his ankle. Charles grunted, and shook his head to clear it.

Suddenly from the house came a cry. He looked to see Julia speeding toward him across the grass. The flying figure, a cloak streaming out behind, was undisputably, gloriously Julia!

While Charles was drinking in the welcome sight of his approaching love, Arnold clipped him one at the corner of his jaw, and Charles slid gently to the ground.

Julia was not alone. She was followed by several others, notably Ferguson and his wife. Ferguson was shouting, "I'll save you from him!" Mrs. Ferguson panted, "Ferguson, you fool!"

Julia reached the arbor. "Where . . . where . . .?"

Arnold pointed dramatically toward the ground. "There's your seducer! There's the villain!"

"Oh, Charles!"

On her knees beside Charles, she stroked his face, murmuring small sounds of comfort.

Arnold was incensed. "How can you bear to touch that evil man!"

Julia turned blazing eyes on her would-be rescuer. "Arnold, how silly you are. You're not fit to shine Charles's boots!"

Charles groaned. She sat beside him and brought his head to rest on her shoulder. Putting her arm around his broad shoulders, she was hard put to bring her cloak to cover him, but she managed.

"Oh, my dear love," she crooned, oblivious of the others standing agape around her. "Mr. Ferguson, pray send for the surgeon. Arnold, for goodness' sake, don't stand there! Go get Diggs to help us."

Mrs. Ferguson stated the obvious. "Then you know the gentleman."

"Of course I do. Dear Mrs. Ferguson, I know what it must look like, but truly, all is as it should be. Charles and I—"

"No need to say more. I can see how it is with him and you," said Mrs. Ferguson. "Come, you fool"—referring to her husband—"get that manservant."

"Not possible," said Ferguson. "He's dead out. That milk you give him. I doped it."

"I never!" cried Mrs. Ferguson, leading her husband back to the house.

Julia watched them go. Suddenly she was aware that an alteration had taken place in the man she held in her arms. She could feel warm lips nibbling at her neck. She held her breath, savoring the new and delightful sensation.

She caught sight of Arnold. "Go on, Arnold," she said vigorously. "You're the cause of all this. Go send for the doctor."

Wordlessly Arnold stared. Then, defeated, he turned and trudged toward the house.

Mischievously she said, "Now, Charles, I really think . . ."

"I think, my dear love," said Charles's beloved voice in her ear, "you did not quite finish your sentence."

"I really think . . .?"

"No, no, not that one. The one that started 'Charles and I . . .' "

"Oh."

"Come, now. Charles and I *what*?"

She turned shining eyes to him. "Whatever you wish, dear heart."

"My intentions are honorable," he persisted.

"I am not quite sure," she ventured, "that mine are."

"Julia, you shock me!" he said, laughing.

He pulled her down to him, and found her lips. After a suitable interval, he released her. "How much time we have wasted!" he said. "I'll never let you run away again."

Suddenly practical, Julia agreed. "Time wasted, dear Charles. And it occurs to me that the doctor will soon be here to see to your ankle. Perhaps even in a few minutes!"

"Well, then, love, I suggest we pass the time profitably."

"You are right, as always, Charles."

She offered her lips eagerly, and they slipped away into their own private dream.

24

On the third day from the accident which destroyed Charles's conveyance, a spanking new curricle, drawn by a high-bred pair of Welsh grays, stood before Lord Charles Langley's fashionable Mount Street door, an agent of Tattersall's at their heads.

Various urchins, drawn by the irresistible magnet of prime horseflesh, gathered at a respectful distance. It could have been expected that his lordship himself would appear momentarily and take the reins. The ragged boys waited in vain.

Instead of the languid Corinthian whose superb handling of his chestnuts they had frequently admired, only a groom came out to receive the reins, mount up to the seat, and with a mere touch of the whip tool off purposefully down the street.

The impromptu and appreciative juvenile audience were not the only persons who took note of the event.

Eugenia, Duchess of Knebworth, suffered from a sense of uncertainty over the results of her most recent conversation with Charles. He had, in no mild terms, told her to mind her own business. She was not truly affronted, for her mind was singularly devoted to one object at a time, and was not broad enough to accommodate more than one train of thought simultaneously.

Eugenia had decided that she must take matters into her own hands, this time without allowing Charles to evade her well-reasoned suggestions. At Harriet's, he had simply left the house. She had not obtained his agreement to Knebworth's instructions, nor had Charles returned to Minton House in the intervening three days.

Nor, upon inquiry of her cousin Lady Pyatt, did it appear that he had been seen in any of his various haunts. Her single-minded, if misplaced, optimism suggested that he had indeed taken dear Edward's advice and abandoned London in favor of one of his country houses.

It was shabby indeed, she thought, that he had not seen fit to inform her of his plans. She had said as much to Harriet, but that lady had quite simply flounced off without answering.

As always, she reflected, she must perform all unpleasant duties herself. Dear Edward could not be expected to place himself in Charles's way. Only her constant and strong representations to her husband had enabled her to obtain his grudging permission to, as the Duke put it, "speak to Charles."

Edward, she knew, still had an unreasoning affection for his younger brother. Indeed, Eugenia could not be sure that, were Charles to confront Edward, her husband would hew to the line she had carefully laid out for him to follow.

The Duchess sighed. Men were such strange, unpredictable creatures, but, alas, they were also the fountain of all respectability and wealth. It did not do to let Charles's honors and fortune be wasted upon a veritable child who would add naught to the Langley family prestige.

Eugenia therefore set out from Grosvenor Square, walking north on Audley toward Charles's residence. She intended to meet him on his own ground, and she would not leave until this matter was entirely settled.

If he had indeed left London, then Brimm must tell her.

She emerged into Mount Street in time to see a young person, whose name she did not trouble to remember beyond the recollection that she had seen him before and knew him to be in Charles's employ, driving away from Charles's door. She puzzled over the significance of Charles's servant in charge of a vehicle and pair that were clearly too costly for him. The rig, of course, was Charles's.

She advanced purposefully across the street and entered Charles's front door. She was not one to brook evasions or denials from mere servants, even though they were not her own, and it took a substantial amount of time before she confessed herself defeated and took her ruffled leave, without having learned aught of her brother-in-law's affairs.

"I cannot understand it," she told Harriet later, after she had related the morning's odd circumstances. "Where is Charles? Why is he buying a new curricle? Why is his groom driving it? I have known Charles to say he would never let any ham-handed jarvey touch his cattle. What does it mean?"

Minton set aside his newspaper and turned in his chair before the fire. "What it means, Eugenia," he said testily, "is that Charles trusts the groom who drove away with his new grays." He grew puzzled. "Grays? Thought he preferred chestnuts. Always has."

"That is just what I mean," agreed Eugenia. "And why would he need another pair?"

Minton considered the facts as presented to him. "I'd trust Crouch myself with anything with four feet," he pronounced at last.

Eugenia was startled. "Didn't I tell you? It was not Crouch. It was that young man Charles took in when his father the parson died."

"Not Crouch!"

She had her brother-in-law's full attention. "That is what troubles me. Crouch is still at Mount Street. And reprehensibly secretive, I must add!"

Minton was about to say more when he caught a significant glance from his wife. He had been married sufficiently long to understand that, were he to plunge ahead along the lines he intended, he would find himself in a morass that could be unpleasant indeed. Instead, he harrumphed, "Well, no doubt Charles knows what he's doing." He picked up his newspaper again, and retreated within its shelter. But a careful observer might have noticed that he turned no pages.

"Ah, but what *is* he doing?" murmured Eugenia. "Harriet, do you know?"

Harriet denied knowing anything at all. She did not deceive her husband. Later, when they were alone, he taxed her with a certain loose treatment of fact.

"Not at all," said Harriet, with an appearance of calm. "I spoke the truth. I do not know precisely what he is doing. Nor do I know his plans. But he did leave here days

229

ago, with his curricle, to search for Julia. And he took Diggs instead of Crouch, for you must know I inquired yesterday from Crouch himself, and . . ."

Suddenly her face crumpled and she sought comfort in her husband's embrace. "George, where is he? What has happened to him? You know, I sent him to that place Miss Hastings mentioned. What if it was a trap?"

"Nonsense," said George Minton stoutly. "What kind of trap? He's well able to take care of himself."

"George . . ."

"No, m'dear, I shall not hare off after him. He'd not thank me for interfering."

Harriet played her trump card. "George, you know Eugenia informed me that she is staying here until she learns what Charles is up to."

"Good God!" said Minton. "Well, I'll give Charles two days. Then we must see what is best to do."

"Two days!"

"M'dear, use your wits. If Diggs is going to take the new curricle to Charles, wherever he may be, then it stands to reason that Charles could not return before tomorrow."

Harriet was dubious. "But you realize, George, that a new curricle means that Charles has dished the old one some way."

George Minton had hoped that his lady would not arrive at that conclusion quite so soon. "Well, he's not dead, that's certain, or we would have heard," he said.

There was little comfort in that idea, she thought, but it was the only comfort there was. She would simply have to possess herself in patience for two days.

In the event, her anxiety was relieved before Minton's allotted time had passed. The afternoon of the day following Eugenia's advance on Mount Street, Harriet was summoned by a footman at the behest of Yonge.

When Harriet joined the butler, she had a sudden sense that all this had happened before: Yonge thunderstruck in the foyer, peering out the door, stepping aside to allow his mistress a full view of the apparition—he could deem it no less—standing in the street.

But previously it had been the sight of the Duchess arriving in her cumbersome traveling coach that met her eye. This time, the arrivals were a thousandfold more welcome.

Diggs had jumped down from the rear of the curricle and run to the horses' heads. Charles alighted with caution, favoring his right ankle. He turned to place his hands upon his fair companion's waist, to help her to the pavement. Harriet noted that he was in no hurry to relinquish his hold on Julia, and sighed with heartfelt relief.

All was well with Charles.

Her gaze shifted to the small figure beside him. Julia, dressed quite plainly in a round gown that bore no distinguishing marks of high fashion, looked up at Harriet. The expression on Julia's features quite literally—according to Harriet—turned that lady's heart upside down. She nearly gasped, in a sudden pang of wistful envy—yes, *envy*. Harriet dearly loved George Minton and counted herself fortunate above all women in marrying him, but never, *never* had she suspected that such compelling ecstasy could exist. But there it was, blindingly alive, in Julia's remarkable violet eyes.

Harriet drew a deep breath to steady herself. Instead of the words that reflected her suddenly chaotic state of mind, she murmured conventionally, "How glad I am that you have found her, Charles. My dear Julia, I shall send at once for Miss Moray."

At that moment, Eugenia was sitting calmly in the Gold Salon to the right of the foyer, unaware of momentous events occurring on the very doorstep.

She had been witness to the odd behavior of Charles's servant, driving off a pair of spanking Welsh grays and a smart new curricle. She had followed that spectacle by a judiciously inquiring visit to her cousin. Informed that Miss Maria Sutherland had also been absent from her usual haunts, Eugenia, always listening only to her own dearest wishes, could not help but hope that Charles and Maria had come together, if not in body, at least in intent.

While Lady Pyatt expressed her opinion that Maria had retreated to the country to sulk over her loss of Lord Charles, Eugenia returned to Minton House filled with an elevated sense of anticipation. Surely an announcement of Charles's marriage would soon be forthcoming.

Calmly, now, she drew her needle in and out of the cloth she held, hardly aware of what she was doing. By chance she glanced through the window, and her gaze fell upon Charles, outside on the pavement. He had returned, then, apparently alone, and her hopes seemed confirmed. From her angle of vision she saw nothing of what was transpiring on the steps.

Harriet, with murmured incoherency, at that moment was reaching out to enfold Julia in her arms. George Minton, drawn by the sound of voices, emerged from his study at the back of the entrance hall to join his lady at the front door. One glance at his brother-in-law and the fetching child he had brought was enough to inform him of the approaching happy event. "Charles, my good fellow! How pleased I am! And you, miss . . ." He turned to Julia and took her hands in his. "All's ending well, I see! Couldn't have done better myself, Charles!"

Aware of his misguided tongue, he glanced at Harriet. "M'dear, except for you, of course."

"Of course," said Harriet absently.

"Best get inside, hadn't we? No need to make the neighbors privy to our affairs!"

From the salon, Eugenia watched Charles move toward the entry. Setting her sewing carefully aside, she enjoyed a feeling of gratification that she had waited until Charles's return. She had not quite liked to return to Knebworth Castle with a confession of failure. Now, of course, she was justified in the event.

She emerged into the foyer, and reached a hand out to Charles. "At last, my dear Charles, I see you have come to your senses. The Duke will be most pleased."

Her olive branch was greeted with some surprise, even astonishment. Most uncharacteristically, her grating voice died away into silence.

Then she caught sight of Julia. It was as though, Eugenia thought, her eyes had suddenly blurred, and then sharpened again to reveal that all previous landmarks had vanished. However, Eugenia was made of strong fiber. She forged on, unvanquished.

"Charles, pray tell me . . ."

But Julia's instincts served her well. Whether on purpose or not, she was never to be clear in her own mind. She turned impulsively to her prospective sister-in-law and smiled dazzlingly. "How good of you to say you're

232

pleased," she said sweetly, if inaccurately. "Indeed I am most happy, and I shall hope that Charles will be, too."

Eugenia stared icily at her, and then turned her frigid gaze to her wayward brother-in-law. She was clearly on the verge of withering speech, when Minton cleared his throat, preparatory to speaking. "Don't know what maggot you've got in your head, Eugenia—"

Harriet, belatedly spurred to her social duties, broke in. "Eugenia, this is dear Julia. But of course, I had quite forgotten, you met her at the Victory Celebration in August. I do remember that now. And of course, you must have met at other times. I am sure you are not strangers." Harriet realized that she was spouting nonsense, and fell silent.

Charles said warningly, "Eugenia, you will want to wish us both happy."

Minton's remark, spoken in an undertone, still carried regrettably far. "I doubt that."

Suddenly they were all anxious to prevent Eugenia from giving voice to the words that obviously clamored to be said.

Harriet said, "Our dear Julia is—"

Charles's clear voice interrupted, "—to become my wife, Eugenia."

Julia, who had lived in a state of exaltation for some days now, until Charles's ankle healed and Diggs returned with a new curricle to replace the one smashed by Charles's contrivance, now quietly enjoyed a state of bliss which promised to be never-ending. *Wife*, she reflected, when she had been agreeable to be . . . whatever Charles wanted. How fortunate, but not truly decisive, that he wished to wed her! A minor detail, for what she really could not live without was Charles himself.

She had been terrified of Eugenia—once. Now, with Charles beside her, and assured, quite frequently, that he thought she was as nigh perfect as mortal woman could be, she was well-disposed toward every living creature.

"Please," said Julia winsomely to the Duchess, "can we not become friends? I do *so* wish it!"

The shocked silence of held breaths was palpable.

The Duchess glared at the upstart who had captured her fool of a brother-in-law. But Eugenia, while proud and self-centered, was at times a realist. She was now vis-

233

ited by a sharp-focused vision of the dear Duke, as prone as any other man to be beguiled by a pretty face. She dared not let herself be put in the wrong.

"I must welcome," she said with obvious difficulty, "any new member of the Langley family."

What her remark lacked in cordiality, it made up for in sheer power to stupefy.

Julia's hands reached out and Eugenia was forced to take them. Harriet was heard to mention something in a stifled voice.

Minton said, in a low voice, to Charles, "Good God! I never would have believed this!"

Charles, besotted with pride in his darling Julia, smiled complacently. "Forgive your enemies, George. It's the sweetest revenge on the face of the earth!"

ABOUT THE AUTHOR

Vanessa Gray grew up in Oak Park, Illinois, and graduated from the University of Chicago. She currently lives in the farm country of northeastern Indiana, where she pursues her interest in the history of Georgian England and the Middle Ages.

Her lips were still warm from the imprint of his kiss, but now Silvia knew there was nothing to protect her from the terror of Serpent Tree Hall. Not even love. Especially not love. . . .

DARK SPLENDOR

ANDREA PARNELL

Lovely young Silvia Bradstreet had come from London to Colonial America to be a bondservant on an isolated island estate off the Georgia coast. But a far different fate awaited her at the castle-like manor: a man whose lips moved like a hot flame over her flesh ... whose relentless passion and incredible strength aroused feelings she could not control. And as a whirlpool of intrigue and violence sucked her into the depths of evil ... flames of desire melted all her power to resist. . . .

Coming in September from Signet!